# Blood Moon
# Dragon

Shelley Munro

Munro Press

**Blood Moon Dragon**

Copyright © 2024 by Shelley Munro

Ebook ISBN: 978-0-9941483-5-3
Print ISBN: 978-1-99-106359-5

Editor: Evil Eye Editing
Cover: Kim Killion, The Killion Group, Inc.

Munro Press, New Zealand.

First Munro Press electronic publication May 2017
First Munro Press print publication August 2024

# DEDICATION

For Paul: my husband, partner in crime, and fellow adventurer.
Every day is a good day.

# Introduction

Curvy country star Cassie Miller-Pope lives and breathes music until the fated day when betrayal boots her in the backside and leaves her flailing for balance. She completes her obligations, then demands her manager-ex-boyfriend give her time off to visit her home country of New Zealand. No, she's not licking her wounds. She's checking out her unexpected inheritance from her grandfather. That's her story, and she's sticking to the script.

Hone Taniwha is a bad boy—a reputation he's earned honestly and doesn't deny. After all, his rules aren't hush-hush. He makes his anti-marriage and attachment opinions clear before each sexual encounter. But what he does keep secret is his true identity. His surname indicates his shifter personality. Hone *is* a taniwha—that's dragon to you non-New Zealand readers—and to help keep his human form and his tribes' otherness under the radar, sex and lots of it, is a necessity.

Cassie is enamored with Hone from the beginning, despite

warnings from her best friend. Hone experiences the same lethal attraction and struggles to avoid the woman who wears happy-ever-after on an invisible billboard above her head. Unbeknown to Cassie, the second she gives in to her desire for the charming rogue, she's placed herself in jeopardy, and it's not just danger to her beleaguered heart. This time, it's her life on the line...in a battle that's the stuff of legends.

*Contains a voluptuous, girl-next-door heroine with a wounded heart and a sexy, happy-go-lucky alpha hero with a rebellious dragon. Both have secrets, so let's see how things shake down...*

# Pronunciation Guide and Glossary

Taniwha – a dragon from Māori mythology. Some—water dragons—live in lakes, rivers or the sea. Legend says a taniwha lives at every bend of a river. Other taniwhas are cave dwellers and have the ability to fly. Some are benevolent while others are mischievous tricksters or true villains. Taniwha is pronounced tun-ee-far.

Hone – Māori for John, and a very common Christian name. Hone is pronounced Hon-knee.

Manu – Māori, meaning man of the birds or a person held in high esteem. Manu is pronounced Ma-noo

Tane – Māori, meaning a god. Tane is pronounced Ta-nay.

Kahurangi – Māori, meaning sky blue or precious. Kahurangi is pronounced Ka-who-rung-ee

Motel – a motel in New Zealand and Australia is accommodation for holidaymakers or people from out of town, usually of a nice and decent standard. They provide excellent family accommodation and provide self-catering facilities. Some are on par with hotels.

## CHAPTER 1

# Summer, early January, South Auckland, New Zealand

"I want *you-ou* to show me the way!" Cassandra Miller-Pope, Cassie for short, beat her palms on the steering wheel of the in-your-face red SUV and cast a sideways wink at her long-term friend Emma Montrose.

Their grins ricocheted off each other, toothy and comfortable and perfect, as Cassie sped along hedge-lined country roads. The city of Auckland was cosmopolitan these days, but the proximity of true countryside never failed to astonish her. And now, she owned a slice of that green herself.

"I'm so glad you could join me." Cassie pressed her prescription glasses up her nose, mentally high-fiving her transition lenses that had battled the glare and won. After staying away for so long, she'd forgotten the intensity of the New Zealand sun.

"I'm thrilled you're here, even if it is for merely a month."

"Me too. Letters and emails aren't the same as an in-person visit." Her good cheer took a nosedive. "I wish I could stay longer. With the business and Kevin..." She lowered her speed to pass a horse and rider and wished she could slow her life in the same way. "It was difficult carving out a month in the schedule Kevin wants to set." A problem because suddenly, her enthusiasm had waned for her singing, her upcoming year, her life. "I'm not certain of the farm cottage condition since no one has lived in the place for months. Not since Grandad died."

"Probably full of rodents. Mummy mouse and Daddy mouse and groups of baby mice." Emma tightened the black-and-red scarf tying back her sun-kissed brown hair. Curls rippled through the strands now that it was longer, highlighting her friend's oval face and pursed lips.

"Ugh! Don't tell me that." Cassie overtook a pack of cyclists, sleek and trim in their colorful cycling gear. Tight Lycra. Not anything she'd consider wearing with her determined—overweight, according to her mother—curves. In her peripheral vision, she caught a flash of Emma's white teeth, the twinkling I-got-ya-good blue eyes. "Oh, you're winding me up."

"Can you feel the key in your back?"

"Yes," Cassie spoke crisply, broadcasting affront in a perfect mirror of her mom's lectures. "Don't you remember I'm a famous country star? You can't tease me."

"Huh!" Emma wrinkled her nose. "Hate to burst your bubble, but you're famous in the US. In New Zealand, you're plain Cassie."

A groan—half-laugh, half-despair—rasped her throat before it emerged, victorious and loud. "Don't remind me. Kevin keeps telling me to record a pop crossover song, that other artists are doing well jumping genres, and I'm missing the proverbial bus. But the truth is I kinda like being anonymous at home. It's a treat to shop at the mall or hire a zippy SUV without people gushing over me." She paused for a calming inhalation and shoved her manager's face from her mind. "Don't get me wrong. I love my fans, but this normalcy is pure gold. Enough about me. What about you? I can't believe you finally wore down Jack. I still have your letters, full of studly Jack and his supreme hotness, how he didn't register your presence. Good on you for ripping off his blinders." She peered at the faded road sign and indicated to turn onto the gravel surface. "Ah, this *is* the road. I recognize the stand of trees and the dam."

Emma craned her neck. "You're a long way from anywhere."

Pleasure suffused Cassie at the expanse of green. No strangers she had to play nice with. No bossy, demanding manager. No disappointed parents. Just a landscape of farmland and trees, paddocks of sheep. *Oh!* Cute, shaggy Highland cattle. Fresh air. Peace. "Clevedon township is ten minutes in the other direction. I have a phone. It will be fine. *I'll* be fine. The peace and quiet will be good for the songwriting I plan to do."

"Fair warning, I intend to drag you out to socialize. Shopping excursions. Dinner. A fruity cocktail or two at my favorite nightspots."

"Done deal, but don't tell Mom." Cassie paused, her mind busy, thoughts shooting to the last crazy *discussion* with her mother. "Huh, when in New Zealand...don't tell Mum. When she pauses to take breaths between her high-power business meetings, she mentions grandchildren. Yep, grandchildren! I asked her what she was drinking, but that didn't go down well."

Cassie caught Emma's grimace and returned it with a wrinkle of her nose. During her childhood, before the family had left New Zealand to chase business opportunities in the States, her parents had kept busy with their careers. Later, as a teenager, she'd wondered how her parents managed to conceive her since they never spent much time in the same vicinity. Weird her mother would ask about grandchildren when she'd cheerfully handed over child-rearing duties to staff. Her mom had missed birthdays, school functions, lots of firsts.

And when she had spent time with her parents...

Cassie blinked rapidly to push away the onset of tears. "This is

Grandad's place."

She pulled up outside the single-level weatherboard house, the air exploding from her in a silent O as she studied her inheritance.

"You can't stay here." Emma broke the oh-crap silence first.

Cassie eyed the peeling paint, the gap-toothed baseboards, the overgrown grass and weeds surrounding the house like a gang intent on robbery. The bushy trees loomed, creating dark shadows of neglect and gloom and creepiness. "I didn't think it would be this bad."

"Perhaps the inside will be okay." Emma's voice held doubt.

"Fingers crossed." *Please let it be all right.* She exited the rental vehicle and groped for calm. She refused to stumble at this obstacle, not after she'd informed her mother of her plans.

Her mother had scoffed, but in her polite and firm manner that left most people unclear if they'd been slighted or not. Cassie knew better. The silk-wrapped words reeked of insult and the harsh memory steeled Cassie's spine. She'd rallied her troops—Emma in this case—and sailed forth with her plans.

She lassoed her panic, forced herself to analyze. *Yay. One childhood lecture had stuck.* Her second scan took in the gigantic spider web, the cracked windowpane, the moss on the faded red roof. Not much of an improvement. "I hoped I was seeing things."

"Nope. It's a sad, run-down house," Emma confirmed.

"Once the lawn is mowed..." Happy memories of holidays spent with her grandparents had driven her here. Failure was not an option.

"I'll ring Jack." Emma pulled out her phone. "He won't mind helping. Clevedon Oysters isn't far away, and my man has a weakness for shellfish. That will work as a bribe."

"Done deal." Cassie took two steps and skidded on the dew-slick grass. Her feet shot from under her, and she landed on her well-padded butt, the air exploding from her in a loud *oomph*.

Emma rushed to her aid. "Are you okay?"

Cassie waved her away and pushed to her feet with a groan. "Nothing a clumsy pill wouldn't fix." She rubbed her backside and winced at the dampness seeping through her favorite blue vintage sundress.

"Is your mother still telling you to lose weight to cure your clumsiness?"

A strained chortle burst from Cassie. "She blames you. She says you instilled bad eating habits in me."

Emma pulled a face that would make a Māori warrior proud. "Your mother is a witch. You don't listen to her, do you? Jack loves my curves. All you need to worry about is staying fit and healthy. You look great."

"You're my friend. You have to say that."

"I wrote to you about Jack. You know how hard I had to work to get his notice. Consider it this way. You wanted to sing, right?"

"Yes."

"You wanted it so bad you ignored your parents' wishes. If you find someone who interests you, fight for him in the same way."

"And if I fail? Or he rejects me?"

Emma linked arms with her. "I'll wipe your eyes, ply you with carrot sticks, and you'll start again. None of us needs a man to be happy, but they can be handy with mice and long grass."

"And for sex."

"That too."

The reason Emma was her best friend. She never treated her like a superstar or expected Cassie to buy her things. She kept up their longstanding correspondence and indulged Cassie's love of receiving mail by writing regular letters.

"Just an aside, Emma. Chocolate ice cream works much better than carrot sticks. Oh, and a bottle of wine would go down well."

"Gotcha. Chocolate. Wine. Ready to explore?" Emma winked—an exaggerated blink that boosted Cassie into an I-can-do-this determination.

Cassie sucked in her stomach, straightened her shoulders, and lifted her chin. "Does Jack deal with rodents too?"

"He might lend you his cat."

"I'd love a pet, but I'm on the road so much it wouldn't be fair. That's part of my man problem. I meet someone promising and have to leave. When I get back to base, I find another smart woman has snapped him up."

"You put too much pressure on yourself. This is a holiday. Sun. Fresh air. My company."

"Duly noted. I have the key." She retrieved the key, still thankfully in her pocket, and fit it into the lock. It turned, and she pushed. Nothing happened. She twisted the key again and shoved. The wooden barrier flew open and, taken by surprise, Cassie toppled through the doorway.

Something big—huge—bounded from the nearby sitting room. Cassie screamed as a second jumped at her with a panicked *baa*.

"Cassie? Are you okay? Holy Hannah. Where did those sheep come from?"

On hands and knees, Cassie peeked into the sitting room and saw it was clear of sheep. "The door wasn't locked." She groaned as she shoved herself upright.

"Is the back door open?"

"Let's see." Cassie picked her way down the passage and stepped over a soldier-straight line of beer cans, her heart breaking at the destruction. Witty curses in lime-green spray-paint adorned the walls. Sheep manure peppered the faded blue carpet. A sheep—well, a lamb, since it was small—leaped through the kitchen doorway and disappeared through an open door. "Mystery solved." She shut the door.

"Wait, we'd better check all the rooms."

"Good point." Cassie turned and stood in poop. "Ugh, my favorite shoes."

They searched for more sheep, but luckily, they'd departed en masse.

"Cassie, you can't stay here tonight."

"No." Cassie sighed, slumping as she watched five sheep burst through a gap in the fence and disappear. "The place needs TLC first. Since we're here, I'd like to make a list of what needs doing. I have paper and pen in the SUV."

"Still resisting computers?"

"Digital has its place. I use phones. I read e-books. I Google as much as the next girl, but the tactile sensations of paper and pen help me to focus."

Emma laughed, her blue eyes alight with mischief. Happiness and contentment radiated from her, and without warning, an envy-bomb pierced Cassie's chest, so painful she rubbed the spot. Comparisons sprang to mind, a woe-is-me attitude shoving forward like a whiny child. Heck...

Aghast at the surge of jealousy, Cassie forced a pained grin and fled to collect her notebook while bitch-slapping her shrill inner child.

"Most of the mess and damage inside is superficial," Emma said on her return. "Painting and cleaning up the rubbish. I rang Jack. He said he wouldn't mind oysters and wasn't busy. He's bringing Hone with him."

"Who's Hone? I don't remember you mentioning him."

"He's George's oldest son. Hone works at George Taniwha and Sons with us."

"He's a private investigator too?"

"Yes. Don't worry. You'll like him. Where do you want to start?"

Cassie, who, after her harsh self-lecture, had re-entered the friend mindset, scanned the kitchen. "Might as well start here. New kitchen units, definitely. It's a spacious room. Grandma always used to have a table. I have no idea what happened to that." She jotted in bullet points. *Table. Units. Breakfast bar?*

"The place has good bones. You'll need to chuck the carpet since the sheep have made a mess. Should we pull up a piece to see if you have wooden floorboards?"

With those words of encouragement, Cassie's residual envy slipped away, and excitement replaced the destructive emotion. Grandad had never updated, especially after her grandmother died. A project might settle the angst that had trailed her during her last tour. At the very least, it would give her a base to use when she wanted to recharge.

"That was Emma. Her friend's house is a mess, and she asked if I'd mow the long grass for her." Jack speared his spade into the ground. He ran a hand through his straight black hair, cut on a regular basis now that he'd married Emma, and picked up his black T-shirt. "I said I'd go and help. You want to come?"

"Why? That sounds like more work. Why are you digging up perfectly good lawn again?"

"Emma wants a vegetable garden."

Hone stretched, not minding the physical labor but complaining for form's sake. He grounded his spade and wiped the sweat off his forehead.

"Emma's friend is paying in oysters."

Hone reached for his T-shirt. "I haven't had a feed of shellfish for ages. Where are we going?"

"Clevedon. We can hit the beach once we're finished. If the tide is right, we can collect cockles at Kawakawa Bay."

"Throw in a beer at the pub, and you're on."

Jack eyed him. "You look disgustingly satisfied. Thought you'd complain more or say you have a hot date."

"Nope. At present, my taniwha is a lazy slug. You have Emma to satiate your dragon's appetite for sex. I had the Geraldine twins. Many times," he added with a wink.

"Hell. Don't tell Emma."

Hone shrugged. "So shoot me. My taniwha and I love sex. Full moon last night. I needed the sex to maintain control. Aunt June doesn't approve of dragons flying through the sky letting off flares of fire. Says it upsets the authorities. Dad reiterates her lectures so it's either rebellion or sex since Manu's invention isn't working yet."

"Yeah, sucks being a taniwha sometimes. At least I can swim if necessary, and Emma knows what to do if that ever happens."

"You're a lucky man." Nothing less than the truth, but Hone didn't add the rest of his thoughts. He loved sex and wouldn't apologize for it, but at the back of his mind, he'd started to yearn for more. A partner with whom he could be himself. That hadn't, however, stopped him from trotting out his rules to every woman he *dated*.

One—technically, he didn't date, and what he had was fun, consensual encounters.

Two—leave them as friends. No drama and angst that way.

And three—make rules clear at the start.

Jack turned toward his garden shed. "I'll load the mower."

His friend pulled Hone's mind from women and rules. "If the grass is long, a slasher might work better. A chainsaw might come in handy. Stop at home on the way. Dad won't mind if we borrow his tools."

Jack's phone rang. Emma again. Hone heard her sultry voice as she spoke to Jack. Something to pry up old carpet and mouse traps.

Soon, they were on their way to Clevedon.

As always, leaving the city excited his taniwha, but after the indulgences of sex in many positions, it wasn't difficult to keep his human form. Instead, he opened the passenger side window and stuck out his head, inhaling the fresher country air.

Jack shot him *the look*, his dark brows scrunched in disapproval. "Quit acting like a dog."

Hone let the insult roll right off him, content with his world. "Does Emma's friend realize how many oysters we'll eat?"

"Behave," Jack warned. "Cassie and Emma have been friends since they were in primary school."

"She know about taniwhas?" He held up a hand and spoke before Jack could reply. "Scratch that. Emma wouldn't blab." Hone stuck his head farther out the window and dragged in myriad country scents—animals, grass, trees, a few people—ignoring Jack's grumbles to delight in the crisp air.

Jack drove fast but with expert control and the journey didn't take long.

Hone straightened, his eyes narrowing at the idea of a woman—any woman—living in such isolation. "This place is in the middle of nowhere."

"This place is a dump." Jack stated the obvious as he parked beside a red SUV.

Hone studied the wooden bungalow. The building had a sturdy frame. Sure, it was missing a few boards and needed repainting. "It will be better once the grass is cut. You go and tell Emma we're here, and I'll start unloading. Glad we brought the chainsaw. Those trees will need trimming. Take away the gloom."

"Might take more. Depends what the inside is like." Jack climbed from the vehicle, his ground-eating steps taking him to the door.

Hone, used to Jack and his abruptness, didn't take offense. He set to work unloading the mower and tools. The thump of Jack's knock on the door, his call, and the feminine response brought warmth to Hone's heart, a sense of rightness. At one time, he'd considered hooking up with Emma, but anyone but an idiot could see she wanted Jack. Hell, Jack had been an idiot. Oblivious until a case on Waiheke Island in the Hauraki Gulf forced them together. Add in a full moon, and Jack hadn't stood a chance.

Not that his friend seemed unhappy. Emma was good for Jack, jerking him from his taciturn behavior. These days, he smiled more readily, behaved more human.

Hone adjusted the mower to a high setting, ripped off his T-shirt, and began his attack on the long grass. No need for a catcher. Hopefully, the mower wouldn't have a spastic attack and refuse to work.

He started on the right-hand side and discovered an overgrown concrete path on his third round of the lawn. The sun beat down overhead, and he paused to wipe the sweat from his brow with his forearm. Jack trotted outside with Emma and another woman. Emma waved, and he returned the greeting. He recommenced his mowing pattern.

Jack said something to the women and strode to his work vehicle. He handed Emma a hammer and a crowbar. Hone chortled as Jack offered a comment to his wife. Advice probably. Emma with tools. He couldn't wait to see what she intended to do with those.

On his next circuit, Jack gestured at the trees. The friend nodded, and she and Emma retreated. Jack hadn't mentioned the friend was attractive, although to be honest, he hadn't asked because an innocent question might make Emma consider matchmaking. Women did that stuff. Not gonna happen.

But from what he could see, the friend rocked some serious curves. Not as tall as Emma, which meant she would reach his shoulders in height. Long black hair gathered in a messy ponytail. Too far away to see the minute details, such as whether she had freckles or white teeth or an agreeable scent. Not that it mattered. A short-term involvement with the friend would make his interaction with Emma difficult and would piss off Jack.

Yeah, he'd quell his natural inclination to flirt. Keep his boots firmly planted in the friend zone.

# CHAPTER 2

**M**atthew Jamieson scanned the neighboring property through binoculars. Two men. Could be innocent. Could be trouble. Could be a pain in his arse. One man mowed the grass and the other cut back trees and the encroaching undergrowth. He cursed under his breath. This might interrupt the harvest, muck up his retirement plans.

Damn, he'd known he shouldn't use the land, but it had been the best solution. Hell, a brilliant answer to his problem. He'd made an offer to purchase via his solicitor and been summarily rejected. The owner vetoed his second increased offer. He hadn't liked to make a third and arouse curiosity.

Place was a dump, the land acreage too small for economic farming. None of his investigations turned up details about

C Miller-Pope, other than his name. His inability to extract information from the law firm handling the property had irked him, but after almost nine months of inactivity, he'd decided it was safe to make use of the land to increase his drug production area.

Mistake.

He'd sensed it in his gut yet forged ahead anyway. Taken a calculated risk.

"Fuck." Matt placed the binoculars on the nearby table and rubbed his face, mind racing, playing the angles as he paced. He halted at the desk in the corner, spinning to return to the cluster of chairs arranged to take advantage of the view.

Yeah, that might work.

He plucked his cell phone from his pocket and rang Herbert, his top man. In a crisp voice, he issued instructions, then disconnected. He stared through the window of his upstairs lounge, his gaze trailing the man mowing grass.

With a harsh sigh, he settled in his favorite chair and reached for the bottle of imported beer he'd opened earlier.

The ability to roll with life's punches had turned him into a successful businessman. This was nothing but a small bump on the road to his empire. His plan to retire with his son would go ahead. He refused to allow an alternative.

"You could have warned me about his Supreme Hunkiness. *Just a workmate,* you said. His panty-wetting grin…" Cassie broke off, unwilling to share the extent of her instant arousal. She cleared her throat. "All that hotness needs a license."

"He's a flirt. Women adore him," Emma agreed. "But a warning. As much as I love Hone, he's not interested in settling with one woman. If you want a holiday fling, Hone is your man. If you're looking for more, and I suspect you are, try man-shopping in another market."

"He's almost as sexy as Jack." Cassie's gaze followed Hone's progress as he cut the overgrown grass. Tall, over six foot. Messy black hair in need of a cut to tame the curls. Probably brown eyes, given his Māori descent and coloring. Muscles that rippled with each circuit of her lawn, a hairless chest, and intriguing tattoos on his back and left biceps. Not an ounce of surplus flesh on him. Easy to see this since he'd whipped off his T-shirt and wore only shorts. She sighed. "It might be worth a dented heart to spend time bumping uglies with him."

A choked gasp came from Emma, and Cassie turned to gape at her friend. She'd turned red in the face attempting to hold back her laughter. Well, Cassie couldn't have that. She gave a thumbs-up sign, waggled her eyebrows, and worked to hold back the giggles tickling her throat.

Emma exploded in an unladylike guffaw. Seconds later, Cassie let her own amusement loose. They chortled and gasped until they held each other to stay upright. Cassie hadn't laughed this hard for ages, and as she wiped away her mirth and replaced her glasses, she was glad she'd insisted on taking a break, even if it had left Kevin pissed and grumpy.

She picked up the hammer and the crowbar. "We'd better get started on this carpet."

"Oh no, you don't," Emma said, taking ownership of the tools. "You haven't outgrown the clumsy gene yet."

Funny, when her mother commented on her habitual clumsiness, Cassie bristled enough to resemble a hedgehog. When her friend did the same thing, she handed over the tools without argument.

"All right. You pull out the tacks, and I'll roll up the strips."

They set to work with much chatter to catch up on the things each of them had done since their last letter.

"It must be fun traveling to new places," Emma said, pausing to wipe her forehead.

After the usual unsettled December weather of muggy temperatures and precipitation, summer had arrived with a roar in the New Year, the dry conditions and lack of forecast rain setting farmers grumbling about drought. Cassie didn't care about the weather, happy to be back with her friend and in the place she called home.

"It was exciting—for a while—but one hotel room resembles the next. It's lonely," she confessed. "I sing at a venue, pack up, travel to the next city, and repeat. The constant travel is exhausting. The promo events are nerve-racking. You'd think they'd get easier. They don't. My bubbly blonde act has a price, even though it offers me anonymity when I step back for a break." At first, her wigs and costumes had been a coping mechanism for stage fright. A smokescreen when she became confident. A diva. A star. Now, fatigue weighed on her shoulders. Exhaustion had left her questioning her path and she had no idea of what to do to make things better.

"So, what have you decided to do?"

"Kevin wants me to try some crossover songs. More pop than country. Then, once I break out, he wants to do a world tour."

Emma shot her a look of concern. "You don't sound keen."

"It's the touring part. It's isolating and strenuous, physically and emotionally. Kevin wants to sign me with a bigger label."

"Can you do that?" Emma returned to ripping up carpet tacks.

"My contract is almost at an end with Kevin and the label. I've fulfilled my obligations. I have new contract offers from both, but I haven't signed anything yet." She shrugged and stood to stretch abused muscles. "That's something else to worry about."

"What do you want to do?"

Cassie chuckled, amused and impressed. "You're the first person to ask me that."

"Do you know?"

"I want to write new songs."

"Genre?"

Cassie cocked her head, considering. "I have the urge to write more upbeat stuff. That part gels with Kevin, but I'm sick, sick, *sick* of syrupy-sweet ballads about cheating and broken hearts. Kevin wants the pop version of syrupy-sweet."

"Would you like my opinion?"

"What?"

"You've already decided what you want to do, but you're scared of Kevin's reaction."

"How do you figure that?"

Emma stood. "Because you're my best friend. I understand your thought processes almost as well as my own."

Speechless, she gaped at Emma. "Kevin wants me to change up my image."

"Wait." Emma held up her hand. "Don't tell me. He wants you to lose weight."

"Yes."

"What do you think about that part?"

"I'm tired of people commenting on my weight. I've always been big, but I do eat healthily, especially when I'm on the road. I exercise, and my weight stays the same. I feel good. That's what I told him. We argued about it."

"I see." Emma's expression hit enigmatic, but Cassie understood her views on busybody know-it-alls.

"Kevin keeps leaving me messages. I'm not talking to him."

"I see."

Cassie scowled. "What do you see?"

Emma applauded, mischief illuminating her like a diva in a spotlight. "That you're finally getting a set of balls."

A snort escaped Cassie. It was true. She'd started standing up for herself with Kevin and not letting him steamroll right over her or rush her into decisions. A recent occurrence, and one that gave her a measure of pride. She should've found her backbone much earlier.

"What did your stars say?"

Cassie blushed. "I can't believe you remembered I read my stars every day."

"Nothing wrong with that. It's a fun quirk."

"Last month, the forecast that slipped into my inbox implied I had a big decision to make and I should trust my gut instincts. Later that day, Kevin hit me with his vision of my future. I said I'd consider it instead of agreeing."

"Good for you."

"Can you help me roll up this piece of carpet? It's huge."

"I'll help," a husky masculine voice said from behind her.

Cassie let out an *eep* and twisted too fast. Her feet tangled, and she landed hard on her butt. "Ouch." She flicked down the skirts of her dress and surreptitiously rubbed her abused behind. "I thought padding was meant to help cushion clumsiness."

"Sorry." Hone's amusement flooded his face—lips, wrinkled

nose, and ended in his magnetic chocolate-brown eyes. He shot a quick, searching glance at Emma before crouching beside her.

Yep, sex-on-a-stick, and she badly wanted to lick every inch of bared skin. When Cassie realized her mouth gaped, she clamped her jaw shut. She'd been right about the eye color. However, his charisma and sex appeal, the lustful jolt to her nerve-endings when she stared at him... Nothing could prepare a woman for that sizzle.

"Not a thing wrong with your padding." Hone winked and stroked his finger over her cheek. "Cobweb. You don't want to walk around with spider silk on your pretty face."

"Stop flirting with her." Emma's expression held disapproval. "Have you finished the lawn?"

"Ran out of petrol."

He stood and prowled—there was no other word for it—across the room to squat at the far edge of the big piece of worn blue carpet. "Ready?"

Cassie blinked from her reverie and readied herself to roll her end. With Hone's help, the process ran smoothly. They stacked the last piece with the others against the wall and moved into the next room, where Emma was already busy lifting tacks.

"Why is there sheep shit everywhere?" Hone eyed the graffiti on the wall. "The tags are recent."

Cassie scowled at the slogans. Red in this room. "There were sheep here when we came inside. The vandals left the back door open, or at least that's my assumption."

"How did they get in?"

"The front door wasn't locked."

"You're not staying here tonight," Hone said.

Not a question. A statement.

Cassie lifted her chin to give him attitude. Her scowl bounced right off his flirtatious grin.

"I have no idea what they did with the furniture," she said. "I had intended to stay, but the house has been stripped. The lawyer organized someone to clean the house. At least that was my assumption. I'll have to ask him about Grandad's private stuff."

"He didn't tell you?" Hone asked.

Cassie exchanged an I-bet-I-know-what-happened glance with Emma. "My parents probably had a hand in the house clearing. They assumed my father would inherit but Grandad left the property to me."

Hone's gaze skimmed her, their surroundings. "You said the front door was unlocked?"

"The lawyer made a point of giving me the keys, so it should've been locked."

"I'll see if I can find where they broke inside." Hone stalked from the room, his exit as quiet as his entrance.

"That man needs bells," she said to Emma, surreptitiously rubbing her butt again.

"Where will you stay?"

"I'll book a motel room in Papakura until I can replace furniture and have new locks fitted."

"I can sort out the locks for you," Hone said.

Cassie started and clapped her hand to her racing heart. "Will you stop creeping around?"

"I'll wear my bells tomorrow," Hone deadpanned.

"You heard that?"

"He has the hearing of a bat," Emma said. "So does Jack. It's a PI thing."

"My Auntie June runs a motel in Papakura. I'll give her a call if you want a room," Hone offered.

"You heard that too?"

Hone full-out grinned. Yep, lethal, and she'd become a victim. Heat spilled into her cheeks, and she had to focus on hiding her unease.

"Should I ring Auntie?"

"Yes, please. I'd like to book in for a week."

"You want the carpet lifted in the other rooms?" Jack's voice came from behind her.

Cassie whirled. "What is wrong with you two? My pulse rate is still erratic after my unexpected meeting with the sheep. I don't need men creeping around giving me a heart attack on top of that."

Jack lifted a dark brow. "Carpet? The other rooms?"

"Yes, please." Cassie watched them leave, admiring the view.

A sharp nudge in her ribs jolted her from the mesmerizing sight.

"Stop ogling my man."

"Sorry. Jack makes me nervous, but the view is fine." She double-checked for possible eavesdroppers. "Mostly, I was gawking at Hone."

"He's charming, but he's a player." Emma's brow furrowed. "I can tell he's interested in playing with you, so be careful. He *will* break your heart."

"Kevin already broke my heart."

"You wrote you'd broken things off, but you never said why. I didn't ask because I figured you'd tell me when you were ready."

"And that is why you're my best friend. You understand when to push or hold back. I...Kevin had asked me to marry him. I was ecstatic. I decided to surprise him in his hotel room with a home-cooked meal. I walked in on him in bed with a man and a woman."

"A couple?" Intrigue played over Emma's features.

"A backup singer and her boyfriend roadie. The three of them were having a fine old time when I pranced into the bedroom."

"What did you do?"

"I tipped the dinner over them. I'd like to say I did it on purpose, but there were clothes everywhere. I tripped over a pair of jeans and lost my balance."

"Oh." Emma's lips quirked. "What did you cook for dinner?"

"Hungarian goulash with noodles, steamed carrots and broccoli. The bright colors contrasted nicely with the white bed linens. I chucked the ring at Kevin." Her shoulders slumped as she recalled that part. "I missed and hit the backup singer. Gave her a black eye."

"She deserved it. Why haven't you sacked Kevin?"

"He's good at his job and we had a contract. All the shows were sold out. I couldn't bail."

"You mentioned the contract."

"It runs out a week after my label contract. Kevin didn't want to chain himself to me if I wasn't a success. He was taking a chance on an unknown. I understood his caution."

Hone listened to the rise and fall of the women's voices as he and Jack lifted strips of carpet to reveal dusty wooden boards. Native kauri wood. Once treated and polished, they'd gleam and last for years.

"What does Cassie do for a job?" The woman made him curious, and he wanted to learn more.

Jack didn't lift his head but continued yanking tacks from the floorboards. "Emma said she works as an assistant to a country singer."

Hone wrinkled his nose. "Country? Broken hearts and such?"

"Yeah, I don't get the appeal either."

"Cassie is more intriguing by the minute."

Jack lifted his head, his jaw clenched. "Don't mess with her, Hone. She's like Emma. A keeper. She's not for a man like you."

Hone battened down his irritation, confining himself to a jerk of his chin. He pulled out his phone to call Auntie June, the matriarch dragon of the Auckland tribe and businesswoman with property. "You know me. I don't do permanent. I have rules."

"Yeah, yeah." Jack went back to ripping up tacks. "As long as you stick to your bloody rules with Cassie."

# CHAPTER 3

"Auntie June invited me to dinner." Hone ended his call. "I told her I was with you, and she said to pass the invitation to you and Emma."

"I heard. What about Cassie?" Jack paused ripping up the carpet to study him. "You gonna ask her? Could open a can of matchmaking worms."

"Too late now. Cassie is invited."

"Your auntie still trying to marry you and your cousins off?"

"Didn't you hear her sly tone? She'll have better luck with one of her sons 'cause I am wise to her ways. Or I could take Cassie myself," he mused, his dragon making a purring sound of approval.

"Don't hurt that woman, Hone. I won't tell you again. The next time I'll lead with my fists. Don't hurt Cassie. Emma will get upset, which, in turn, will make me unhappy. You hear me?"

"Yes," Hone snapped. "I'm not a damn monster."

"Not true," Jack contradicted, and this time his voice held sympathy. "We're both monsters, and right now, yours is showing more than mine. Your irises are glowing red, and your claws are visible beneath your fingernails."

*Crap.* Jack was right. He worked at mentally caging his taniwha. "I'll check with Cassie and ring Auntie June back outside. Fresh air always helps me with control."

He left Jack tearing up carpet and scowled at the red paint on the wall as he strode from the room. *Bikies rule.* Little pricks. Cassie seemed like a nice lady. He might put out a few feelers when he saw his cousins. They had their ear to the ground and would have a good idea of who was responsible for the vandalism. If it was a local gang.

He ducked into the room where Cassie and Emma labored over carpet rolls and prayed his control would hold long enough to issue the invitation.

"Are you sure it's all right?" Cassie asked.

"It's fine." Emma aimed a furtive scowl at him. Her tone remained light for her friend. "You'll like June and Samuel."

"Okay. Thanks," Cassie said.

"I'll tell Auntie June." Pressure built in Hone's chest—his taniwha pushing for release. Hone slapped him back with a testy growl. At this rate, he'd need to find a willing woman for sex. Again. Either that or go for a clandestine flight, which was more problematic in these days of modern technology. Luckily, they had a few inventors and gadgets of their own to confuse satellite imagining and navigational equipment, or at least they would once his cousin, Manu, perfected his latest invention. He strode outside.

Once his claws bled back into his skin, he rang his auntie to confirm they would all be there for dinner.

"Hone! Should I invite Irene Wharerau? She said she hadn't seen you for a while."

"I'm dating, Auntie," he said in a stern voice. "I'm not interested in anything other than friendship with Irene."

"I see," his Auntie said, her tone designed to raise his guilt.

He could picture her face, her unusual light green eyes that came from the mixed European and Māori blood in her ancestry, her furrowed brow and the determined jut of her jaw. Auntie June considered herself a matchmaker with an excellent result rate, and as matriarch and leader of the tribe, she didn't accept gainsaying.

"I haven't known her for long, so don't make any smart comments about marriage. I don't want you to scare her off." Hone heard himself say the words, his mind screaming at him to stop before the hole he dug engulfed him. Meanwhile, his inner dragon purred again, the contented sound making his human side itch with discomfort. What the hell?

"Depends," Auntie June said. "Who is she? Why haven't I

heard? Bring her with you."

"Auntie," he growled. "Please. You want babies to cuddle, you work on Jack or one of your sons. I'm not ready to settle with one woman. I'll come alone." He refused to take a date to his aunt's home.

"Humph."

Not impressed. Too bad. He enjoyed his single lifestyle. "What time should we arrive?"

"Whenever you're ready. Tane and Kahurangi will be here around six. You'd better be careful one of my boys doesn't steal your new girl from under your nose. At least they have open minds about settling with one woman."

Hone held back a snort. His auntie wouldn't appreciate his feedback on this particular point. His cousins told June what she wanted to hear and went their own sweet way. They weren't stupid, but it took skill to keep ahead of their mother.

"Thanks, Auntie. We'll see you later. Anything you want? We're in Clevedon and stopping by the oyster place."

"Get me two dozen oysters in the shell," she said, her voice less strident now. "You're a good boy. If only you'd take advice in the spirit it was offered."

Hone grimaced at his aunt's last shot and slipped his phone into his pocket. His skin itched in a slightly different way, telling him someone was watching him. He bent to check his shoelace, casually glancing around at the same time. A flash caught his eye, but he didn't make the mistake of staring. The knowledge was enough. Someone was spying on him with a pair of binoculars.

Interesting.

He'd mention it to Jack and perhaps investigate the owners of the neighboring property. Of course, the binoculars might mean curiosity, but the snoopy neighbor might have seen something useful.

When he wandered back inside, he found everyone in a bedroom. A bedframe and a mattress bearing nasty stains, plus several beer bottles and empty crisp packets, told an interesting story. "A trysting spot?"

Jack's brows rose, his somber face lightening. "A tryst? Who says that word?"

"Auntie June," Hone said. "She said lots of other words just now. Most of them involved subtle matchmaking."

"Aw, that's so sweet," Emma cooed.

"Jack, am I allowed to smack her butt?"

"Hell, no. That's my job."

Emma winked at her man. "You're very good at it too."

"Do they carry on like this all the time?" Cassie sidled closer to Hone.

Hone grunted. "Isn't it disgusting? I'm glad you're here to save me. Auntie June wants us to buy her two dozen oysters in their shells. She said to turn up around six."

"I'm dusty and grubby after lifting the carpets. I'd like to go swimming. When's high tide?" Emma asked.

"Later this afternoon," Jack said. "It should be on its way in now."

Hone watched Cassie. He couldn't explain his fascination with the woman. Although he enjoyed women of all shapes and sizes, Cassie's robust frame and abundant curves did it for him. She wasn't traditionally pretty with her strong features and bold eyebrows, but the black-framed glasses gave her a cute librarian look, and he adored the sun dress. It cupped her full breasts and fell in a swish of frothy fabric to her knees. The woman had serious legs—long and supple—and her toenails sported bright pink nail polish. His gaze zapped back to her dress. The fabric was blue and covered with cat heads, almost cartoonish since each sported a pink bow and pink-framed glasses. His lips twitched as he fought a full-out grin. Any woman who wore a dress like that didn't take herself too seriously.

"This is the only furniture," Cassie said. "Would you help me put it outside before we leave? And the old carpet too? Then I can organize someone to dump them for me."

"You want the stuff out front?" Jack asked. "Near the vehicles?"

"Yes, please."

"Mattress first?" Hone asked Jack.

"Yup."

It was almost an hour before they cleared the house.

"Are we done?" Hone asked. "I'm ready to hit the beach, and

I'm starving. What say we drive to Maraetai and get fish and chips? We can grab our oysters on the way back to Papakura."

"Works for me," Jack said. "Cassie?"

"Great idea. I'll buy lunch. It's the least I can do after you've helped me all morning."

"We'll meet you there," Emma said. "We're going to lock the doors."

Hone's taniwha growled, and he rushed into speech to cover the sound. "You need new locks. The existing ones aren't worth shit."

Jack narrowed his gaze, probably as a warning to him to get a grip on his beast. Unfortunately, Cassie fascinated his dragon, enticing him to play. Fine for his dragon, but he—the man—hesitated at the idea of confining himself to one woman. His taniwha had turned contrary and seemed to have a permanent arrangement in mind. No wonder confusion rode him, yanking him over to his taniwha's point of view. He shook himself and planted his feet over the line to the bachelor side. Immediately, a growl vibrated through him.

Hone cursed under his breath. He foresaw turmoil in his future. Probably best if he followed Jack's advice and stayed the hell away from temptation.

"Thank you for helping," Cassie said to Emma as she turned onto the coast road. The sea sparkled beneath the overhead sun, and even though summer was well-advanced, some of the gnarled pohutukawa trees still bore their crimson flowers. She'd missed this while she'd lived in the States. Once the pohutukawas bloomed, it truly felt as if summer was on the way.

"No problem. It beats doing laundry and housework at home. What's next for the house?"

"New locks and deadbolts on the windows. A security system. If the local youngsters have taken to using the place as a knocking shop, I need a deterrent."

Emma spluttered. "Is that what they taught you in those posh schools in the States? Words like knocking shop?"

"I didn't spend all my time at school," Cassie said primly. "Some of my friends came from England and taught me the slang."

"Good to hear. What about inside the house? Decorating-wise, I mean?"

"The walls are in good condition, apart from the graffiti. I'll paint everything a neutral color, if I can get paint to cover the spray-paint. The floors are great. I'll scrub them and coat them with a clear seal. I still love to sew and might buy a machine to make curtains. Once that's done, I can buy furniture and move in, sooner if I can finish the main bedroom and get the kitchen sorted. Maybe a bit ambitious for a month, but I'll do as much as I can before I leave."

Emma frowned. "You're so isolated. What happens if those yahoos turn up in the middle of the night?"

"From memory, there are three farms farther down my road. I

might go and introduce myself to the neighbors. Clevedon has a community cop. I'll stop by and report the vandalism and ask if anyone else has had problems."

"All good ideas," Emma said. "The place doesn't seem as creepy now that Jack has trimmed back the undergrowth and the lawn is cut. Obvious signs of habitation might do the trick with the vandals."

"True. Are you going swimming? I didn't pack my swimsuit and no way am I swimming in my underwear. I'll stick to paddling."

"Jack loves the water. He taught me to swim. At least I manage to stay afloat for longer now. If it's too cold to swim in the sea, we go to the public pool. It's heated in the winter. Anyway, long story short, Jack has probably grabbed my swimsuit for me."

Cassie studied her friend. Easy to perceive her happiness, her spark, her satisfaction with the status quo. From their regular letters, she'd known Emma had a crush on Jack, and given her friend's descriptions, she'd wondered if they'd last. But now, seeing them together, her concern dispersed. Jack adored Emma and touched her often in a casual manner. He lit up whenever he looked at her friend. That spear of envy struck again, and she focused on the road.

"I wish I could meet someone like Jack."

"You will. You want my advice?"

"No."

"Too bad. My advice is to take advantage of your break while you make decisions about your future. Get out and meet people. I'll introduce you around. Accept a few dates and live. Enjoy yourself, and even if you don't find a man, you'll probably get material for your songwriting."

Emma was right. She had to stop worrying about getting hurt again and take a few risks. At the very least, she'd make new friends, which was something she sorely lacked, given the amount of time she spent on the road.

They rounded the corner, and Maraetai beach came into view. The wharf appeared more dilapidated than the one in her memory, and the old homes had gone, replaced by modern two-level houses designed to take advantage of the sea views. The beach, however, remained the same as it had during her childhood visits. A long expanse of foreshore, covered with broken shells and sand, looked pristine. Small waves tumbled and rushed over each other, racing toward the high-tide mark. A mother and two toddlers played at the edge of the waves, the children's high-pitched squeaks bringing a smile to her face.

One day she'd like to have children. Her mouth firmed as she climbed from her rental. She'd be a good parent—not an absentee one.

Huh, perhaps that was part of the reason she was digging in her heels when it came to committing to another long tour. Something to consider...

"I'm going to get my swimsuit," Emma said. "The guys will

want to eat first."

Cassie's belly rumbled at the idea of food. "I'll come and take orders, then go and buy our lunch while you're changing."

Four hours later, Cassie dragged her two bags from the rear of her rental and hauled them into her motel room. Jack and Emma had offered to pick her up and drive her to the barbecue, but she'd decided it was better to drive herself. Give herself an escape route.

Right now, she could do with a hot bath since her muscles screamed, her body protesting her morning's exertions.

Spotlessly clean, the motel room had one room dominated by a double bed and a kitchenette to do basic cooking. A square, two-person table with chairs rounded out the amenities in the cream and brown room. Like many motels she'd stayed in over the years, it lacked personality. A few photos around the place would help since she intended to stay here for at least a week.

She dumped her bag and strode into the bathroom. A shower. Well, that would do. She unzipped her dress and peeled it off.

A knock sounded on the door.

"Just a sec!" *Ugh.* She scooped up the dress and yanked it back over her head.

The knock sounded again.

"Coming," she repeated, a fraction louder.

Of course, she tangled her arms, jamming them in the wrong gaps, and she cursed under her breath as she fumbled to right the material and put her arms in the sleeve holes.

Out of breath, hot and bothered, she jerked open the door. A gorgeous man stood there holding a carton of milk. Of Māori descent, he had golden skin and brown eyes beneath jet-black brows. His features combined to give him eye-popping male beauty. This man would never be short of a date. He did a slow body scan, gestured at her dress, and she glanced at her feet.

The hem was tucked up, displaying an abundance of winter-white thigh. She flicked the fabric back in place, uncomfortable with the heat that filled her face. She'd bet she glowed like a child's night-light.

She coughed to clear her throat. "Can I help you?"

"Ma sent me to deliver the milk." He handed over the small carton. "My name is Manu. I'm the oldest in the family. And just so you know, Ma could have left the milk in your fridge earlier, but she's a matchmaker at heart. She must've taken a liking to you when she checked you into the motel."

"Thank you. I'm Cassie."

"Ma said you're coming to our place tonight. She told me to ask if you needed a ride."

"Jack and Emma volunteered to pick me up, but I said I'd drive myself."

"Ah, giving yourself an exit strategy." Manu squinted over his shoulder. "Do you have a minute to talk?"

"Um, I was just about to jump into the shower. I brought half of the beach home with me."

"Please. Just a few quick words," Manu persisted. "It will help us both."

"All right." Clutching her milk to her chest, she stepped back and gestured for Manu to enter. She didn't think he'd be a threat, given his mother owned the place.

"As I said, Ma likes you, and she has decided you and I would work well together. I'm gonna be truthful here. You're Emma's friend, and you seem like a nice woman, but I'm happy with my single status. I'm not looking for serious, but I do enjoy women. I wondered if you'd agree to go to the barbecue with me. We could get to know each other, and even if we don't click, I'm sure we'd make good friends. Ma would be happy because she'd think I'd met someone suitable, and she'd stop her matchmaking, at least for a while."

"And why should I agree to this?"

"Since Ma approves of you, you're in danger of her machinations, too. We could help each other."

Humor snaked through Cassie, but she restrained her impulse to smile. She didn't want him to decide she was a pushover. "I understand you have three brothers."

"Yeah. Kahurangi, Tane and Haurahi. If you give me the heave-ho she'll aim you toward Tane or Kahurangi or my cousin, Hone. We need to stomp on this maneuvering before she gets out of control."

"Your mother seemed very nice."

Manu hesitated as if he was weighing his words. "She liked you too. She knows people, has the instinct to sense the good ones, and she's never wrong. She's convinced you'd make an excellent addition to our family."

Cassie raked his expression, searching for truth. Manu meant every word. He wasn't spinning a line. "I'm here for a month before I fly to Los Angeles. I told your mother that, but okay." She held out her hand. "Friends."

He cocked his head. "Only friends?"

Funny. She hadn't experienced the same blip of lust she had with Hone. "Yes, you're pretty and charming. Sexy. I bet you have a lot of lady friends."

"You think I'm sexy?"

Cassie snorted. "And that's what he distills from my words. Thank you for the milk. What time should I be ready to leave?"

"Six-thirty," he said. "The others will start arriving around six, but we want Ma to pay attention and decide her scheme has a good chance of success. Do you have jeans?"

"Yes," Cassie said, wondering what clothing had to do with anything.

"Good. Wear jeans and bring a jacket because it will get cooler later tonight. The farm is on the estuary, near a river mouth. It's a beautiful spot, but it can get a bit cold." He switched up his charisma, his features glowing with bad-boy charm, and leaned closer. "When you're in the shower, don't forget to wash your face." He tapped a finger on her cheek, then the tip of her nose. "You have dirt right here. See you later, beautiful." And with a wink and a flash of white teeth, he strolled away, whistling.

With her right hand pressed to her face, Cassie stared after him. No, she ogled his butt. Might as well be truthful to herself.

She sighed. Nothing more compelling than a confident bad boy, and she had a feeling that the Taniwha cousins prided their membership in the bad-boy club.

# CHAPTER 4

At six-thirty, she checked her appearance. Smart but casual. At one minute past the appointed hour, she admitted to nerves as she wiped sweaty palms on her jeans. Manu had laid out the truth. He wanted friendship and nothing more. According to Emma, Hone attracted women like a magnet on steroids. He loved women, and they loved him in return. Both men were sexy and had that bad-boy vibe going for them.

That was what she needed. A holiday fling. It wasn't something she'd done in the past, but that was because of a lack of opportunity.

A slow grin worked across her lips. Fun and a research opportunity for her songwriting. Win-win. But then, the good-girl part of her—the sector of personality inherited from her mother—spoke up. She'd get hurt. She didn't do casual sex because she needed an emotional connection to function.

A vehicle pulled up outside, and a knock sounded. She grabbed her bag and opened the door.

"I like a woman who doesn't keep me waiting."

Cassie's brows rose, and she pushed her glasses up her nose.

He flashed her another of his panty-wetting grins. "Don't get me wrong. Unhurried and slow is good for some things, but for dinner at the family home. Not so much."

Her mind trotted right along where he led it—like a well-trained pet lamb. "Did you just mention sex and your parents in the same sentence?"

"A woman with a quick mind. Nice." He kissed her cheek. "It's a mild night. I brought my bike."

Her mouth opened. Bad timing. A bug took this as an invitation and flew right on in. She coughed, spluttered, and turned to her right to spit into a pot full of red petunias.

Manu took a giant step back, watching her act with interest. "A new mating dance?"

"A bug flew in my mouth." She shoved her fingers inside and managed to extract the very dead insect. "Yuck."

He held out his hand. "I brought a spare helmet for you."

Aware she'd already behaved with her usual gaucheness, she locked the door of her motel unit, took his hand, and followed along.

That pet lamb thing again. Something about this man brought out her clumsy in a big way.

"You ridden on a bike before? Here, I'll take your bag." He packed it in a compartment as he waited for her reply.

"No."

"You'll like it." He studied her hair. "It might be easier if you loosen your hair. You can fix it again when we get to the farm."

"Will my glasses be okay?"

"Depends if you want to see." The corner of his mouth twitched, that bad-boy smoothness making a reappearance.

Heck. A challenge. With trembling fingers, she tugged off her scrunchie. The glasses would stay. Song-writing opportunity, so she needed color and details during the ride to their destination.

"You have pretty hair. Is the color natural?"

"Yes." She saved the wigs and other artifices to improve her appearance for the stage. Katie-Jo's territory.

"Hard to tell these days," he said. "This is your helmet. Put it on, and I'll fasten the chin strap for you."

Bemused, she followed his instructions. Somehow, she guessed this man liked and cherished women. He also said what he thought, so she didn't have to second guess every nuance of their conversation. This idea pleased her.

He straddled the bike. "Get on behind and put your arms around my waist. Your feet go here." He indicated the spot for her feet. "When I lean into a corner, you lean the same way as me. Got all that?"

"Yes." She flung her leg over the back of the bike, did an awkward hop in between, muttered under her breath, but finally got her butt on the seat.

"Closer," Manu shouted. "I don't bite. Much."

She snorted. Even though she hadn't known Manu for long, she *knew* him. Charming flirt, yet his core of honesty made her comfortable, made her laugh. She inched closer and placed her arms around his waist. Warmth greeted her touch. He reached behind and yanked her nearer until her breasts flattened against his back.

The next second, they were off in a rush of wind. Her hair blew behind her and only his muscled strength and the competent way he drove kept her screech of panic behind closed lips.

Recalling his instructions, she held tight and didn't move an inch, except when he leaned into a corner. By the time they sped through country lanes, past a paddock of grazing thoroughbreds and an alpaca farm, she'd relaxed enough to enjoy the ride and actually use her glasses to see.

He shot down a series of roads and finally turned onto a long driveway.

He stopped outside a sprawling old house with six vehicles of various ages parked out front. The rumble of the bike ceased, and quietness filled the air.

"Everyone is here."

"Will I meet all your brothers tonight?"

"Not Haurahi, my youngest brother. He's married and lives in the South Island, not far from Lake Tekapo. He's Ma's favorite because he and his wife are expecting their first child."

Cassie recognized Jack's vehicle and was pleased she wasn't walking into a total room of strangers. Even after her time performing, meeting strangers made her uneasy.

"Hey, don't be nervous. My brothers only bite when asked politely. You've already met me, and I'm the troublemaker."

Cassie was still chuckling when she entered the house. The man radiated devilment—a carefree charm—and she could see why women would flock to him.

June, tall and robust, with long black hair and a stern face, approached them. "*Ae*, son. What am I going to do with you? Late again. We've been waiting."

"Cassie made me wait," Manu said.

Cassie gasped. "I did not."

"You've met my mother—June Taniwha."

"Thank you for inviting me, Mrs. Taniwha." Easy to see where Manu got his handsome genes. June Taniwha with her height and lithe figure would always draw a second glance, her light green eyes stunning against her long black hair.

"I told you to call me June, dear, when I checked you into your room."

Manu curled an arm around Cassie's waist and pulled her to his side before she could reply. "Cassie agreed to go out with me."

June Taniwha beamed. "I forgive your lateness, number one son."

Manu puffed out his breath in an audible *pffff*. "Haurahi is your number one son because he's busy making grandchildren."

June's beam didn't shift. "There is hope for you yet." She made a shooing motion. "Take Cassie outside and introduce her to your father and brothers."

"Yes, Ma," Manu said obediently.

Cassie took in the details of the house. The wallpaper was a neutral cream but bore an embossed pattern. Bright jewel colors—so many of them—should have clashed but gave the rooms a cheerful and lived-in atmosphere. The scents coming from the kitchen reminded her she hadn't eaten for several hours. Garlic bread, if she wasn't mistaken. Yum. Her favorite. Despite hearing her mother's squawk of horror rattle through her mind, her taste buds stood and saluted.

At least Emma wouldn't look askance when she consumed her dinner with gusto.

"Would you like a drink before I take you around and introduce you to my family? We have wine—sauvignon blanc because that's Ma's favorite, beer and juice or water."

"A glass of wine please."

With drinks in hand, Manu introduced her to his two brothers, Kahurangi and Tane. They were younger editions of Manu, both with longer black hair, handsome features, and broad, flirtatious grins. Kahurangi wore a form-fitting black T-shirt and sported a sleeve of tattoos—all Māori in origin. Tane wore a royal-blue T-shirt advertising a local beer, and the ends of tattoo spirals peeked beneath the sleeve on his upper right biceps.

"This is my father—Samuel Taniwha," Manu said.

Okay, he'd contributed to his sons in the looks department too. His hair was short and pitch black. Warmth and welcome wreathed him as he stretched out his hand. Big and tanned, it engulfed hers as they shook in greeting. "Hello, dear. June told me about you. Welcome to our home."

"Thank you, Mr. Taniwha."

"Call me Samuel. I'm sure we'll be seeing a lot more of you." His gentle smile warmed her through.

"Thank you." Cassie checked on Manu and saw his gaze had narrowed. Without amusement painting his features, he appeared stern and imposing. When he noticed her watching him, he relaxed, but he focused on his father and the two seemed to communicate without words.

"I suppose you want to say hello to Emma and Jack and my grumpy cousin," Manu said.

"Hone isn't grumpy."

Manu swiveled in Emma and Jack's direction. "Could have fooled me."

"You didn't tell me you were coming with Manu," Emma said

as Cassie and Manu joined them.

"He persuaded me." Cassie studied her surroundings. A large wooden deck extended the living area and took advantage of the view. Trees grew along fences, giving the illusion of privacy and directing the eye toward the estuary. She'd bet the sunsets from here were stunning. With luck, she'd see one later.

A strange growl sounded—the warning of an animal about to attack. Cassie froze and scanned the area for a dog.

Manu removed his arm from her shoulders, and the growling faded, leaving an uncomfortable silence.

"How is the motel?" Emma rushed the words, and the tension retreated.

"It's comfortable. It won't be a hardship to stay there while I'm fixing up the house."

Manu and Hone were talking quietly together. Both studied her, and the hackles at the back of her neck rose. Too far away to eavesdrop, she was certain they were discussing her.

"Jack said he'd install an alarm system for you—if you're okay with that."

Jack wrenched his attention from Hone and Manu to focus on her. Every muscle in his body rippled with tension.

"Which alarm would you recommend?" she asked.

"I thought you'd prefer uncomplicated. Something you can set when you go out and reset at night while you're at home. We can organize a firm to monitor your alarm and ring the local police in the case of problems."

"That sounds perfect. Are you sure it's no trouble? You and Hone helped so much today."

"You're Emma's friend," Jack said. "That makes you our friend too."

"Oh." His intense brown gaze left her groping for understanding. She turned to Emma and found her friend pensive as she glanced from Manu and Hone to Cassie.

"What?"

"Nothing. You're in for a treat. Can you smell the garlic bread? June makes it with loads of garlic and adds cheese. It's delicious."

"I considered bringing a salad or dessert, but I didn't have enough time to grab anything."

"Don't worry. If June wants you to do something, she's not shy in asking. She rang me to make a salad."

"Emma. Cassie. I need help in the kitchen," June called.

"Told you." Emma spread her hands in a see-what-I-mean gesture. "She'll want us to carry out salads and the rest of the food because Samuel is pulling the steaks off the barbecue."

Emma guessed right, and June organized them to ferry food from the kitchen to the wooden tables outside on the deck.

"Okay, ladies. Grab a plate and get your dinner before my sons decimate the table and leave nothing for us to eat."

"But there's so much food."

Emma grabbed two plates and handed one to Cassie. "Watch

and learn." She headed straight for the platter of garlic bread.

With her plate loaded, Cassie followed Emma and sat at a long table with bench seats.

June arrived minutes later, carrying a bottle of white wine to top up their glasses.

"This smells wonderful. I'm starving," Cassie said. "It must be all the fresh air and hard work today."

June tutted, the sound vibrating in the air for long seconds afterward. "Emma and Jack told me about your house. Terrible thing to arrive and find it vandalized."

Manu sat beside Cassie. One of those weird growls sounded again. Cassie frowned, glancing around for an agitated dog. Not one canine in sight. *Weird.*

June coughed, and the noise ceased.

Hone rounded the table and claimed the seat opposite her.

How could one man eat that much food? "Wow, I must have worked you too hard today."

Her words fell in a slice of silence. One of Manu's brothers made a smart-ass remark, and a blush suffused her face. She felt the crawl of heat and knew—just knew—she glowed like a firebug. "I didn't mention sex." She sought June's attention, mortified. "Tell your sons and nephews I wasn't talking about sex."

June reached over and patted her hand, her light green eyes twinkling. "You're a good girl, but if I tell my sons anything, they do the opposite. You'll learn that when you have children of her own."

"She needs a man for that first," Emma piped up.

"Not helpful. Be careful, or I'll cross you off my friend list."

"Me?" Emma batted her eyelids and aimed for innocent. She missed by a country mile.

"Emma said you've recently returned from the States," Samuel said. "You've lived there for a while, I understand."

"Yes. My mother is American, and we left New Zealand when I was eight," Cassie said, careful with her words but not wanting to appear uncivil given the Taniwhas' hospitality.

"Oh? What part of America?" June asked.

"We moved around a lot since my parents work for a big company. My parents are currently in Washington DC. I work as a personal assistant, but I'm taking a break at present."

"What type of personal assistant?" June asked.

"For a country singer. It's not as glamorous as it sounds," she added when everyone stared at her.

"Will we have heard of them?" Manu asked.

Cassie shrugged. "Perhaps. I'm sorry, but I can't tell you who because I signed a confidentiality agreement. I'll lose my job if I blab."

"The girl has integrity." Approval emanated from June. "Not enough young people have that quality or can keep a secret."

To Cassie's relief, the talk turned general after that, and she applied herself to her meal.

Manu bumped her lightly with his shoulder. "Ma really has taken a liking to you. You'll never escape her matchmaking now."

"But it's not true," Cassie whispered.

Manu leaned closer to murmur in her ear. "We'll keep that secret between the two of us."

## CHAPTER 5

H one struggled to control his dragon from the second Manu arrived for dinner with Cassie in tow. His cousin liked her—he could tell—but he'd seen her first. Should've gone with instinct and asked Cassie if she wanted a lift. Instead, he'd vetoed the idea. As jealousy sank its talons into his flesh, he tried to tell himself he didn't want a woman, didn't want *this* woman.

He enjoyed his single life.

His taniwha refuted each mental argument. It whined. It flexed his muscles. It growled, the rumbles becoming louder until they echoed through his head and bled free.

Cassie heard him. Hell, his cousins, his auntie, his uncle heard and made their disapproval clear. Jack glared at him, but he was rapidly losing his grip, his taniwha becoming increasingly out of control.

He'd have to leave early, give his regrets. Unable to eat while he was in this state, he set his cutlery down with a clunk. His entire being acknowledged the presence of the moon, hovering just out of sight, the *tug-tug-tug* almost too much for him to bear. His gaze swept the sky, darting to the invisible moon. *There.* A sliver came into view, and it glowed red. *Blood moon.* Maybe it was his sight coloring the moon, or it was a bad portent. A shiver racked him.

Given the amount of sex he'd had recently, he should have no problem controlling his beast. Hell, he had to get out of here.

Hone stood abruptly. "I'm not feeling well. I might head home." After he stopped at his usual haunts and picked up an agreeable woman for the night. A growl bled free, despite his gritted teeth. "See you tomorrow. Thanks, Auntie."

"Cuz, I'll walk out with you," Manu said. "I wanted to ask you something."

Hone gave a clipped yeah-tread-easy nod and emphasized it with a dragon snarl. Manu was the last person he wanted to speak with. His cousin had handled Cassie. Handled her soft skin. His taniwha scent still clung to her sexy curves. A snarl burst forth and claws dug into his clenched palms. Pale gray-black scales glinted on his forearms, tinged with red to go with his fury.

"Hone, wait up."

Hone ignored Manu and lengthened his strides, desperate to escape before his urge to pummel his cousin or vaporize him with dragon's breath got the better of him. Now that would cause a scene.

Manu grabbed his biceps and hauled him to a halt. "Quit that damn snarling. I had no idea you were interested in Cassie."

"I'm not," Hone spat.

"Could have fooled me." Manu scrutinized him, his powerful dragon sending off calming vibes. "What about your rules?"

Hone struggled to halt his shift, which had progressed enough for his clothing to strain at the seams. They were his rules. His taniwha wanted them to change.

Manu manhandled him down a long passage. He opened a door with his free hand and thrust Hone into a Spartan bedroom bearing a bed and not much else. Manu's, judging by the scent.

His cousin shoved him toward the double bed. "Listen to me, moron. Cassie and I are going to be friends. I asked her to come with me tonight because Ma was busy scheming. Cassie isn't interested in me. I amuse her, but she agreed to play a part to foil Ma's matchmaking attempts. That is all. We rode here on my bike, which is why her scent is all over me."

"I'm not interested in her," Hone spat.

"Let me rephrase. Your taniwha wants her. You should surrender now." Manu remained calm, which made him a natural leader. Cool under pressure and heir to the leadership of the Auckland tribe should anything happen to June.

Surrender? *Hell, no!* "My taniwha isn't the boss of me."

"No?" Manu's brows rose.

Yeah, that was irony right there. He'd taken one look at Cassie and wanted to fuck her. His dragon had picked up his interest and magnified it tenfold, liking—no, loving—the concept.

"I can't go home like this." Hone gestured at the scales still glinting on his forearms.

"Want to go flying later? I've worked on the bugs in the cloaking system and wanted to test it anyway." Manu waited for his reaction, his expression enigmatic.

"Yeah, thanks." Hone hadn't flown for months. None of them had while Manu attempted to perfect his cloaking system. Instead, the taniwha population—those who flew—had increased the frequency of their sexual encounters to calm their beasts.

"I'll tell Ma you're lying down, and I'll sneak you dessert. That always appeases my taniwha when he gets unruly."

"Thanks." Hone sighed and parked his butt on the bed. He wasn't sure he'd manage the same magnanimity given the same circumstances. "I'm sorry."

Manu squeezed Hone's shoulder. "No worries."

He left, shutting the bedroom door with a click, and only then did Hone sigh again. What a fuckin' mess.

He truly didn't want a permanent relationship. He'd seen what had happened with his friends and other cousins when they'd let their taniwha blindly lead them. Chaos. Broken relationships, and in two cases, humans who had blabbed to the press. Luckily, the reporters hadn't trusted the women who approached them. Thought they were gaga crazy. There had been social media posts, but since then, no one had snapped photos to prove their existence. June had threatened the next taniwha to break protocol would forfeit their life. Her proclamation settled the community and fortified Hone's rules about no ties with women.

He didn't intend to be the dragon who tested June's resolve.

Luckily, Jack's situation had occurred before the big drama and June's decree. Human Emma had accepted Jack shifting to taniwha to save their lives. She'd been more pissed at Jack for making her swim from Waiheke to the mainland. Of course, Jack was a river and lake dragon. Hone was of the flying variety, and if anyone irked him while in taniwha form, Hone reacted with fire.

Manu arrived with a tray of meat, a plate of pavlova and strawberries, a generous serving of lemon tart, and a piece of chocolate log. After his cousin left again, Hone tucked in, starting with the dessert. A sugar coma might quieten his taniwha.

The sweet treats did the trick and pushed his dragon into slumber. Hone tugged off his boots and relaxed on the bed. If he and Manu were flying, he'd rest now. No telling when he'd have a chance to fly again. He should make the most of this opportunity.

"Did you have to grope Cassie?" Hone's dragon woke with a jealous snarl of displeasure since Cassie's scent covered Manu.

Manu grinned, a broad smirk that held not a shred of apology. "We rode on my bike. What would you have me do? Tow her behind?"

"Change your clothes. Take a shower and use soap unless you want my fist in your face," Hone ordered.

"All right. All right." Manu backed away in capitulation. "I'll shower."

"Go and chill with a drink. Ma and Dad have gone to bed. Jack and Emma left as I arrived back here. It's just Kahurangi and Tane out there."

Perfect. His cousins would tease the crap out of him. He might as well gulp down his pride and man up. He pulled on his boots and stomped out to face his cousins.

"Ooh, it's the jealous one," Tane cooed.

"Don't you mean the fallen one? The mated one," Kahurangi corrected.

*Deny everything.* "No idea what you're talking about."

Tane snorted. "You were growling like a guard dog. Ma's not pleased with you."

Kahurangi cocked his head, regarded him like a bug. "She's earmarked Cassie for Manu."

His dragon's snarl of displeasure bled free, and his cousins chortled.

"Stop taunting him." Manu pushed his dragon through the order, and his younger brothers ceased their teasing, both stepping back to give Manu space. He carried his modified cloaking systems, although, to Hone's untrained eye, they appeared unchanged from the last time he'd helped Manu. Small—square boxes with two controls and straps.

"Okay." He handed a unit to Hone. "It's the same as last time. This goes around your right wrist. The unit will shift with you, and once you're airborne, should cloak your presence. Did you see the news item about the guy who has developed a diving suit that allows divers to approach crocodiles and sharks without causing them alarm or to attack?"

"No."

Manu strapped on a unit. "The suit cloaks a human's magnetic signal. I've designed my unit along the same lines. It's like stealth jet technology."

"You left me in lost and found the minute you started talking about magnetic signals. As long as it works. My scales have a reddish tinge at present, the ones on my arms at any rate. I suspect I'll be more red than black when I shift. Will it still cloak me if I'm a flashy color?"

"The purpose of this test. Kahurangi and Tane will monitor us and listen to air traffic. I've designed the units with a beacon, so those at base can check our location. They'll alert me to problems, but I'm confident the unit will work this time."

"I hope so," Hone said.

"Our brother is a genius. If this works, he can put it on the market. It will mean other shifter species can shift without discovery too," Kahurangi said with pride. "We'll all be rich."

"Me more than you," Manu said dryly. "You ready? We'll take off from here, fly toward the Manukau Heads do a circle 'round and over Ardmore. If the planes landing at Auckland International Airport or Ardmore Airport don't see us, and air traffic control doesn't register our presence, we'll be one step closer to marketing the unit."

"Are you sure? We normally avoid those areas. There will be hell to pay if we're seen. What about your mother? She wasn't kidding in her threats."

"The test is necessary."

"Did you tell her you were doing another trial?"

"No."

Living dangerously. "Okay. Whatever you say. Anything else I should watch for?"

"Nope. Enjoy the flight but pay attention. I'll be in contact with Kahurangi and Tane. If there's a problem, I'll signal you. Stay close enough for telepathic communication."

"Will do." Hone tugged off his T-shirt. He removed his boots and tossed the rest of his clothes over the back of a wooden outdoor chair before moving away from the others to shift.

His taniwha burst forth, the sharp pain of bones and skin

rearranging sucking away Hone's breath. He groaned, slumping forward as limbs changed to clawed feet. As he'd assumed, his hide was redder than normal. The scales on his chest remained glossy black, but his legs and tail glowed scarlet in the subtle outdoor lighting.

Not far away, Manu pushed through his own shift. Although he was mainly black, the spines along his back and the tip of his tail shone a regal purple.

*"Ready to go?"* Manu sent the thought winging to his mind.

*"All set."* Hone lifted his wings, beating them to warm up muscles not used during the months of lockdown. Pleasure roared through him as he took to the air, every sense greedily drinking in the magnified sensations. He hated to admit it, but flying beat sex. Using the prevailing wind currents, he lifted and rose higher until the estuary spread out below him. The scent of mud and mangroves ebbed, and instead, he smelled someone's dinner—a roast of beef—and animals.

In the past, the dragons had an uneasy peace with the Māori tribes inhabiting the country. Some taniwha had stolen or attacked the tribes, while others had brokered peace in return for a frequent tithe. A pity the moa birds had become extinct. Legend said they'd been tasty morsels, the giant ones large enough to feed more than one dragon.

Life for a modern-day taniwha had its benefits. Food was plentiful, but the need for secrecy was a concern. He wondered if he'd live long enough to experience the day when the shifter population came out to humans. Commonsense said that day would arrive soon.

"*Head over toward that party,*" Manu instructed. "*We'll do a low swoop. They sound drunk, but it will still be a good test.*"

Hone smelled the beer and the sweet scent of drugs, the pungent smoke from their bonfire. He chuckled, his humor emerging as a *huh-huh-huh*. If the units failed or didn't work as Manu predicted, these men and women would assume they were hallucinating.

Following Manu's lead, Hone maneuvered lower. He gave a lazy flap of his wings and flew above the group. Their loud chatter, punctuated with colorful curses and the *thump-thump-thump* of heavy metal music, never faltered. Manu flew in a tight circle above the property, and Hone followed, rejoicing in the movement of muscles and the wind blowing across his scales.

"*Good. They don't see us. Let's fly to the head, do a circle over the sea, and come back via the airport. Watch out for planes.*"

"*Don't have to tell me,*" Hone replied. "*Last thing I need is a sheared off wing or tail.*"

The briny fragrance of the Tasman Sea seduced him into swooping low and flying mere feet above the churning waves. He reveled in the spray against his face. God, he hoped this unit continued to work. It would make such a difference to their people and to other shifters who found it increasingly difficult to maintain secrecy in this modern world.

*"Stop playing, cuz. You haven't flown for a while and you'll be sore tomorrow. Airport now. That will be our big test."*

Hone heard the strain in Manu's voice and snapped to attention. He wanted to encourage his cousin but remained silent. This trial was important.

He trailed Manu as his cousin headed toward the airport. Long before the terminal came into sight, the rumble of airplanes vibrated in the air, and the scent of fuel filled his nostrils.

*"We'll follow the trajectory of the incoming planes and keep away from those taking off,"* Manu sent.

*"I'll stay behind you in tight formation."* His cousin's tenseness came through clearly, and Hone battled the teasing words trembling for release.

Manu slowed the beat of his wings, then rose steeply to follow an Air New Zealand flight coming in to land. Once the plane taxied, they banked and waited for the next—a flight from Singapore. They repeated the exercise a third time, flying closer, near enough to the cockpit to see the pilots at work. Neither man shifted their attention from their instruments.

*"Nothing coming through on air traffic control."* Excitement radiated through Manu's words. *"I'd like to test at Ardmore Airport now."*

Hone bared his teeth in a celebratory chortle. *"Well done, cuz. Are your units waterproof? You could give one to Jack to test."*

*"Jack promised to test one for me, but he wanted us to do our checks*

*first because the water dragons get stuck in their natural forms for longer after they shift."*

They repeated the checks at Ardmore airport, following six small planes in as they landed.

*"Kahurangi said there is a break in the arrivals. We can land here."*

He could do with a rest. His muscles were screaming at him, but he wouldn't have missed this experience for anything.

They landed beside a hangar on the far side of the airport. Although the airport at Mangere was the main airport, Ardmore airport was the busiest, with numerous private planes.

*"Kahurangi and Tane say no alarms have been raised anywhere."*

*"That's great. What's the next step?"*

*"I'll get Jack to test a unit out in a gulf. If none of the ferry passengers, yachties or fishermen see him, that's a good sign. I need to check the unit remains waterproof for an extended time."*

*"Can you calibrate it to work for us in our human forms?"*

*"That would be a good test, but I wouldn't want the units to get in the wrong hands. Something like that would be invaluable to the criminal element."*

Hone considered the problem and agreed. *"You probably should make the adjustments and test it in this way, but have you considered offering only rental units on the market? Get Dad to investigate those who wish to rent the units to vet them first and have them sign an agreement to say they won't use them for criminal purposes."*

"Hell, good point. I haven't thought much beyond perfecting them. The last thing I want is to create problems or, even worse, some type of clandestine war."

"I can help," Hone offered. "I'll talk to Dad and Jack. We'll come up with a plan for when you want to go to market. You've devoted a lot of time and money into perfecting your unit, and you should profit from your investment."

"Let me think about it," Manu said. "I'll need to discuss it with Ma. Let's wander over to those hangars and in front of their main building where those people are working. I don't want to get in their way, but we'll venture close enough for them to see us if they're not blind."

"Then we head home?"

"Yup."

Half an hour later, they touched down at the farm. Hone visualized his human form in his mind, and his tired taniwha subsided without a whimper. His body quivered with fatigue, yet satisfaction throbbed through him. He'd sleep well this evening.

"You look as bad as I feel," Manu said. "You'd better crash here tonight."

"Not gonna argue. Thank you for taking me with you. Even though I'm tired, there's a sense of exhilaration as if I've had a sex marathon. Your invention...I just wanted to say I'm in awe of your talent."

A whoosh of red rushed to his cousin's face. So unusual, Hone wanted to make a joke. He resisted because this was a momentous occasion. Manu deserved praise. Those taniwha who scoffed at his cousin's inventions, called him a nerd, and alleged he wasn't up to his position within the tribe would stand in line to get an invisibility unit.

"Do you have a costing available? How much will it cost to produce each unit?"

"Probably close to two thousand. A little more to make sure the unit is robust and will survive someone dropping it."

Hone clapped his cousin on the shoulder, proud of his accomplishments. "I doubt any shifter will quibble at the expense. Which room should I take?"

Manu yawned. "Share my room. That's probably easiest since it's late. I'm so tired I'll drop off the second my head hits the pillow."

"Thanks. I'm not even gonna offer any smart-arse comments about sleeping with you," Hone said, and they trudged the final steps home.

# CHAPTER 6

C assie woke early and arrived at the local hardware store at one minute past nine. She headed straight for the paint samples.

"Good grief." Overwhelmed, she gaped at the countless paint pots and the sample sheets. Who knew white came in so many shades?

Luckily, an assistant came to her aid, and soon, she was on her way with two cans of cream paint, another of white, a paint roller and tray, tape, and an assortment of brushes. June had given her two old sheets the previous evening when she'd said she intended to spend her day painting.

Her cell phone rang, and she pulled over to the side of the road to answer the call. Kevin. She considered ignoring the summons.

No, dodging his calls was childish.

"Hey, Kev. What's up?" She suspected he intended to push his agenda again for an overseas tour.

"Would you be interested in joining a summer vineyard tour for two concerts? One of their acts has pulled out due to illness. The venues are Matakana and Auckland, so the concerts are close to you."

"But no one knows me here." Did she want her two lives to intersect? That was the biggest question.

"You'd be a supporting act. It would be an opportunity for you to test your songs in a different market." He dangled the suggestion like a juicy carrot. "And you could do me a favor by testing something in the pop genre."

Actually, the idea of going in as a mainly unknown act appealed to her, now that she thought about it. Kev was right. She could test new songs and material, do some covers, and stay far away from most of the Katie-Jo stuff her fans in America clamored for. "Just the two nights?"

"Yes, they're hoping the lead singer will recover to finish the last two concerts in Napier and Martinborough."

"All right. I'll do it. Send me the details."

There was a pause. "That was easier than I assumed," Kevin said finally.

"You dangled the right carrot. I'll do a few covers, two or three Katie-Jo songs and I have two new songs I might try."

"You didn't tell me you had new songs." Distinctly accusing.

"They're not the Katie-Jo brand," Cassie said. "There is no point showing them to you when I know they're not the direction you want for me. How come we were approached with this?"

"An old girlfriend."

Cassie took in that info and rapidly backpedaled. "Stop. Forget I asked."

"She was before you," Kevin said. "We're still friends and I always make contact at Christmas. I told her you were in New Zealand and she rang me yesterday. Gotta go. I'll email you the details."

Wow, she hadn't seen that coming. Okay. So, she'd have to work out what to do in her set. She checked her rearview mirror and pulled out again. At least there were no cyclists hogging the road today. The sun shone with the promise of a hot day, and not a cloud filled the blue sky.

Ah, summer in New Zealand.

*Hmm, which songs would work best?* She mentally riffled through her material as she drove sedately down the country roads.

The blast of a horn made her start. Heart thudding faster than seconds before, she checked her mirror and fear tensed her muscles. A large truck barreled up behind her, going way too fast. She steered to the far left of the road, her left tires going off the tarmac to strike loose gravel.

The truck kept coming. Closer. Closer. Closer.

She clenched the wheel, eyed the rearview mirror.

The truck nudged her rear bumper, and the impact shot her right off the tarmac. She gasped and attempted to muscle her vehicle back onto the road. A second shunt propelled her against the steering wheel before the seatbelt ripped tight against her chest. Her vehicle roared as her foot pressed the accelerator and bumped through a pothole. For an instant, she was airborne, then a heavy jolt struck as her rental plowed into a watery ditch, screeching and revving on impact. The truck driver blasted his horn again and sped past.

Cassie groaned as the seatbelt dug into her boobs. *Ow!* Her ribs throbbed as if she'd gone several rounds in the boxing ring, even though the impact hadn't deployed the airbags. The engine noise reverberated through her head, and she turned the ignition key to silence her growling rental. Soon only her harsh breathing broke the blissful silence. She repositioned her glasses and sat for a moment longer, breathing. Just breathing before she decided what to do next.

Not another sound disturbed the country quiet. Not a friendly farmer. Not another vehicle.

A hard shudder jerked her body, and she fumbled for the door. It opened a few inches before hitting mud. Far enough to squeeze out, surely. She struggled, panic a hungry beast, feeding on her predicament. Her arms flailed, her breathing hoarse, then the truth hit her.

Seat belt.

*Ugh!*

Trembling fingers managed the release and the tightness around her chest eased. She crawled from the car, desperate to stand on solid ground. Her feet hit water, right up to her ankles. Cold water that seeped right through her sneakers and socks in seconds.

God, what should she do?

*Assess the situation.* Her mother's exasperated words flooded her mind with parental disapproval. She splashed to the front of the vehicle to check the damage. Apart from the nose kissing the far side of the ditch and the gleaming paintwork sporting mud and chunks of grass, she couldn't see any visible dents.

She splashed back and climbed out of the ditch. It wasn't a big one, but the banks were too steep for her to get the vehicle out herself. Cassie stood on the road and surveyed the rear of the SUV. The bumper hung at a weird angle, and metal buckled out of shape as if the vehicle scowled at her. The rear doors wouldn't open in a hurry.

She reached for her phone and realized it was still in her handbag. With a sigh, she started back down the bank. Her right foot skidded in the mud, her arms windmilled but she remained upright. Just. Her giant splash left water dripping from her nose and glasses, obscuring her vision.

"Ugh." She wiped her hand over her face and carefully removed her glasses to wipe the lenses. That done, she retrieved her handbag and clambered back onto the road.

Her first call was to the rental company to explain her predicament and how the shiny red SUV happened to be sitting in a ditch.

"Someone rear-ended you? I'll ring the police. They'll need to do a report. I'll arrange for one of the servicemen to collect the vehicle, but he won't be able to touch it until you've filed a report with the police. Are you injured?" the woman asked belatedly.

"No."

"Sit tight. I'll set things in motion." She hung up.

By the time a police car arrived three-quarters of an hour later, Cassie had composed part of a song about a clumsy single woman in a car crash. She gave her statement to the police officer while attempting to ignore the quirk of his mouth. The muddy water in the ditch had dried on the bottom of her jeans, but she suspected her splashing around had put mud on her face too. Difficult to see without a mirror.

"A truck rear-ended you?"

"Yes."

"Did you get the registration number?"

"No, it happened too quickly."

"Make of truck?"

Cassie paused. "Um, a blue truck. Not big like a stock truck, but the type that does deliveries. Bigger than my SUV."

"Did you see the driver?"

"Not really. It was a man, and he wore dark sunglasses and a cap. That's all I saw."

The policeman, probably in his thirties, had military-short black hair and bright blue eyes, which were emphasized by his navy-blue uniform. He surveyed the vehicle from all angles, and his long legs let him jump the drain with ease.

"Okay. It's obvious someone has rear-ended you because I can see traces of blue paint. Sign here."

Cassie started to say she'd already told him that before she realized the cops were used to people lying to them. Instead of arguing, she scrawled her signature on the statement.

"Here is a copy for you. You'll need it for the rental company. They told me they'd arranged for a tow."

"Yes, I don't suppose you could give me a lift?"

"I'm heading to Clevedon."

"That's fine. I can ring my friend from there."

The rental people arrived, and Cassie retrieved her paint and brushes before leaving.

The policeman dropped her at the café, and her face burned as several locals witnessed her climbing from the vehicle with her box of painting equipment. Even though she'd done nothing wrong, she felt like a criminal.

Her first stop was the restroom at the café. She groaned. No wonder she'd amused the cop.

Once she'd cleaned her face and ordered a coffee, she called

Emma to ask if she'd be able to come and collect her.

"Are you sure you're all right?"

Cassie grimaced. "My jeans are muddy, and my feet are still wet. I amused the cop who came to take my statement. Apart from that, I'm fine." She didn't mention the sore muscles where the seat belt had dug into her as she jerked to a halt in the ditch. Those were nothing and would heal.

"Hang on," Emma said.

Cassie heard her talking to someone in the background.

"You there, Cassie?"

"Yeah."

"I'm over the bridge on the other side of Auckland. Jack is working a case in town and can't get away."

"Oh, I'll see if I can call a cab."

"Hone is in Papakura. He said he'll come and get you."

"Don't worry. I can get a cab."

"Too late. He's already on his way. Are you sure you're all right?"

"Yes."

"Did you take photos of the damage?"

"Good gravy, it didn't occur to me. I have the police report to give to the rental company."

"Take a copy of it first," Emma said.

"Will do. Thanks, Emma."

"No thanks necessary."

Cassie heard voices in the background.

"Gotta go," Emma said. "See you later."

Cassie set her phone on the table with a loud sigh. Hone had been so grumpy last night. Although initially attracted to him, she'd put up with Kevin's moodiness and didn't intend to do it for another man. She drank her coffee, her mind drifting as an idea for a song came to her. She grabbed her notebook and started scribbling down random lyrics while humming under her breath.

"Cassie."

She glanced up to find Hone, his big frame practically vibrating with tension. He hauled her to her feet as if she weighed nothing and wrapped his arms around her in a tight embrace.

"You're okay," he murmured against her ear.

Her muscles, already abused, protested the fierceness of his hug, but it felt good to have his support. Tears burned in her eyes—delayed reaction from the accident.

She tried to suck in a breath. Couldn't. "Too tight," she gasped.

Hone released her, and she half fell back onto her seat.

"Thanks for coming to get me."

"Are you okay?" Hone pulled out the other chair at her table and sat. "What happened?"

His expression darkened as she told him about the truck. "What did the cop say?"

"He said the specks of blue paint proved the driver rear-ended me. He took samples and lots of photos. I didn't get the license number." Cassie pulled a face. "It happened so quickly. I didn't see much at all. I was too busy trying to keep the SUV driving straight."

Hone's expression didn't relax. "What do you want to do?"

"Start painting some of the rooms. I'd like to move in as soon as possible."

"I don't like the idea of you staying on your own."

"I have my phone. I'm sure this was a random accident. No one knew I would drive along that stretch of road at that time."

"You didn't notice anyone following?"

"I didn't see any other vehicles once I passed Ardmore Airport."

"All right. How about I drop you off at the house? I have to go and do a job in Karaka, but I'll be back to install an alarm for you."

Cassie studied his hard features. He resembled the portraits of fierce Māori warriors she'd seen in the Auckland art gallery. All he needed was a feather cloak and facial tattoos to complete the picture. "I thought you'd argue."

"You're an adult."

Pleasure suffused her at his words. Someone who treated her as an equal with her own mind. "Thank you."

"Have you met your neighbors yet?" Hone changed the subject.

"No, it's on my list of things to do."

Hone surprised her with his laid-back attitude. Most other people of her acquaintance—her mother and Kevin, for example—would have lectured her, although Hone's behavior did verge on bossy. She drank the last of her coffee and stood. Pain scored her ribs, and she grimaced. When she caught Hone's gaze and noticed his scrutiny, she attempted to smooth her expression.

"I'm trained in first aid," he said as he scooped up her box of decorating supplies without effort. "I'll check your injuries once we get to your house."

"I don't need—"

"It's either that or I'll set Auntie June on you."

It didn't take much imagination on her part to realize she'd come out second best in an encounter with June. Still, she'd had enough of Kevin bossing her around. She didn't intend to set a bad precedent and let Hone ride roughshod over her either.

"If this is an attempt to get a better ogle of my boobs..." Cassie trailed off on seeing his amusement. This was the Hone she'd glimpsed during their first meeting, and his smile tugged at her, making her want to share in the exchange.

"That's a side benefit," he said as he urged her to the door. "As well as making sure you're not injured and perving at your stunning breasts, I'll learn if your skin is soft and breathe in your sexy scent."

Cassie opened and closed her mouth. For once, words failed her. Instead, she concentrated on putting one foot in front of the other. She wouldn't get much painting done today. At least she had her notebook, and she could use the time to decide on song choice. Or at least she could once she learned the time allocation for her performance at the vineyard concerts.

Hone ushered her to a big black utility vehicle. He set her decorating supplies down, fished his keys from his pockets, and a peep indicated he'd unlocked it. Unexpectedly, he cut in front and opened the door for her.

"Not going to comment?" he asked, seconds before he closed the door.

Cassie blinked at his gentlemanly conduct. Her lips did that opening and closing action again while her mind took a detour and considered Hone checking her body for injuries. Her torso tingled. He seemed different this morning, more agreeable. At least he'd relaxed once he'd seen she was unharmed. She watched him stride around the front of his vehicle. No stride wasn't quite the right description. The man was...strutting, and that was a broad grin.

Hone climbed behind the wheel and winked at her. Heat collected in her cheeks and seeped down her neck toward her breasts. Her nipples did a funny tightening thing that made her oh-so-aware of her body, aware of this man.

"What would I do with a smartass man?" she muttered, verbally fighting the temptation whispering in her ear.

Hone shot her a blast of glee, sensual lips pursing. "I've heard we can be helpful when it comes to sex."

*Cripes!* The accident had affected her brain, or at least the connection between her brain and mouth. "You misheard. I said, what will I do with *the* man. You are outrageous."

"Maybe, but I'm also trained in first aid," Hone said. "Emma told me to take you to see a doctor."

"I don't need a doctor."

"Emma said you'd say that, which was when I volunteered to make sure you were okay."

"Look, no blood." Cassie held out her hands. If Hone touched her, she feared she'd lapse, give in to impulse during a weak moment.

"I saw the pain on your face as you stood. You winced when I hugged you. You seem coherent and you're right about the blood. I can't see any." His gaze drifted to her, perused her face, swept down her neck, and lingered at her breasts. He returned his attention to the road. "I bet you're bruised from the seatbelt. You'll be sore for a few days."

"I concur. Nothing a hot bath or an ice pack won't cure."

"Being a medically trained type, I have ice packs in my freezer, and I have a spa pool on the deck. Once you've given up the battle to paint, we'll stop by the motel to grab your swimsuit and go to my place. You can soak for a while."

"I'm surprised you didn't suggest going straight to your place and not worrying about the swimsuit," she said tartly.

He beamed approval. "That would work too, but I didn't want to rush things."

"What things?" Cassie winced at the snap in her tone. She'd dreamed of both Hone and Manu during the night, pondered stripping them naked. Guilty heat collected in her cheeks again as she recalled her X-rated fantasies. Both men, for goodness sake! Thankfully, not at the same time because that would've been weird. Time to steer the conversation into other channels. "Never mind. Don't answer that. I thought you had work to do."

"I have the job I mentioned, then a break before the next job at two. I'll install the alarm for you and drop you at my place so you can soak in the hot tub."

Cassie swallowed. "Thank you. You and your family have been kind to me."

"You're Emma's friend." Hone pulled up in her driveway. "I'll unload the paint for you, then be off after I check your bruising."

Cassie slumped in the seat on hearing his determination. Emma had warned her about Hone and his cousins. None of them wanted anything permanent. Her lusty dreams had to cease. As did the neediness to have the same love and happiness as Emma. Big girl panties along with a dose of reality. She sucked in a breath to shore up her restraint. "Fine. Let's get this done."

## CHAPTER 7

Chuckling, Hone let her lead the way to the front door. An itchiness between his shoulder blades told him they were under scrutiny. Again. He hated the idea of leaving Cassie alone, yet he sensed she intended to stay, no matter what his argument.

"Where do you want the tins of paint?"

"The lounge, please. The words on the walls in there make me grit my teeth."

Hone checked his watch. "I have ten minutes before it's time to leave. Anything else before I go? After I check your ribs."

"Humph."

Hone suppressed his smile at her harsh exhalation. He set down the box of painting equipment. "Show me your war wounds."

"I stubbed my toe."

"Cassie." He remained stern, fighting his instinct to laugh.

She avoided his gaze, instead focusing on her feet. "You're not going to go away, are you?"

"In ten minutes."

She bared her straight white teeth at him. Then a chuckle escaped, a surrender, her hands darting to her blouse buttons. "I am glad I didn't go with my first instinct to wear a dress."

"I like your dresses." Hone made a sweeping gesture to indicate her clothing. "The one with the cats wearing glasses."

"You noticed them?"

"It told me you have a sense of humor. I enjoy that in a woman."

"Oh." Her eyes grew as wide as her mouth.

"Clock's ticking, babe."

Her breasts rose and fell with her gusty sigh, and his taniwha perked up for the first time since his flight-exhausted slumber. The faintest rumble of a purr vibrated through Hone's mind.

With trembling fingers, she unfastened the top two buttons of her pale blue blouse. Hone's gaze drifted to her bra and her creamy curves pushing against the restraint.

"Hey." She clicked her fingers under his nose.

"I didn't say I wouldn't look."

"You're in first-aid mode."

Hone spotted the red mark above her left breast. No broken skin. He prodded the area with light fingers, watching her expression the entire time. She winced.

"How sore are you? Honestly."

"I tensed once I knew I was going to crash. My neck and back are okay, but I have general aches and pains. Nothing too major."

Hone wanted to pull her into his arms, hold her. Just hold her against him until his racing pulse slowed, until the trembling of his knees ceased, until his taniwha stopped struggling for freedom. "Tell me if that changes. I'm serious about the hot tub. That will help." Fighting his taniwha, his need to touch, his urge to protect, he stepped back and watched her refasten her blouse.

"Thank you."

"You're welcome. I'd better go. I'll be back in two hours. Pace yourself, okay?"

"I will."

Hone hesitated, biting back his words of caution, the urge to say more when he had no right. His hands clenched at his sides, and he forced himself to turn away since he didn't do permanent. No women. Cassie was out of bounds.

"See you later."

Cassie didn't breathe properly until the rumble of Hone's vehicle faded. Her skin tingled at the spot he'd touched, and the memory of his masculine scent lingered. She shook her head, the resulting jolt of pain jogging her brain back to sensible. It was easy to see Hone Taniwha and his cousin Manu were charming players. Rogues. Men of the most dangerous kind. Emma was right. She should stay far, far away from both of them.

Forcing her mind to practicalities, she plucked her phone from her bag and checked her email. As promised, Kevin had sent a contract plus details of her concert slots. The segment before the main act at each venue. Five, perhaps six songs, a little chat with the audience, and an encore if she had time. Six songs, she decided. Two covers, two Katie-Jo songs, and two new ones. She'd adapt them to make them fit.

While she considered her song choice—always the most important part of preparing for a concert—she spread out the sheets and taped the skirting boards. Crap. She hadn't considered a ladder. Perhaps Jack would have one she could borrow.

Half an hour later, with the low skirting boards taped, she began painting, taking satisfaction in covering the rude graffiti. The roller meant the work went quickly, and she hummed different songs while she narrowed down her choice of cover songs.

A thump froze her mid-stroke. Crap. She'd forgotten to lock the door after Hone left. *Stupid.* Basic security if she was on her own.

The knock repeated. "Hello? Anyone home?"

An unfamiliar voice. Cassie frowned as she placed her paint-splattered roller in the pan, tension simmering in her belly.

"Coming!" Cassie couldn't see through the door and opened it cautiously with Emma's and Hone's warnings ringing in her ears. "Hello?"

A man dressed in an open-necked white shirt with black trousers turned and acknowledged her presence. "Hi, I'm Matthew Jamieson, your neighbor. I thought I'd pop in and say hello." He extended his hand, his boyish face wreathed in a polite smile.

Cassie relaxed and accepted his hand, approving of the solid yet non-bruising handshake, his business casual attire. "Cassie Miller-Pope. I was intending to drop by and say hello. Do you have time for a cup of tea?"

"Not today, I'm afraid. I'm on my way to a meeting, and later, I must pick up my son. It's my week to have him." His blue eyes crinkled at the corners, his sandy-blond hair and clean-shaven cheeks giving him the boy-next-door vibe.

Cassie bit back a burst of humor. Funny. He *was* the boy next-door. "Have you lived here long?"

"Almost two years. It's a smallholding. We grow Christmas trees."

"That's cool. I noticed the pine trees. I guess it will be quieter for you now that Christmas is over."

"These trees aren't big enough for harvesting yet. My family owns other farms. One in Pukekohe and another in Waiuku. We were busy there in December. It's a relief to have a quiet month. Well, I'd better head off to get to my meeting on time." He extracted a card from his wallet. "These are my numbers if you want to get hold of me for any reason."

"Thanks. I arrived to find the place vandalized. I don't suppose you've noticed any people loitering around the house?"

"That's terrible. I'm sorry to hear that. I haven't noticed anyone, but I'll keep an eye out and pass the word to my employees to do the same."

"Thanks. Have you met the people who live at the farm farther up this road? The Pattersons, from memory?"

"A young business couple owns the farm now. They run alpacas, and both work. They have a family member who lives in the village and keeps an eye on their stock during the week. Are you planning to stay here full-time?"

"Undecided at the moment," Cassie said. "I'm here for a month, but it depends on my work."

"What do you do?"

"I'm a personal assistant." The fib rolled smoothly off her tongue since she'd repeated it often. It was a good way of keeping her anonymity, and she was glad of the white lie since it let her live a relatively normal life when she was away from the stage.

"Is that an American accent I hear?"

"It is," Cassie said. "Although I was born in New Zealand."

Matthew's watch peeped—an alarm of some type. He pushed a button, and the noise ceased. "Sorry, I have to go. Nice to meet you, Cassie. I'll probably see you around. I'll let you get back to your painting."

"How did you know I was painting?"

"Apart from the smell?" He grinned. "You have paint on your nose and one cheek."

Cassie groaned and slapped her hand to her face. "I'm mortified."

He chuckled. "Don't worry. Paint looks good on you." And with a wink, he strode to his navy-blue sedan and drove away.

Well. Cute. He hadn't been wearing a wedding ring. He could be her possible fling. He'd seemed personable...

Matt tapped the driver's wheel as he drove toward Auckland. So, the mysterious C Miller-Pope was one of the women he'd seen earlier. Good. Easier for him to scare, and if she was here short-term, things might not be as grim as he'd suspected. She'd responded to his subtle flirting. Another plus.

The land had been let go since the old guy died, and Matthew had increased his property line into her plot, planted his weed, and enclosed the crop by several rows of pine. She might not notice or be aware of the official boundaries of her land.

Herbert had said he'd run a woman off the road. Cassie, judging from Herbert's description. He'd continue with the same tactics. At best, it might scare her away and at worst, his men had an excuse to loiter since he'd promised to watch for trespassers.

Yes, things might work out, despite his fears. The crops would grow to maturity, they'd shift the drugs, and his bank account would grow by a healthy amount—enough to secret his son from New Zealand.

Yeah, nothing like risk to raise the adrenaline.

# CHAPTER 8

C assie groaned as she slipped into the warm, bubbling water. The hot tub—an excellent idea. Far from the messy bachelor pad she'd expected, Hone's place in Papakura was a house. Rented from a school friend who'd met a woman and moved to the nearby country town of Sloan, Hone had told her. Native trees, punga, karaka and manuka gave the property a sense of privacy from the nearby neighbors and provided a screen for the deck without limiting exposure to the sun. Birds sang from the trees, and somewhere in the distance, a lawnmower droned busily.

Hone had said she'd have privacy and didn't need to wear a swimsuit. Not that she'd gone with his teasing, punctuated with a sly wink, suggestion.

Her tummy did a funny shimmy as her mind fixed on the sexy

rogue. If only he were a keeper. Manu had confirmed he and his cousin weren't relationship material. The little voice at the back of her mind tempted her to ignore Emma, her negative-Nelly friend.

"I'm not a casual kind of woman," she muttered, going for the crux of her problem. No matter how much that little voice warbled at her, she preferred a permanent relationship with an end in sight. A man to hold her in good times and bad. She needed snuggling and arguing and make-up sex. Unfortunately, a luxury with her career.

*Huh!* Work. Time to concentrate on music and her upcoming slot at the vineyard. She hummed a few bars of one of her more upbeat Katie-Jo songs. Gave a decisive nod. Yes, that one would work. A breakup song as a contrast. She sang a recent hit, penned not long after her split from Kevin. Ah, yes. A reminder of the fickleness of men.

Her two new songs, of course, and she'd choose two popular covers. If she alternated them with her stuff, that would keep her audience guessing. Perfect.

Costumes... She frowned. Since she was singing as Katie-Jo, she was stuck with her persona, and she hadn't brought stage clothes with her. Dang it. She'd have to buy a blonde wig, the necessary makeup, and clothes. Two sets of clothes.

And musicians. That one was trickier. A, she wasn't acquainted with the local musicians, and B, if she hired someone, she'd jeopardize her identity. She tapped her chin, pondering alternatives. Huh, the obvious solution. Play her guitar and do a stripped-down, unplugged version of the songs.

Her skin had started to prune by the time she clambered from the tub. She grabbed her phone to text Emma.

*Need an emergency shopping trip. When can you help?*

Her phone remained silent, so she retreated indoors out of the sun, donned the spare set of clothes she'd grabbed—one of her vintage dresses—and picked up her guitar. She worked through her mental list of six songs.

A thump on the door came midway through her he-did-me-wrong song. Her fingers paused on the strings, a burst of fear tensing every muscle in her body. Should she answer?

"Hone, you home?" a familiar voice called.

Her alarm dissipated immediately. Cassie set her guitar aside and answered the door. "Hone isn't here."

Manu straightened from his sprawl against the wall, not blinking at her presence. "Did he say when he'd be back?"

"A few hours. He didn't give a specific time."

"I'll wait." Manu strode forward, reminding her of a bulldozer with his powerful build and flexing muscles, displayed to perfection in a plain black T-shirt.

Cassie retreated before he mowed her down or, worse, stood on her bare toes.

"Want a cold drink? Hone will have beer."

"Ah, sure." Cassie followed him to the kitchen. She supposed it was okay for Manu to make himself comfortable. Hone had told her to help herself to anything in the fridge. "Did Hone know you were coming?"

Manu paused, a bottle of beer in hand. "Nope. Do I make you nervous?"

"Of course not."

He handed her a beer and ambled past her into the lounge, just off the deck. "Hone must have a new guitar. He didn't tell me."

"It's mine."

"You play?" He cocked his head, studying her as if she'd grown an extra head.

"Why are you looking at me like that?"

"Nothing. Play me a song." His chin lifted in challenge as if he suspected she'd refuse. She would've bet he was aiming for innocent. He missed by a mile, and since she'd played for thousands of people in packed-out arenas, singing for one person—no problem.

Cassie set down her drink, picked up her guitar and settled. She glanced at Manu, who now smirked, shrugged inwardly, and started playing her first Katie-Jo hit.

"She sings as well," Manu said as she began crooning the first verse. The song started slow and swelled with emotion. She reached the end and played the final soft notes.

"Wow," Manu said. "That was incredible, though I didn't recognize the song. The girl has talent."

"Thanks. The song was big in the States." She didn't mention it was her own—a song she'd written and her breakout single. "You probably know this one." She broke out into an old Beatles tune.

Manu flashed her a grin and joined in, their voices melding well. She clapped once they finished.

"Wait, let me get Hone's guitar. He won't mind." He disappeared and returned with a guitar. Seconds later, he settled beside her on the brown leather couch. "What about this one?"

One song flowed into another, and Cassie couldn't remember having such a fun jam session.

They finished the next song, and Manu wrapped an arm around her shoulders, hugging her close.

"Well." Hone stood inside the room, his arms folded across his chest. His gaze fired salvos of anger. "This is cozy."

Cassie jumped and gave an *eep* of fright at his unexpected appearance. Manu's arm tightened fractionally before he released her and stood.

"I stopped by to see if you could help me with work stuff." Manu paused as if he wanted to say more but couldn't because she was present.

Hone folded his arms over his chest. "I have a phone."

"I tried to ring you. I figured you were in a blind spot, and I'd catch you here."

"So you made yourself at home."

Hone's flat tone had Cassie frowning. What was with him? All they'd done was play music together.

Manu lifted his chin. "Yeah. I didn't think you'd mind, not after our *discussion* last night. Plus, you have rules, remember?" The strange emphasis on his words raised curiosity as to the content of their chat.

Hone prowled closer, tension broadcast in his tight jaw and rigid shoulders. "I mind."

Manu's quick scrutiny lurked with devilment, like a child intent on skullduggery. "I've changed my mind. I'm entitled."

"You understood my position," Hone snapped.

"Snooze and you lose."

Hone sucked in a breath, and somehow, he swelled, his face and arms changing color.

Cassie blinked. Was that red?

"Cuz, your temper is on display."

Hone roared and sprang at Manu. They grappled. Fists swung. Hone growled. The coffee table tipped over, clipped by a foot.

Cassie jumped to her feet, rescued her guitar, squeezed against the wall. She gawked at the pair, heart misfiring at the fierceness of their clash, the fury pulsing in the air, the lash of danger.

A chair went flying. A big chair.

They weren't mucking around.

"Stop it," she shouted.

They ignored her entreaty.

Hone punched Manu, grazed his jaw. Manu toppled and hit the

floor. Hone sprang at his cousin, growling like an enraged dog.

Blood. There was blood. She swallowed, spied her handbag beside the couch and scooped it up. Handbag and guitar in hand, she retreated, not understanding the cause, the fierce fighting, the brutality.

Cassie strode out the door and left them to their bloody war.

# CHAPTER 9

"Hone. Stand down. Stand down, damn it."

The growl of temper in Manu, the compulsion from a leader pierced Hone's rage. The human part of him wrested back control. With a harsh breath, he straightened, released his grip. Manu's nose spurted blood. He suffered aches himself, his cheekbone smarting where his cousin had struck a lucky blow. He shook the sluggishness from his brain. The coffee table sat on its side and several bottles littered the floor. The scent of beer accompanied the coppery tang of blood. A chair—no, make that two—required repairs.

Manu folded his arms, that irritating mocking to the fore again. "Cassie?"

Hone growled at both his cousin and the situation they'd

created. Explanations. Crap. He swung to survey the kitchen and dining area, visible due to the open plan layout of the room. Long strides took him on a quick tour of the rest of his home, but his nose told him the truth.

She'd left.

"She doesn't have a vehicle." Manu tipped back his head to stem his nosebleed. "Maybe she took yours."

"You told me you weren't interested in her."

"I might have changed my mind."

Hone's taniwha snarled, low and mean and menacing. To hell with Manu's status as tribe heir. Cassie belonged with him. *Him.* Not his cousin.

"All right. All right." Manu held up his hands in surrender, despite the power radiating from his watchful gaze. "I like her. It's true, but my taniwha isn't driving me like yours."

Tension eased from Hone, allowing him to breathe. "She's not your potential mate?"

"No. You'd better go after her."

"Why are you here? Did you realize Cassie was alone?"

"I wanted you to help me with more tests. Cassie's presence was a lucky break. She's good company. I like her," Manu repeated. "There's no pretense. She doesn't flirt or giggle or act coy. She's different from other women."

"Stay away from her." Fury gripped Hone's throat and obstructed his breathing. Anger at his cousin. Frustration at himself because he couldn't decide what to do when it came to Cassie. Not that it mattered. He'd probably blown any chance with her. "Straighten the furniture. I'll find her. Give her a lift to the motel." Hone stomped outside. Ground-eating strides took him to his vehicle, parked haphazardly in the driveway, driver's door still open because his taniwha had snatched control from the second he'd glimpsed Manu's vehicle. He patted his pockets, coming up empty. Ah, the keys were in the ignition.

He zapped from the driveway and scrutinized the road to the left, to the right. No Cassie. For all he knew, she'd called a cab.

Where the hell was his phone? He slapped his pockets with one hand, came up empty. Where had he left it?

Right. He'd try right. If he didn't find her, he'd wait at the motel, hopefully under Auntie June's radar. He scanned the footpaths, the bus stops, the road as he drove.

He didn't see Cassie.

He reached the motel and pulled into a guest parking spot. His phone rang. He located it under the passenger seat. "Yeah."

"Is that the way you answer your phone with customers?" Manu asked.

"The call identity came up with Dickhead."

"Ouch." Manu snorted. "Good one, cuz. Did you find her?"

"Not yet. I'm at the motel."

"Ma is home today."

"That makes things easier."

Manu's chuckle riled Hone's taniwha. A growl emerged, harsh enough to sear his throat.

Manu ceased with his hilarity. "Ma has spies."

"Who?" Hone scanned the motel forecourt. The cleaners had finished for the day.

"Haven't sussed that out yet. I'll tell you the second I discover the traitor's identity."

God, where was she? He scanned the road, releasing a pent-up breath when she came into sight. "I see Cassie."

"Good luck."

Hone's irritated rumble filled his vehicle. "You don't mean that. You like Cassie."

"She deserves better than you."

Hone grunted. "She could do better than you too, Dickhead."

"Just remember, cuz. You screw up, I'll be there to pick up the pieces."

Hone hit end call and shoved his phone in his pocket. He wanted to go to her, wrap his arms around her, beg her forgiveness. Instead, he waited until she unlocked her door and entered her motel room. His breath eased out in a husky sigh. A good man would leave her alone, get back to his rules.

No one had ever called him a good man.

Cassie unpacked the ice cream, the chocolate, the bottle of wine. Classic he-done-me-wrong cures, purchased at the local shop on the fast walk back to her motel. A bunch of bananas added the fruit component. Sort of healthy. Maybe the treats would calm her disquiet. She'd spent the entire hike glancing over her shoulder, looking for goodness knows what, but her skin had itched something fierce as if someone was spying on her.

The freezer door slammed, the back of her eyes stung.

She blinked. Once. Twice. Three times.

The friggin' truth. Her judgment ran amuck when it came to men. They'd been fighting. *Fighting*. And she had no idea why. The pair had spoken in code, no decipherable meaning to their cryptic man-speak. Oh, she'd understood some, but the context. The context escaped her translation.

A tap on her door had her swinging around. She stomped over and flung it open wide.

"You." She glowered at Hone. His right cheekbone bore a cut. A red splotch discolored his jaw. "What do you want?"

Hone swallowed, his usual lightheartedness absent. His hands fisted at his sides, and the sleeve of his black T-shirt gaped open to display his biceps. A faint growl came from him, and he gritted his teeth, sucked in a breath. "I've come to apologize."

"I'm on holiday. I don't have to put up with stupid cavemen males." Normally, Cassie tiptoed around confrontation, preferring a head-in-the-sand approach rather than a skirmish. The dinner-tipping moment with Kevin had been her turning point.

"You're right. I don't normally behave like that. Manu was being a smart-arse."

Her brows lifted.

"And I wasn't far behind," he mumbled, clearly uncomfortable with the confession. "Can I come in?"

Cassie noticed June Taniwha standing outside the motel office, regarding them with hands on her hips. She gestured Hone inside and glimpsed June's fierce frown. "Your auntie is scowling at us."

"What? Manu said she was at home. Crap, she's convinced I'm moving in on her son's girl. Quick, shut the door."

She complied and moved past the kitchenette to stand by the brown couch. "Manu and I are friends."

"I know. He told me. Twice."

"Did it take that long to get through your thick head?" The snide question hovered between them, and Cassie's face heated. "Sorry. That was mean."

"No more than I deserve. Look, I came to apologize. I saw you and Manu, cozy and happy. Jealousy got me. I reacted before my brain kicked into gear."

"Manu and I are friends. How many times do I have to tell you?"

"Obviously, a few more." Hone grimaced, his wry smile brittle at the edges. Tentative, as if he feared this conversational outcome. "Would you have dinner with me? Tomorrow night?"

"A date?"

"Yeah." He watched her with laser-intense regard, waiting for her decision.

"I...okay." Cassie had no idea what had come over her. A breathlessness, yet her pulse raced. A smidge of trepidation but mostly excitement—an impulse to jiggle her hips in a celebration dance. This gorgeous man had asked her out for dinner. "What time?"

"Seven? I'll pick you up."

"I'd like that."

"Okay. Good." Hone shuffled his feet, his gaze not settling. "I'd better go. I'll see you tomorrow at seven." He made his escape, almost running to his vehicle. He lifted a hand in farewell and sped from the parking lot.

Cassie waved goodbye. The man acted as if he were torn about the idea. Weird. She could ask Emma—no. Emma had warned her about Hone, and here she was, stepping out on a date. She'd take things slow and enjoy the getting-to-know details. Keep her heart protected. Have fun. Everyone should spice their lives with fun.

Her phone buzzed, and she shut the door before checking the text.

*Shopping tonight? L8 night at mall.*

She rang Emma. "I need Katie-Jo outfits. Will the mall have something suitable?"

"You told me you were on holiday."

"Kevin rang with an offer of two shows for the vineyard tour. One of the acts canceled due to illness, and they needed a last-minute replacement. It will give me a chance to sing my new material, so I agreed."

"Don't you wear a wig for your act?" Emma asked.

"Yeah, I'll have to buy one."

"Sounds like fun. You want me to pick you up?"

"Yes, please. I still don't have a vehicle."

"Sorry, I forgot. It's been a weird day. Are you feeling up to going shopping?"

"I not only have the inclination to shop, but I'll spring for dinner."

A brisk knock sounded on the door. "Gotta go, Emma. Someone at the door."

"I'll be there soon."

Cassie slipped the phone in her pocket and answered the summons.

"What was Hone doing here? I thought you were going out with my son."

Cassie blinked at the steely disapproval emanating from June Taniwha. "I was in an accident earlier today. Hone came to pick me up because Emma and Jack were busy. I left my phone in his car." She wasn't sure why she tacked the lie at the end of her speech, but it seemed to appease June.

"I wondered where you'd left your vehicle."

"I have to ring about a replacement," Cassie said and pulled out her phone in a subtle hint for June to leave. Those eyes of hers were freaky.

"Manu will help you if you ask."

"Yes, thank you. I saw him today."

June's instant smile dazzled. "I'll let you get on with your call. I'm glad you're all right."

"Thank you for dinner last night." Eyes. *Still creepy.*

"You're welcome, dear." June patted her arm and left her alone.

Well, that was weird. Alone in her room, Cassie scowled, tapped the top of the couch in a one-two, one-two beat. Should she seek Emma's advice? Or at least tell Manu his mother was acting strange about her spending time with Hone. Yeah. *Nah.* She'd let life happen and go with what felt right.

The shopping excursion—a huge success. Thanks to Emma's brilliant suggestion, she now owned a bright pink wig to wear with jeans and sparkly tops. Instead of her trademark cowboy boots, she'd purchased two pairs of pink shoes. One with chunky heels. One with spiky. She'd still appear like Katie-Jo instead of plain Cassie Miller-Pope, but she'd sport an edgy look to match her new, upbeat songs.

"Where do you want me to put these bags?" Emma asked.

"Dump them on the table, and I'll unpack them later. Want a drink?"

"No, I'd better head home before Jack sends out a search party. Thanks for the invitation. It was fun. Is there any chance of getting tickets to go to your show? I'd love to see you live."

"I'll try," Cassie promised. "Will Jack keep my secret?"

"Jack is excellent at secrets."

"Wait to see if I can score tickets before you tell him, okay?"

"Fair enough." Emma hugged Cassie. "Thank you."

Cassie winced, and Emma released her at once.

"You sore?"

"A little. I'll take a hot shower and painkillers before I go to bed. That should help. Busy day tomorrow. I want to do more painting, rehearse for the first show, and pick up my replacement rental car. Oh, I forgot to tell you. I met my neighbor this morning. He seems nice."

"Dateable?"

"A businessman. A little buttoned-up for me. I have a weakness for the bad boys. Always my downfall."

Emma chortled and patted her shoulder in commiseration. "At least you know they're bad. See you tomorrow."

Cassie locked the door after her friend. She padded to the tiny bathroom, deciding to remove her makeup and have an early night.

Five minutes later, she stepped from the hot shower. The whiny fan wasn't coping with the surplus steam, so she opened the frosted-glass window above the vanity unit. It bore a security lock and opened a scant five inches. Music, something about bringing on the clowns, drifted on the air. She shivered and drew her towel around her naked form. A creepy song about creepy beings.

Without warning, a gloved hand shot through the window gap.

A white hand.

Cassie screamed and lurched backward. Her spine hit the shower stall. The door vibrated with the force of her weight.

"Send in the clowns," a voice rasped.

Clammy fear slithered down Cassie's spine. A whimper broke free. The strange voice, the tone of the words worked on her psyche like fingernails on a blackboard. "G-go away. I-I'm calling the police."

A face pressed close to the gap. A white face. A red button nose.

Cassie's legs quaked. The clown chuckled. Maniacal. Cray-crazy. She moaned, edged toward the door. Her phone. She had to get her phone. The door was locked. He'd have to break a window, the door, something to gain entry.

"Where ya gone, girlie? Just acting friendly. Where ya be?"

Cassie's breaths came in harsh pants, her fingers quivering as she reached for her phone. Her fingers shook so much she misdialed once before she rang 111.

"111 emergency, fire, ambulance or police?"

"Police. Please, I need the police," Cassie gasped out.

Immediately, a tone sounded in her ear. Her gaze darted toward the bathroom, she cocked her head to listen.

"This is the police. How can I help you?" a calm feminine voice asked.

"Someone is trying to break into my motel room."

"What is your address?"

"167 Great South Road, Papakura. The Montville motel." She cried out. Cringed as the notes of the clown song blasting loud. "Oh, heck."

"What is happening? Are you safe?"

"He's playing a creepy clown song." Great. Now her voice shook in concert with her limbs.

"Are you safe?" the woman repeated.

"T-the doors are locked."

"Is he still there?

"I d-don't k-know. All I can hear is the creepy clown music."

Sirens sounded in the distance, faint at first but coming closer and closer, eventually drowning out the disturbing music.

A vehicle pulled up outside, blue lights, red lights flashing.

"I-I think the police are here."

"Don't open the door until they identify themselves."

"'Kay."

A knock rattled the wooden door. "Police."

Quick steps took her to the window to double-check. Yep, the friendly neighborhood police. Thank you. Thank you. *Thank you.* Relief solidified her knees, cleared her mind, allowed her to calm, to breathe.

"It's them." She answered the summons, despite wearing nothing more than a damp towel.

One male and a female policeman displayed their identification. "You reported an intruder?"

# CHAPTER 10

H one started in his chair, the strident demand of his phone wrenching, dragging, yanking him from sexy dreams of the curvy Cassie.

"Hell." He swiped his hand across his brow, adjusted his track pants before lowering the chair footrest. He snagged his phone off the wooden coffee table.

"Yeah."

"Something's up at the motel. Cassie's unit," Manu said without preamble. "My security system beeped. Bad enough to call the cops."

Fully awake now, Hone grabbed his keys, fiercely glad he'd fallen asleep fully dressed. Saved time.

A fast trip later, after superb driving—even if he did say so himself—he screeched into the motel parking lot. A cop car had parked outside Cassie's unit. Cassie stood at the door with the police.

A growl rumbled through him, his taniwha exerting displeasure. Hone straightened, slapped his beast down, because he needed to speak with the cops. Cassie.

*Calm down. We need Cassie.*

His taniwha growled and fell silent.

Hone approached the cops—one male and the other female. "Cassie, you okay?"

"Who are you?" the female cop asked before Cassie could reply. The male cop circled the motel wall and disappeared.

"I'm her boyfriend," Hone said.

Luckily, Cassie scarcely blinked.

"Where were you half an hour ago?"

"Asleep at home in my chair. My auntie owns the motel. She heard about the trouble and asked me to come and check," Hone said.

The suspicion didn't lessen on the cop's face. She turned to Cassie. "He really your boyfriend?"

"Yes. I haven't known him long, but he works with my best friend. Besides, the man I saw wore full clown makeup."

"A clown?" Hone grimaced. No wonder she looked freaked. Was this a copycat of the clown craze sweeping the world, or was it connected to Cassie's earlier accident?

Hone weighed the information, factored in coincidence, and kept coming back to instinct. Someone wanted her frightened. Someone wanted her pain. Someone was stalking her.

Unobtrusively, he sniffed the air, sorting through the layers of smells. Petrol. Perfume. Aftershave. Grass. Nothing out of place in the parking lot.

The male cop reappeared. He wagged his head, an imperceptible shake, and the female cop turned back to Cassie. "We have your statement. If you have any other problems, call us."

"You okay, Cass?"

Relief flickered over her face as she flew at him to burrow against his chest. His arms wrapped around her, and she shuddered, her breathing harsh. Not far from breaking point. He didn't feel much better, his heart racing, but the weight of her body against his calmed his angst. She was safe.

A long moment later, she pulled back, tear-stained gaze behind her smeared glasses. "I can't stay here tonight. I can't."

"Would you like to come home with me?"

"Yes, please," she said in a small voice.

"Okay, let's get your things." He propelled her into the motel unit. "I'll ring Manu while you pack. I'll be right here, okay? You don't have to worry."

"Why are you ringing Manu?"

"He told me the police were at the motel. I said I'd check on you. He'll want to know what happened."

"You're not arguing with him again?" The strident note in her words had him smiling.

"I've apologized to you and Manu. Besides, we're cousins and friends. We argue, and we move on."

"Oh. Okay." Cassie pulled open drawers and placed clothes in a pile on the bed. "Um, can you come with me to the bathroom?" Her chin wobbled, and he closed the distance between them to offer comfort. Her vulnerability dragged out the protective caveman. Something new, but an action he didn't shy from with Cassie.

"What do you need? I can get it for you."

"My toothbrush and other toiletries."

"All right, babe. You finishing packing. I'll get them for you."

Hone strode into the bathroom, noted the window—open scant inches due to the security lock—the black dusting of fingerprint powder. After sucking in a deep breath to test for scents, he scowled. An out-of-place smell polluted the air. Greasy. Paint-like. It could've come from the cops. He'd question Cassie once she'd calmed.

He secured the window and gathered the toiletries into the blue toilet bag sitting on the vanity top. "I think I have everything. Are you ready to go?"

"Yes." She stood by the bed, arms wrapped around her torso.

"You've had an eventful day." He tossed the toilet bag into the open bag on the bed and zipped it shut, then picked it up with his left hand.

"I don't want a repeat, that's for sure."

An understatement. Run off the road this morning and an intruder tonight. "Any enemies you know of?"

"I haven't been back in New Zealand for long." A furrow formed between her bloodshot eyes, and she gnawed her bottom lip like a champ. "I haven't had time to make enemies."

"Ex-boyfriends?"

"I spoke to Kevin earlier today. While we didn't part on good terms, we still work together. It's not him since he's still in Los Angeles."

"I see." Not really, and neither did his taniwha. The idea of another man with hands-on privileges brought the beast to growly life. Hone—the man—disliked the thought too. "Are you sure?"

"I've no reason to suppose otherwise. I need my guitar," she said without warning, balking at his gentle guidance toward the door. "I can't go without it." She darted away, grabbed the instrument, and returned to his side.

"Where is the case?"

"Still at your place."

Guilt roared through him in a dizzy rush. His fault. God, he hadn't experienced the longing to pummel Manu since his teen days when he was learning to control his taniwha. His father would've been horrified. His uncle too, but he figured Manu wouldn't blab because that would draw June's attention. No one wanted the matriarch angry, spurting fiery punishment.

"Did the police have any idea of the prowler's identity?"

"They said they hadn't received reports of clowns breaking into properties." She pulled a face. "Clowns are creepy."

"You ain't wrong." Hone scanned the motel grounds as he hustled Cassie to his vehicle. The back of his neck tingled, dragon spidery senses roaring, and he didn't doubt someone skulked in the darkness. Watching. Calculating. It would be interesting to see if that Peeping Tom followed them—not that he'd make their location easy to discover.

His vehicle unlocked, and he placed Cassie's bag in the rear. He opened the passenger door for her, half his attention on their surroundings. If he could pinpoint the vicinity, he might have a chance of catching the bastard.

A chuff of approval rippled through his mind, yet the human part of him tempered the eagerness with a mental order.

*We need to keep Cassie safe.*

"Have plans for tomorrow?" During the drive home, he scrutinized other vehicles while doing the small-chat thing with Cassie.

"Same as earlier. The clown doesn't change anything."

"Who dresses up as a clown?"

"Yeah. I know. Who does that?" She yawned, white teeth flashing before she clapped a hand over her lips. "Sorry."

"Nearly home," Hone said. "You can sleep without worrying

about clowns."

Cassie lay in the comfy bed in Hone's spare room. Each of the four windows was locked. Hone had set the alarm. She should feel safe, but every clock tick, every car rumble, every unfamiliar creak had her bolting upright, fear rioting, cold sweat bursting across her skin. Every time she closed her eyes, the clown did a *cha-cha-cha* across her eyelids. White face. Scarlet lips. Bubble nose. Creepy. The lyrics of the song resounded in a loop-de-loop. Creepy. *So creepy.*

A harsh squeak had her halfway to the door before the order from her brain. At the repeat of the creak, she darted through the doorway, down the passage to Hone's bedroom—the one he'd pointed out earlier. She skidded through the doorway despite the darkness, despite her lack of glasses, despite the skimpy nightclothes, the bad boy danger. She blundered forward and barked her knees on the bed.

"Oomph." She caught her weight on her hands and straightened to rub the sore spots.

"Cassie, what's wrong?" His husky voice guided her.

"Noises." Like a heat-seeking missile, she headed for safety.

"What sort of noises?" The covers whispered as he changed position.

"Groans and thumps. Squeaks."

"Get into bed to keep warm while I do a security check." The floor creaked, and she widened her eyes to see the blur of Hone and what he wore—or didn't wear—to bed.

"I...um..."

His voice. It got to her—strummed and plucked her nerves in a different way. This time the quakes working through her body had nothing to do with her crazy day, everything to do with *him*.

"Cassie." His voice soothed, a gentle calm-the-wild-animal inflection. "Do as you're told. I'll be back once I've done recon."

She shuffled, still night-blind, lack-of-glasses blind, using her hand to guide her to the head of the bed. Tension kept her shoulders stiff, and she strained to hear. She'd never forgive herself if danger had followed her to Hone's home.

"Cassie?"

She let out a shriek.

Without warning, light flooded the bedroom.

"Cassie, it's me."

"Did you find anything?" She tried not to focus on his naked chest. Her gaze skittered down to his form-fitting boxer-briefs. Not much better. She wrenched her gaze away and settled for watching his face. He sported a grin.

"Nothing out of the ordinary," he murmured.

For a naughty second, she speculated if he meant outside or in his boxer-briefs. "I..." She wrapped her arms around herself again, pressing her oversized T-shirt to her unbound breasts. "Um...don't look at me like that. I can't concentrate."

"Me neither," he whispered. "Go back to bed, Cassie."

"I can't sleep," she wailed. "I close my eyes, and I see clowns. C-can I stay with you?"

"Is that a good idea?"

"You won't hurt me."

"That's not what I meant. If you keep up the silent invitations, I will forget myself and kiss you. You've had a rough day."

Before she could answer, he pulled back the covers and gestured for her to get into the bed. The light switched off the second she cuddled into the duvet. While she'd experienced a chill earlier, now heat raced across her skin.

The mattress dipped, and her breath caught. "I'm not imagining clowns now."

"Good."

"I'm thinking about you kissing me."

Was that a groan? It could've been a tetchy sigh. "Cassie, you've had a hard day. You're bruised, and someone tried to frighten you. Go to sleep."

Cassie flopped onto her side, huffed out her frustration. Emma would never believe this scenario. She'd offered herself to Hone and received a rejection.

The bad boy had scruples.

# Chapter 11

Hone recognized the moment she fell asleep because her breathing deepened and her body relaxed. Kissing. Hell, he had to open his big mouth and tell her he wanted to kiss her. Do more than kiss. Both human and taniwha thought about Cassie Miller-Pope far more than advisable.

He stared into the darkness. She inhaled softly, and her floral fragrance wafted in the air. His taniwha hummed in approval. Would Cassie wake if he left the bed? Self-preservation drove him to think of drinking, despite his dragon's delight in her presence.

If he didn't move soon, he'd end up doing something stupid...like waking her, like ravaging her lips with his, like rolling her under him.

Without warning, she turned over, minimizing the distance

between them. She snuggled. Snuggled against his chest. Snuggled until his groan filled the air, yet she didn't wake.

Maybe he could...

Before he took action, she flung her arm over his hip, effectively trapping him. If he moved, chances were he'd wake her.

Perhaps if he mentally arranged his calendar for the rest of the week. The quote for a burglar alarm at a residential property. Yeah. And the off-site meeting for a clothing factory to halt staff pilfering. *What next? Crap.. What next?*

The...the cheating husband. Following him. Snapping telltale photos for the wife after revenge. Yeah. She aimed to nail his arse to the wall. The cheaters met for lunch. Had to organize his day around this assignment.

*Huh!* Better. Along with not wanting to hurry into a serious relationship, watching the stream of imploding couples during his workday made a man cynical. His muscles relaxed until he recalled his friends.

Jack. Emma. They experienced the same phenomenon.

Cheating. Sneaking around. Lies.

Neither had hesitated. They seemed happy. No. They *were* happy.

Man, this relationship stuff confused him. Things had been easier before Cassie exploded into his life. Only two days ago. His life—simpler pre-Cassie.

He puffed out a hard breath and checked to see if Cassie

stirred. So much in a short time. He recalled Jack's grumpiness with Emma. His avoidance. His other women before he gave up running. Fleeing. Hiding.

Was that what he was doing?

His dragon growled. At him, this time. Off-balance. Out-of-sorts. He kept screwing up simple things.

Not too late to walk away. Run away. Sprint.

He hadn't kissed her yet.

Trouble. A human came with trouble. Big and chaotic and worrying trouble.

*Emma had handled the knowledge of Jack's otherness.*

Cassie...

*No!* No, getting close and personal with Cassie.

Hone grunted. Frustration. Longing. Hope. His beast pounded him with contrary emotions, refuting every logical argument.

Sex.

Hot and sweaty sex.

He squirmed now. Cassie's weight restricted movement, merely suffusing him with awareness. His dick grazed her leg, and his moan of pleasure-pain squeezed free.

It was gonna be a bloody long night.


Hone woke. Instant awareness zapped him into sexual frustration. Cassie's warm body draped him like a comfy blanket. Must've gone to sleep after all.

His cock ached. Ached so bad. He pushed out his senses. Not long 'til daybreak.

Cassie stirred. One moment she was relaxed and fragrant and perfect in his arms. The next, every muscle grew rigid.

"Cassie?" His dick throbbed. Just the slightest touch...

"Hone!"

He growled at her shocked tone. "Who'd you expect?"

She jerked away, putting space between them. Her naked eyes, different without her glasses, blinked at him. "Did you have to make a move on me while I was sleeping?"

His laugh scratched his throat as it emerged. "I was lying here wondering how to get out of bed without waking you. You were on top of me."

Delicate pink flushed her cheeks. "I've always been a bed hog."

A picture popped into his mind—one of Cassie with a faceless man.

*Hell to the no.*

His taniwha swelled with fury, push, push, pushing against his skin-and-bone cage. A growl escaped, rippling in the air between them.

Her swift inhalation caught. She stared, wide-eyed. Easy to read her thoughts. Fight or flight. Damn his impertinent animal side.

"W-what was that?"

Hone refused to lie. Nah, avoidance to survive. Deny. Deny. Deny. He reached for her and dragged her close in one efficient

move. Her curves fit him like perfect puzzle pieces. Soft to hard.
She opened her mouth.

Hell, women liked to talk. No talking. Talking was bad.

He kissed her.

A mistake.

He acknowledged it the instant her lips softened against his.

His taniwha purred, glorying in his human half following his
program.

Warning. Warning. *Warning*. Pull back. Pull back. *Pull back
now.*

Instead, Hone deepened the contact, diving into the kiss. He
inhaled, dragging in her floral scent. His tongue dragged across her
lower lip, and he nipped her, her sharp gasp indicating surprise.
The second she opened to him, he went all-out, tasting and
learning her as he'd craved since the first time he'd spotted her with
Emma.

She gripped his shoulders and pushed to separate their bodies.

Hone froze. Did she not want this? *Hellfire.*

He pulled back a fraction. "I-I'm sorry. I didn't mean to force
myself on you."

"You didn't. I can hear a phone."

Cassie's red, swollen lips drew his gaze. *So pretty.*

"The phone?"

Finally, her words pierced his fog-brain, and he, too, heard the
summons.

"Stay there. I'll get it." He threw back the covers and stalked from the bedroom, mentally cursing himself for not placing his cell phone by his bed. He normally did. Cassie's fault.

He licked his lips, located the offending phone, and barked into it, "This had better be good."

"It's Jack. Emma says Cassie isn't answering her call."

"What time is this to ring?" Hone demanded.

"Six isn't early."

"It is when you have a willing woman in your bed."

"That better not be Cassie," Jack snapped, his attitude reminiscent of the Jack of old, before Emma smoothed his rough edges.

"There was trouble at the motel last night. A prowler. Cassie had to call the cops."

"Crap. She okay?"

Hone heard Emma prattling in the background. He wasn't surprised to find himself speaking with her instead of Jack. Knowing she'd want to talk to Cassie, he returned to the bedroom. Cassie was propped against his pillows. He took a moment to savor the sight before handing her the phone. Emma continued to prattle and squawk.

"Emma wants to talk to you."

He handed over the phone, and she shivered at the hand-to-hand contact. His taniwha sighed happily. Interesting.

Terrifying.

*No.* No more touching. He stepped back. Away.

"Hi, Emma." Cassie listened, held the phone farther from her ear. "Emma! I'm okay. I rang the police and—"

Emma interrupted. "Why didn't you ring me?"

Hone eavesdropped without shame. Knowledge was power. He *needed* to know this woman.

"Hone came. It was late, and I didn't want to wake you and Jack."

"What will you do about the concerts?" Emma demanded. "Someone ran you off the road, and you had to report a prowler. You've been home days. Days! You shouldn't be on your own. You need security. What if it's a fan? A smart one who's figured out the truth?"

Hone dropped onto the side of the bed, pretending interest in sleep. Fan? Concerts? What the hell was Emma babbling about?

"When is the first concert?"

"Saturday." Cassie dissected his expression until he felt like a nuisance bug. Seemed her vision worked okay this close. He shut his eyes a scant second before her gaze tickled over his face.

"What about security?" Emma demanded.

"Didn't think I'd need protection. This is New Zealand, not the States."

"Hello?" Emma screeched so loud even Hone winced. "Prowler? I'll talk to George, see if he'll give me time off to bodyguard you while you're performing."

While Hone digested this, he heard Jack's curse of protest.

"I can afford to pay for security." She glanced at him, and this time Hone stared back openly. "We can discuss this later. I have things to do today." She hung up on Emma mid-lecture.

"Why do you need security?"

Cassie wet her lips. "I want a confidentiality agreement before I answer that."

Hone froze. "I'm your friend. Emma's friend. I'd never hurt you."

"My last boyfriend—Kevin—I found him in bed with another couple. We'd been together for almost a year. I was planning on forever with him."

"An agreement won't prevent me from fucking around," Hone spoke bluntly, but he took his phone and hit speed dial. "Dad, do you have free time this morning? Good, I need to see you. I'm bringing someone with me, and we need a non-disclosure contract. Nine? Sure, that works. See you then." He hung up and turned to Cassie.

His dragon purred, ecstatic at their proximity.

Hell. Too close.

Her heat. Her feminine scent. Her sexy breathing.

He jumped to his feet and forced his legs to carry him to the end of the king-size bed. "Nine work for you?"

"Yes. Thank you." Her expression veered to weird. "Most people would've turned huffy, demanded answers."

"I'm not most people," Hone snapped. "You want coffee?"

"Please."

"I'll bring in your bag for you. You can use my shower." He gestured to his en suite and left before his dragon pushed the issue, and he climbed back in bed with her.

Oh, sugar.

She puffed out her breath hard enough to stir her fringe. She'd pissed him off when he'd been nothing but kind to her, rescuing her not once but twice. Yet, she didn't know him...

*You kissed him*, a little voice interrupted. Heat rushed through her at the memory. The man kissed...perfect, masterful kisses that strummed her like a guitar. He had a right to ask questions, but what would happen once he learned the truth? She'd discovered it was better to keep her life private—her two lives separate. Less complicated, and she didn't have to make excuses about her absences, her weird hours.

*But you're not happy.* That stupid little voice again.

She was content. She was blissful. She was a box of joyful songbirds.

Yet she'd come home to New Zealand. She'd decided to take a break when Kevin required her to embrace a new direction. The truth. Something lacked in her life...

Hone appeared. "Here is your bag. The coffee is almost ready."

"I'll come out," Cassie said. "I won't be long. I need my glasses to take away the fuzziness."

He offered a curt nod and wheeled, leaving her staring at his spectacular arse, outlined by his boxer-briefs, and his bare back covered by a blurry dragon tattoo. Her fingers tingled as she recalled touching his warm skin, trailing her hands over his muscled chest. She'd touched him and enjoyed the tactile caress.

Emma had the worst timing.

# CHAPTER 12

George Taniwha, the figurehead of George Taniwha & Sons, was a handsome man with unruly black hair and a welcoming, pleased-to-meet-you beam, much like his son. But also like Hone, those eyes held keen intelligence, and Cassie sensed not much got past him. He stood when Hone guided her into the spacious office.

A large wooden desk held a pile of folders, one of which was open in front of George. The office was functional and gave off a busy vibe that would reassure clients.

"It's great to meet you, Cassie. I've heard a lot about you from June and Samuel." He stretched out his hand and took hers in a firm grip before gesturing at the pair of chairs adjacent to his desk.

"Good things, I hope." Cassie sank onto a chair.

George furrowed his brows and studied his son in the way of parents the world over. Hone broke and shifted his weight.

"June said you were dating Manu," George said.

"No," Cassie spluttered, her spine going poker-straight to hit the back of her office chair. "We...Manu and I are friends."

One of those weird growls emerged from Hone, and George straightened, his features shooting to stern. Oh, yes. Parent-mode in full force. Cassie was glad she wasn't the only one who buckled beneath parental disapproval.

The rumble abruptly ceased.

George studied them with clear expectation. Cassie glanced at Hone, unsure of where to start.

"I need information from Cassie, but she is reluctant to give it to me without a confidentiality agreement in place. She requires a bodyguard."

The way Hone said this made her feel low, but she had to protect herself, didn't she?

"I have one here," George said. "It's the standard contract our clients sign to protect both us and them." He opened a folder, extracted a sheet of paper, and pushed it over the table to her. "Read it, and if you find it suitable, we'll all sign and go from there."

Cassie's phone rang. "Sorry." She plucked it from her pocket and scanned the screen. "It's Emma."

"I'll talk to her," Hone said. "You read that."

"I'm getting tired of people bossing me about." Cassie glared at Hone's father when he had the audacity to chuckle but handed over her phone to read the confidentiality agreement.

Fortunately, it was in plain English and easy to understand. It was typed on George Taniwha & Sons letterhead, the silhouette of the taniwha drawing her attention. She had a thing for dragons and liked to read shapeshifter romances in her downtime between shows. A secret between her and her e-reader.

The document held gaps to fill in names. Seemed straightforward, and it spelled out what would happen if either party disclosed confidential information.

"Pen?"

She filled in the blanks and scrawled her signature as the office door sprang open. The receptionist scrambled after Emma while Jack shook his head in amusement.

"Are you all right?" Emma demanded.

"I told you she's fine," Hone grumbled.

"I wanted to see for myself." Emma strode into the office, and Jack prowled after her.

"Janice," George said. "Can you come in here and witness a document for us?"

"I'd like Jack and Hone to sign the agreement as well, then I can tell you all together," Cassie said. "It will be easier that way."

She watched everyone sign, and the receptionist witnessed the document and left the room.

"Right," Hone said. "Now tell me why you need security."

"I'm not a personal assistant to a singer," Cassie said. "I *am* the singer. My manager asked me to do two concerts at local vineyards. I'm filling in for a last-minute cancellation. With all that has happened in the last two days, Emma has decided I have a rabid fan after me."

"No one recognized you at the beach," Hone said.

"What is your stage name?" Jack asked, expression full of concentration and focus.

This was how Cassie imagined Jack in PI mode.

"It's Katie-Jo," Emma said. "She's big in country music."

"Country isn't as popular here, but I wear stage costumes and a wig. It makes it easier for me to have a private life," Cassie said. "Although it's not impossible that someone has penetrated my disguise, it's unlikely. My agent put out the story that I was going home to rest and take a vacation. My official bio says my home is in Washington DC where my parents live. I usually keep a low profile. The only person who knows my identity is Emma."

"That explains the guitar and the singing," Hone said. "I heard you and Manu before..." He glanced at Jack and Emma, then his father, before shrugging. "You're good."

"Thanks." Her fans enjoyed her singing, but it was nice to have someone who knew her—if two day's acquaintance counted—tell her she wasn't wasting time with her music.

Her mother...

Cassie blanked the rest of that thought. Her parents, her mother in particular, didn't approve of many things. Something Cassie tried to ignore.

"Emma is right," Hone said. "You can't go to the concerts on your own, not until we discover if the clown was a coincidence."

"Clown?" George asked.

"My prowler last night was dressed as a clown," Cassie said. "He played a creepy song about clowns. I used to laugh about people with clown phobias. Considered them precious. After last night, I have sympathy. I'm not sure how I feel about someone tagging after me all the time," she added.

"I'll go with you." Hone leaned back and stretched his arms above his head. He reminded her of a spring-loaded door. "We'll keep it casual. I'll go as your boyfriend."

His words fell into silence loaded with indecipherable undercurrents. It left Cassie drifting and cranky. She hated people managing her and bossing her around. This felt like a takeover.

"Is that all right with you, Miss Miller-Pope?" George picked up a pen and tapped it on his desktop twice.

"Call me Cassie," she said. "I guess we can try that and see how it works. Given the weird things happening to me, it would be silly to refuse your help."

"What about from now until the concert?" Emma demanded. "You can't be alone."

"I don't need a babysitter," Cassie snapped, stung by her friend's words.

"Be reasonable. You could've been killed when that truck ran you off the road. You're lucky you got away with bruising."

Cassie sighed, admitting Emma was right. Things seemed to happen whenever she was alone. "I wanted to go to the house and do more painting. I need to work through my bracket of songs. Rehearse."

"I could probably shift around my jobs. I don't mind painting," Hone said.

"It's settled then," George said. "Hone, a word before you go."

Hone waited while Cassie, Emma, and Jack left the office.

"Shut the door behind you," George called to Jack.

The door closed with an abrupt click.

"June is right. Cassie is a lovely girl." His father grinned at him. "June is gonna be pissed when she learns about you and Cassie."

"Dad, I met her two days ago."

"Your taniwha wants her."

"Rubbish." Hone lied without a blink.

"He flickers in your pupils. You're having trouble controlling him. Jack told me although I see it for myself."

"Jack is a blabbermouth."

"Working as Cassie's bodyguard will give you a chance to get better acquainted."

Hone grunted.

"You play guitar. Rehearse with her. You might need the additional cover, especially if the venue organizers have hired security already. If you can help with her act that gives you a legitimate excuse to be near her onstage."

Hone saw the sense in his father's suggestion. "I'll ask her."

"Your mother will be pleased."

"Dad, I repeat. I've known her for two days."

"I knew your mother for one."

"You were childhood friends."

"But I didn't meet her again until we were in our early twenties," George countered.

Hone grimaced, having heard the story hundreds of times. "Please don't tell her anything."

"Too late," George said. "June has told Irene about Cassie. She was gloating about the wonderful woman Manu had found. Your mother will want to do some rejoicing of her own."

"Auntie June will lose her temper," Hone predicted. "It won't end well."

"You're right," his father said. "We'll wait. Besides, we have the confidentiality agreement now. I won't say anything until this is over."

Hone rolled his shoulders and stood. "I hope we're overreacting."

"You don't think so."

"I don't know, but I'll feel better when Cassie has finished her concerts. I could ask Manu to do a flyover of her property once he is sure his cloaking device is officially working. He said he wanted to do more tests."

"We're lucky to have Manu," his father said. "The boy has talent and strong leadership skills. He'll be a worthy successor once June decides to pass the mantle."

"Our people underrate him," Hone said. "I flew with him the other night. There were no alarms or alerts from pilots or bystanders. His invention works. It's almost ready for market."

His father tapped his pen. "Manu rang me. We discussed marketing and checking the backgrounds of those who wish to buy units. He wants to check his device in different weather conditions. He said your flight was clear, but he wants to run tests in rain and fog."

"I didn't think of that. I guess I'd better get moving."

"Have Janice swap around your jobs. I'll tell her not to schedule you for anything for the next few weeks."

A tap sounded on the door, and when Hone opened it, Cassie stood there. "I forgot to ask for a quote. I mightn't be able to afford your services."

"We'll give you the family rate since you're Emma's friend." His father named a ridiculously cheap rate. "I also expect a signed CD of your latest album. You still have CDs, or is your music only available online?"

"I'll have some sent to you," Cassie promised. "Thank you."

"Nice to meet you, Cassie. Hone, text me Cassie's number. I want you to check in with me morning and night. Call if you need support. I can send Emma or Jack to give you a break."

"Will do. Where to first?" he asked Cassie.

"I'll check out of the motel. There is no way I can stay there now without having nightmares. Will June be okay about it?"

"I'll ring her," his father volunteered. "She'll want to beef up her security anyway."

"Thanks, Dad. I'll talk to you tonight." He ushered Cassie from the office. "Do you need more paint?"

"If you're helping me—yes. I'll need more brushes and another paint roller as well."

Cassie tensed as she unlocked the door to her grandfather's house, half expecting more sheep or something worse. Incredibly aware of Hone behind her, she concentrated on foot placement while her pulse raced. She peeked down the passage. Nothing scary apart from a dust bunny. She put down her bag and the can of paint she carried to plug in the alarm code, suppressing her groan at the protest of bruised muscles. She'd been better.

Once the beeping ceased, she turned to Hone with a grin and more than a hint of relief. "The alarm seems to have done the trick."

"Good. Where do you want me to paint?"

"Could you paint over the graffiti in the kitchen? I've decided to rip out the kitchen units, so don't worry about them. I want to cover all the graffiti first." She wandered into the kitchen and wrinkled her nose. "I forgot. The walls need prep before painting."

"No problem," Hone said. "You're paying my wages."

"I have an idea of how much security guards cost because my manager whines about the expense. Your father gave me a huge reduction."

"You got the friend discount."

"Which reminds me. I should check in with Kevin about Saturday night, and I'll organize the CDs for your parents."

She rang Kevin. "Hi, Kevin. Is there anything I need to know about the first concert? Who do I report to?"

"I'll meet you at the Matakana vineyard. The organizer is Charlie Blake. I'll text you his details, so you can discuss musicians and lighting et cetera."

"You're coming to New Zealand? I thought you said the place is a dump, and you wouldn't be seen dead here." Another contentious subject between them. She loved her birth country and had hated leaving. Kevin, a Los Angeles man, liked big cities and fast action.

A snort escaped her. Probably why their plain vanilla sex hadn't done it for them, and he'd strayed elsewhere.

"You're my client. I'll be there Friday."

Translation: he was worried she wouldn't resign her contract. She grimaced. Jeez, when had she become so cynical about the music business?

She shoved aside her battle of should she, shouldn't she resign with Kevin to concentrate on her upcoming concerts. "Can you bring a selection of my CDs for me?"

"Sure."

"Okay, I'll see you there then. An hour before kick-off, okay?"

"That will work," Kevin said. "What about musicians? Charlie said they'd find someone for you, but you'd need to contact him before the gig."

"I've decided to do an unplugged version of my songs. Just me and my guitar. If I change my mind, I have a few contacts here I can tap as a backup."

"Chosen your songs?"

"Yes, Kevin." She suppressed her sigh. She didn't need micromanaging for this show. In her earlier days, she'd leaned on Kevin, but she'd grown lately and wasn't the same naïve girl. "Don't worry. I'm organized and will do you proud."

"These shows are important, Cassie. Don't make the mistake of taking them lightly. They're a test to learn if your music translates to other markets. You need to pick your songs carefully."

"Kevin." She didn't try hiding her indignation. "I am always serious about my career because I wouldn't have one if I didn't have fans. I won't screw up."

There was a pause, and she pictured the silent counting Kevin did when things weren't going his way, the sweep of his hand through his overlong blond hair. "All right. Give me a call if you need anything. I'll be in touch. Wait—what are you doing about costumes?"

"Sorted." She didn't tell him she had changed up her look, wanting to save herself a lecture.

He paused again, and Cassie fought the urge to giggle. Kevin wasn't sure what to do with this new version of her. Before they'd split, she'd never argued or made her own decisions. She liked herself much better now, even though the changes had come from a place of pain.

"Call me if you need anything."

"I will, Kevin. Thank you." She disconnected and set her phone aside. While her muscles ached, it was time to get painting. If she ran through her songs at the same time, she'd be doubly productive.

Cassie worked for an hour and decided, during that time, to swap the songs around. Yeah, start with the cover song to get the crowd excited. Not a Beatles' song though. A Crowded House song—one from a famous New Zealand band—might go down better with the home crowd. She sang the lyrics of the song, silently giving thanks for her exceptional memory when it came to music. Once she learned a piece, it stuck in her mind.

"That sounds good," Hone said from behind her. "You have a beautiful voice. You want me to play guitar with you? I'm better than Manu."

She laughed. "You both possess impossibly big egos."

Hone shrugged. "I heard what you're singing. You want to go all the way through with music to check your timing or whatever?"

Cassie set down her paint roller. "All right. It would be good to do a run-through. I usually chatter between songs, so I'll add that in as well." She checked her watch as Hone picked up her guitar.

"Hi! I'm Katie-Jo, a country singer from America. Most of you won't have heard of me, but that's okay. I'll let you judge me by the music. This first song has been a favorite of mine for years. You probably recognize it." And she launched into Crowded House's Better Be Home Soon.

As soon as she started singing, Hone added guitar backing. She jerked her chin in approval and yahooed inwardly. He was right. The man had skills.

She continued her songs, adding snippets about the music and with her own songs, how she came to write them and some of her Katie-Jo journey. Even though Hone didn't know the songs, he picked up the melody and had few missteps. He even harmonized in the choruses. When the final note drew out and faded, he grinned.

"I'm in awe." His big hands caressed her guitar, and she grew hot all over.

She averted her gaze before she self-combusted. After their kiss this morning, her imagination jumped ahead in leaps and spurts right into dirty, sexy acts with Hone. In bed. Against a wall. She didn't care. She'd been kidding herself with Kevin. Hone's kiss had left her more satisfied than any sweaty sex with her ex.

"Thanks. Anything to improve or suggestions to change around my selection?"

"No, you're good. Will you let me go onstage with you?"

"If you can manage playing for a crowd. Kevin won't let me hear the end of it if you freeze."

"I can handle myself. You want me to start ripping out the kitchen units?"

"Sounds good." Cassie picked up her roller, her mind skipping ahead. Excitement filled her, and she hadn't experienced this anticipation for a long time. She was right to stand her ground, despite Kevin's objections. While she enjoyed performing, it was the writing and shaping of new songs that made her happy. There was no reason she couldn't do what she wanted—write songs and sell the rights. Kevin could still be her manager. Yeah...she could write a few country tunes and write to please herself—see how that worked. It wasn't as if she didn't have enough money. Her parents had taught her the benefits of saving and prudent investment.

She could do whatever she wanted. Something to consider.

"Hey, boss." A strong thump on the door accompanied the

salutation.

Matthew looked up from his papers. "Herbert." The guy was big with shoulder-length brown hair and cauliflower ears. The oily strands accentuated rather than hid the defect. "You have something to report?"

"I did what you said. The woman has moved out of the motel. She's staying with some guy."

"Still in Papakura?"

"Yeah. Red Hill area."

"Is she scared?"

"Keeps checking over her shoulder. The guy she's with is some kind of private investigator. I followed them to an office. Had to hang back. The guy is watchful."

"Where are they now?"

"At the house in Clevedon. Think they're painting. Leastways they carried in cans of paint. Installed an alarm too. You want me to keep following 'em?"

"Yes, please. Keep back. If you have an opportunity, give her another scare. Don't take risks, but I'd like to keep her on edge."

"Will do, boss."

"Good. Anything else?"

"Nah. Crop's good. Another week, perhaps two, and we should be harvesting."

Matthew tapped his fingers on the desk. "I took a look last night. Another week should do it. Keep me posted about what she's doing."

"Will do." Herbert ambled away.

Matthew stared after him, thankful he'd employed the ex-rugby player. The man might look big and stupid, but he had a brain and the ability to think for himself and make good decisions.

All he needed was time. One month for planning to finesse his ex-wife. One month until he left for South America.

Just one more month until he gained every dream on his bucket list.

His son. Money. Victory.

## CHAPTER 13

Hone stood in the doorway, watching Cassie. So engrossed in her painting, she hadn't noticed his presence. His taniwha hummed, and a surge of lust bolted straight to his dick. Kissing her had been awesome. He'd enjoyed the hell out of himself. He'd craved more, but he'd forced himself to go slow.

No reason he couldn't do more kissing and groping tonight, though. He grinned and pushed away from the doorjamb. "You've been painting for three hours."

She squeaked before turning around to glare at him. She patted her left breast. "There's no need to sneak."

"Wasn't," he said cheerfully.

She rolled her shoulders and winced.

"I knew you shouldn't overdo it after yesterday."

"You never said anything."

"Figured you're an adult and you'd stop if you hurt."

"My mother would have ordered me."

He folded beefy arms across his chest. "I'm not your mother."

"Lucky for me. Yeah, I'm sore. I've overdone things. Pleased with the progress, though."

"You should take a break tomorrow. You want to be fighting fit for your show."

"You're right. I don't like to sit around doing nothing."

"We can find something to do." He winked and laughed at himself because his mind zapped straight to sex. He burned with the desire to touch her. "Let's go. You can soak away your aches in the spa pool."

Less than an hour later, they were back in Papakura. Manu was waiting for them and pushed away from the porch when they pulled up in the driveway. His expression...something wasn't right.

"What's up?" Hone opened the window, battling his urge to find privacy to get to know Cassie better and work out the tangle of emotions buzzing through his head, overshadowing even his dragon's determination to keep Cassie. With foreboding, he climbed from his vehicle.

"My mother's temper. She's poised for battle because, in her mind, you stole Cassie from me. Wanted to give you a heads-up."

"Who told her?"

"No idea, but she's eager for a confrontation."

The slam of the passenger door indicated Cassie was listening. They'd have to be careful of what they said in her presence.

"That makes me sound like a toy. We're adults." She frowned at Manu before turning her scowl on him. "Surely June isn't that angry? A few days' acquaintance doesn't make a relationship. I should talk to her." Cassie grimaced at Hone's low growl. "Stop rumbling. It's not cool. What do you think? Should I talk to June?"

"No," Hone snapped.

"No way," Manu echoed. "I'm going to my lab and not coming out until Dad tells me the smoke has cleared."

"Auntie June is angry at you, too. You heard of fire-breathing dragons? That is Auntie June when she gets riled." The truth as much as he could warn her. He pulled a face at his cousin. "How do you feel about a couple of days up north? We can go to Goat Island, check out the vineyards, and relax on the beach. Do some snorkeling, and it would be nearer to..." He trailed off as he glanced at Manu. Not his secret to tell, confidentiality and all that. "It might give Auntie time to calm down."

"I don't understand why you're tiptoeing around June. Is her temper really that bad?"

"Yes," Manu said bluntly. "The cops didn't catch the prowler. You should leave town."

"I suppose a few days away might be nice," Cassie said. "Emma and I visited the Goat Island marine reserve when we were kids, and I haven't been since."

"Excellent. We can leave tomorrow."

"Head off tonight," Manu prompted. "Ma is irate because your father gloated about your new lady. She connected the dots, even though Uncle George didn't mention names. She's angry enough to visit and voice her displeasure."

"Hell."

"Not even Dad has managed to calm her down."

"We'll go tonight," Hone agreed.

Cassie didn't understand why Hone and Manu seemed almost terrified of June. Manu's mother. Hone's aunt. It was weird. Totally weird. Yet, the truth was she'd be happy to leave Auckland. Ever since the accident, she'd been jumpy and kept looking over her shoulder. It was as if someone was spying on her. She thought back—no, she'd only experienced this creepy itchiness since the truck had run her off the road. The clown episode had compounded her nerves.

On cue, the ants-under-the-skin sensation scraped over her skin. A shiver worked through her, rippling along her arms and legs. Slowly, she surveyed the street behind them. Two children played with a large orange ball in the section opposite, their mother watching them as she hung out the washing. Farther down the street, a woman deadheaded her rose bushes.

Ordinary things.

Nothing to cause her anxiety.

She issued an irritated sigh, impatient with her over-active imagination. Too many late nights or something like that.

"Cassie?" Hone's tone indicated this wasn't the first time he'd called her name.

"Sorry. Zoned out for an instant there. What did you say?"

"Are you okay with leaving now? Did you want to ring Emma before we go?"

Her stomach let out a loud grumble of hunger. "I need food."

Manu and Hone exchanged a look and burst into action. Cassie blinked as Hone hustled her indoors, and Manu strode into the kitchen.

"I'll organize food while you pack," Manu said.

"Better ring a motel." Hone pulled out his phone and tapped several buttons. "That looks good."

Cassie sank onto a barstool at the kitchen counter and watched their frantic hurry. "You two are acting weird."

"Ring Emma," Hone ordered without taking his gaze off his screen.

Shrugging, she did as he said. "Hey, Emma."

"How are you?"

"Fine. Is June really as fierce as Hone and Manu are making out? Evidently, she's crabby with me because she'd decided Manu and I were a couple. Now she's found out that Hone and I—well, I'm not sure what we are since I've only known him for a few days. Hang on for a sec." She slid off the barstool. "I'm going into the spare bedroom so I can talk without ears flapping."

"Are you sure?" Manu asked. "Things were just getting interesting."

Cassie ignored them and hurried to the spare room. She shut the door and sank onto the end of the bed. "I don't hurry into relationships, but I like Hone. When he kissed me...I felt beautiful and desirable."

"Hone kissed you?"

"Yes. He made me feel feminine, and my size doesn't seem to worry him. But now he's behaving strangely. Is he a weirdo? You'd tell me, right?"

"There is nothing wrong with Hone, apart from the fact he goes through women like tissues," Emma said dryly. "Kissing is bad."

Cassie ignored the comment. "Why are they being so odd about June?"

"Because she has a fierce temper, and she holds a grudge," Emma said. "What did Manu suggest you do?"

"He and Hone have decided we're leaving town for a few days."

"Not a bad idea. You seem to be attracting trouble. Where are you going? Wait, don't tell me. Then if June asks me, I don't have to lie."

"You're frightened of her."

"You haven't seen her in a rage," Emma retorted.

"So you think I'll be safe with Hone?"

"Yes, otherwise, I wouldn't have agreed for him to act as your bodyguard."

"That's not what I meant," Cassie said.

"He'll treat you well, the sex will be excellent, and you'll have a laugh. If you want more than that, you should keep your distance and aim for friendship. I've told you that already. Wait, you said there was kissing. It's too late for warnings."

"Yeah." Cassie rearranged her fringe with a swipe of her fingers. "He's gonna break my heart, isn't he?"

"Probably."

"A broken heart won't kill me. I've had one before. As long as you ply me with chocolate, I'll get through it."

"I can do chocolate. That's what friends are for," Emma said lightly.

"I might get some songs out of it too."

"There you go. Silver linings. Look, Cassie. Just enjoy yourself and worry about everything else later."

"It worked out okay for you with Jack."

Emma remained silent for a few seconds. "Jack and Hone are different. Jack wasn't as big a player as Hone and his cousins."

"So if I was interested in Manu, you'd give me the same talk?"

"Yes."

"Right then."

"Have you heard from your mother?"

"Buzzkill," Cassie said. "Now she'll leap into my mind when I'm with Hone. If I were a man, that would give me performance issues."

Emma snort-laughed through the phone. "Go. Enjoy yourselves. Send me a text or two, okay?"

"I've organized tickets for you and Jack for Saturday at the Matakana vineyard. They said to give your names at the gate. My segment starts at eight."

"Cool. We'll see you Saturday night. Gotta go. This sleazeball is on the move. Need to take photos. Bye."

"Right." Cassie tossed the few belongings she'd unpacked the previous night back into her bag. She frowned and removed her glasses to check the lenses. No wonder her sight was fuzzy. She cleaned them, put them on again, and squared her shoulders.

Despite all the naysayers, she liked Hone, and if he wanted to take her to bed, she was all in.

Hone's gut bucked, and his dragon growled warnings and complaints during the drive north from Auckland, despite Cassie sitting in the seat beside them.

"I have this weird feeling." Cassie glanced over her shoulder and studied the traffic behind their vehicle before turning back to scan the motorway in front of them. "I keep looking without trying to be obvious, but my neck is prickling as if someone is watching me. Am I crazy?"

"No, I sense it too." Hone sped up and took the next off-ramp.

"Hope we don't attract a cop."

"A friend lives not far from here. We'll see if we can shake our tail and swap vehicles for the weekend." He darted down a side street, taking the corner fast but competently. Beside him, Cassie didn't squeak or go all girly on him. Instead, she braced and watched the road.

Five minutes later, they shot up a tree-lined driveway and came to a halt behind a wooden bungalow.

"Stay here," Hone said. "My friend is a recluse and doesn't take well to strangers."

"Sure. I'll do some work while I wait." Cassie pulled out her notebook and a pen.

He relaxed a fraction. What he didn't tell her was that Roderick was a handsome bastard, and women gravitated to him. Hone wanted to keep Cassie well away until he'd claimed her as his own.

That he didn't even hesitate told him how gone he was on her. A week ago, he'd have laughed himself silly. He always rolled his eyes when his father and mother reminisced about their courtship. Their short, short courtship. They'd known after one day. Sooner, his mother had insisted. No more smartarse remarks from him because now he understood the magnetic attraction.

Understandably, Cassie was cautious. From the little he'd heard while eavesdropping on Cassie and Emma's conversation, Cassie had suffered bad luck with men and that had made her wary. Now he had a chance to show her how it could be between them—the sex. Hell, who was he trying to kid? His thoughts, prompted by his mulish taniwha, were deviating toward something more permanent.

"Hone, long time no see," Roderick hollered. "How's it hangin'?" He lifted his nose and sniffed. "You've got a lady with you. Bring her in and introduce me." The tall muscular man yanked open the front door. He wore black shorts and nothing else, his black hair loose and past his shoulders.

Hone clasped his hand and pulled Roderick in for a man-hug. "Hell, no," he said once they'd released each other.

Roderick's gaze spewed mirth. "A bro could get his feelings hurt."

"Pull the other one," Hone retorted. "I need a favor. Someone is giving Cassie a hard time. They're following us, but I can't see them yet. Can we swap vehicles for the weekend?"

"Cassie." Roderick rolled her name around his mouth with a dragonish purr. He sniffed, his top lip curling as he processed the layers of air. "Her scent is all over you."

"Yeah."

"She smells divine. Describe her to me."

"No." Hone didn't even try for polite.

"Ah." Roderick cocked his head, his gaze intent. "Interesting."

"Yeah."

"First Jack, and now you."

"Cassie is Emma's friend."

"Ah," Roderick said again.

"Can I take your vehicle?"

"No prob. Let me get the keys, and I'll walk you out." No questions, just easy acceptance. Hone liked that about Roderick.

"Just give me the keys. We're in a hurry."

"You want to borrow my vehicle, then you have to introduce me."

"You touch her, and I won't keep control," Hone warned.

"You've already figuratively pissed on her and claimed your territory. What kind of mate would I be if I didn't say a friendly hello to your girl?"

"How do you keep your pretty looks?" Hone asked through gritted teeth. "Everyone who knows you wants to bash in your face."

"Not the women, my friend." Roderick chuckled. "It's good to see you like this, fighting for a woman instead of using them to sate your taniwha."

"And you don't?"

Roderick fell silent, his amusement fading. "Not while I was with Marina."

Crap. "Sorry, I'm on edge because I'm trying to go slow with Cassie. I've known her for three days—"

"I get it." Roderick disappeared and came back with the keys. "Introduce me."

Hone fought the snarl building in his mind. He curled his hands to fists and felt the prick of claws as they gouged his palms.

Despite his apprehension, he acquiesced with a don't-push-me shrug. Trust. He could give Cassie that, and if Roderick managed to flirt and seduce her away, he'd get over the betrayal. Somehow.

He forced his feet to move and couldn't have described a single item he passed on the trip back to his vehicle.

Roderick strolled to the passenger side and grinned while Hone watched with nerves bouncing around his gut. Cassie had climbed from his vehicle and leaned against the front in the shade. She wore one of her pretty dresses, this one green and covered with red roses. His dragon growled, low and mean, but Roderick didn't hesitate.

"Hello, darlin'. You must be Cassie. I'm Roderick, a friend of Hone's."

*The woman whisperer.* That's what they called him, and now that he was single again, his job was to attract maidens from other tribes. Not many unmated women could resist him, and Hone steeled himself for the fallout.

"Hi." Cassie's gaze flicked over Roderick's naked chest and back to his face. "I'm pleased to meet you. Hone said you'd lend us your vehicle. Thank you for helping us."

"You're welcome, darlin'." He picked up her right hand and lifted it to his lips.

Hone growled the entire time, and he almost lost it when Roderick pressed a kiss to her wrist.

Cassie tugged her hand free. "Are you related to him?"

"Distant relations."

"Figures. You're all flirts."

"You wound me," Roderick said and winked at Hone.

"I doubt it," Cassie said. "Every one of Hone's cousins is a terrible flirt. It must be something in the water."

"It's bred into our genes," Roderick replied.

Hone leaned into his vehicle and grabbed a hat from the glovebox, his pulse lowering to a more regular speed. "Put on your hat, Cassie. I'll grab our bags."

"Hone, I'll park your vehicle in the garage and won't use it unless the weather changes." His nostrils flared as he tested the air. "Won't happen this weekend."

A few minutes later, they were on their way, driving down tree-lined streets, past wooden bungalows that were some of the oldest and most expensive houses in Auckland.

"Want to listen to music?" Hone asked, still not believing Cassie's reaction to Roderick. Deep in his gut, he sensed Cassie was the one for him.

"Yes, please. Actually, I wouldn't mind listening to the news first." She leaned forward and turned the power switch before Hone could use the driver's controls.

A deep male voice came through the speakers. "...a scrub fire north of Whangarei is causing concern. Firefighters and a helicopter are on the scene. Police suspect the fire was deliberately lit..."

"How can people do that? It's so dry at this time of the year."

"We have relatives up there," Hone said. "It can't be too bad yet because they would have contacted Auntie June." He spoke without thinking and silently cursed at Cassie's arched eyebrows. "Auntie June is the organizer in our family. She gets things done," he added before she could ask her questions.

The news ended, and Hone switched to the music system.

He took the turning to the motorway and drove over the Auckland harbor bridge. Yachts and small fishing boats darted across the water, leaving swirling white waves in their wake.

"There's a cruise ship in today," Cassie said as she glanced back at the cityscape.

"Yeah, we get quite a few over the summer months."

"Where are we staying?"

"I've booked a room not far from Matakana. One room."

"One bed?"

"Yes." Hone waited for her reaction.

"We're going to share the bed?"

"I'd like to," Hone said.

"Good. I'd like that too."

And just like that his cock grew full and his balls started to ache. It was a different feeling from when he needed sex to maintain his taniwha shape. This desire came from deep in his gut, seared his heart, and his dragon gave a sexy purr. He couldn't wait to get to their accommodation and was glad he'd listened to Manu and gone for an upscale place rather than a basic motel.

"Boss, I've lost them. They took a motorway off-ramp. I followed, but they vanished."

Matthew frowned. "As long as they stay away from the house. That's the main thing. I'll station Jerry as a lookout and get him to give you a call if she turns up there."

"And if she does?"

"We keep a close eye on her. If she remains at the house, it won't be a big problem, but if she takes it into her mind to wander the rest of her property, that's another matter."

"Pity we can't plant another crop."

"Too risky," Matthew said. "Have another drive around and see if you can locate them. If not, come back to the farm."

"Okay, boss."

Matthew hung up and pondered the problem. The temptation to plant another batch of plants gnawed at him. It was easy money, and once they shifted this current crop, he'd never need to worry about money again. A hazard to contemplate.

## CHAPTER 14

C assie slid a sideways glance at Hone. The motel—no, it was a hotel, really—was gorgeous with views over the sea, even from the car park. Perched on a hill, with a track down to a secluded beach and lots of privacy, it was ideal. Romantic even.

Even as she thought that, Hone reached for her hand and twined their fingers together. Her heart went pitter-patter and a shot of desire pierced her belly.

"Is this okay?"

"It's perfect."

"Good. Still want to share that bed with me?"

"Yes."

"Now?"

Cassie turned, noticed the hint of color in his cheeks, the absence of his usual grin. "Yes." She didn't try to play games or act coy. Not when she wanted him. Bad.

Hone lifted her hand and kissed the back of it, his lips branding her skin and driving heat to the heart of her. "Let's get the bags and check in."

Their room lived up to the promise of the exterior of the hotel. The main building housed reception, the restaurant and a small gift shop while the majority of the rooms were bungalows, located a distance apart to give the occupants privacy. A large bed drew her attention, the plain white covers and paua-shell throw—the combination of teal, turquoise, blues and pinks giving a shot of color—more inviting to her than the stunning view.

Hone set down the bags. He took off his hat and sunglasses, purpose in each careful action.

When she stared at him, he removed her hat and glasses. "I can't see you as well now."

"You don't need to see for what we're about to do." His husky voice promised all sorts of sensual pleasures. "You want this, right?"

"Yes." She never hesitated. She intended to have hot, naked sex with Hone Taniwha without any commitment between them. She hadn't even slept with Kevin for the first three months of their official dating relationship. Stern warnings from her mother crept through her mind—about milk and cows. She flipped them off and took the hand Hone extended to her.

For once, she intended to please herself, and Hone pleased her very much.

His fingers tightened around hers, and a shiver—the pleasurable sort—frisked her nerve-endings. She sucked in a quick breath, puffed it back out.

Hone paused. "Are you scared of me? Because you needn't be. I'd never hurt you."

Physically, maybe. But when he cut her loose... She accepted the truth—Emma had warned her, and she'd decided she could live with the fallout. She *would* cope with the aftermath, because for once, she was following her heart instead of her mother's strictures.

Summoning her inner siren, she spread her arms wide, did a little wiggle of her hips. "Shut up and kiss me, Hone."

She thought he'd pounce, but he surprised her. With his gaze locked on her face the entire time, he drew her nearer until the tips of her breasts brushed his chest. His eyes glowed with a strange red light that should've scared her. Instead, his intensity pleased her, made her feel desirable.

His lips brushed hers, gentle as a butterfly, yet packing more power than any other kiss she'd received. Her lids fluttered shut, enclosing her in a world of sensation. The whisper of his hands over her shoulders and back as he fitted their bodies together. The press of his lips as he deepened the kiss. The scent of soap and aftershave. The shift of his muscles beneath her fingertips.

Then his lips were gone.

Confused, she opened her eyes to greet the reddish heat reflected in his brown irises and his quizzical gaze.

"What?" she whispered, frightened to break the fragile peace in her heart.

"I want to take off your clothes, see those luscious curves of yours, touch them."

Cassie issued a happy sigh and released her inner tension. The open window faced the sea, and although it was designed for privacy with a gray tint, light still blazed into the room. He'd see her. All of her. She sucked in her tummy as every insecurity and Kevin's complaints about her size whacked her over the head.

No, dammit. She refused to let her fears spoil this moment. She chose to believe Hone desired her and everyone else could go hang while she enjoyed the hell out of the coming bout of sex.

"You go right ahead," she pushed out, striving for a sexy purr. Her words emerged on the croaky side, but Hone didn't hesitate.

After another whisper-soft kiss that left her craving more, he turned her and slid down the zipper at the back of her dress. Her bodice gaped, and she fought the impulse to catch it and hide her breasts.

No. No. *No.*

She would not let her mind fix on body image and all the crap that went with it. Last warning. She forced her hands to her sides and let gravity do its thing. The cotton sundress slid down, snaring on her hips. Hone's quick tug sent it swooshing to the floor. She stepped out of the circle of fabric.

"Turn around," Hone said in a hoarse voice.

That weird red light glittered in his gaze. His lips curved up in sexy-man approval. "Gorgeous underwear."

Her shoulders straightened and pride roared through her. She did look good—glamorous even—in her favorite set of black lingerie.

Without warning, he moved, scooping her into his arms. He deposited her on the bed, then sat back to remove her black sandals. Instead of progressing quickly, as Kevin had, he massaged her feet.

"Pretty toes," he whispered.

She made a note to thank Emma for the pedicure suggestion.

His hands moved up her calves, stroking and rubbing until she wanted to melt into the mattress. Arousal stroked over her body, prickling her breasts and standing her nipples to attention.

One of his fingers traced the hi-cut lacy leg of her black briefs.

"Part your legs for me, sweetheart."

Her legs parted before the thought to obey filtered through her mind.

Hone inhaled, and his red-brown eyes drew her slightly blurry attention. "You want me."

"Yes." Nothing less than the truth.

He rose up the bed until he was close enough for the fuzzy edges of his face to come into focus.

"I can see you properly now."

His finger traced the lacy edge of a bra cup. "Have you always worn glasses?"

"Since I was four." She chuckled at the memory, recalling her mother's despair at a less-than-perfect child. "Both my parents have good eyesight. I inherited this from my father's side, per my mother."

"From the little I've heard about your family, your mother sounds like a witch."

"Complete with broomstick at times," Cassie agreed, her lips twitching. "She expects perfection. It's the way her parents raised her, and sometimes she forgets that an imperfect moment or object can have its own charm. I just agree with her, make my own decisions, and live with her disapproval."

"I'm sorry."

"Don't be. In her own way, she loves me. It's easier now that I'm older. Now let's kick her out of this bed because talking about my parents and sex at the same time is slightly freaky."

He ran his middle finger along the edge of her other bra cup, then surprised her again. Instead of whisking off her bra and panties, he settled in to kiss her. Long kisses. Slow kisses. Soft kisses. Passionate kisses.

Before, there had been one type of kiss in her repertoire. The perfunctory kisses made to prepare a body for sex. She clung to Hone, her fingers digging into his T-shirt clad shoulders as lips shaped and tested and learned.

"I can't get enough of kissing you," he said hoarsely.

"You kiss divinely. I should be wary of all that expertise, but wow!"

He laughed, the rough sound coming from deep in his throat. He shifted his body a fraction, notching his erection against her sex. A zinger swept her, stealing her breath, her ability to process ideas. Her lids closed.

"Open," Hone whispered.

She raised her weighted lids with difficulty and stared at him. That weird red light in his irises drew her. Flames. That's what it reminded her of—fire.

"Good girl."

He removed her bra with an expertise that made her blink. Her black panties slid down her legs, leaving her naked while he still wore jeans and T-shirt.

Her insecurities rose to thumb their bony fingers at her. She batted them away with difficulty and focused on Hone's gaze.

"I'm a big man, Cassie. I've never been attracted to petite women. I prefer a woman with shape and curves like yours. Jack, Manu and all my cousins are the same. Why do you suppose jealousy struck me so hard when I thought Manu was making a move on you? Because you're exactly his type." He answered his own question.

"It's not that exactly. Well, not all of it. I feel vulnerable when

I'm the only one without clothes."

"The clothing helps me keep control. I want you, Cassie. I've wanted you since the first moment I saw you. And what I want more than anything right now is to savor you and give you the first time you deserve."

"Oh! Oh," she said once his words sank in to her lust-fogged brain. He grinned that charming, boyish grin of his and a wave of pure lust struck her. "Your eyes are weird."

"Family trait," he replied lightly. "It means I want you."

Hone stopped talking and kissed her. He palmed one breast, shoving her onto an entirely different plane of desire. She gasped as he parted their lips.

"Keep those pretty eyes open. I want to see *you*."

He took the same time with her breasts as he had kissing her. His busy fingers plucked and tugged her nipples and shaped each breast until she trembled. It felt as if a single caress of her nipples would send her exploding into orgasm. The warm heat, the strong suction created a nerve ending path to her pussy.

She moaned her pleasure, raising her hips in silent demand. While his mouth was busy, Hone's hands wandered her ribs, her stomach and her hipbones until she thought she might lose her wits.

"Eyes, sweetheart."

She groaned, unaware she'd screened her sight yet again. It was becoming harder and harder to keep them open when every inch of her body sang to the maestro's touch. She managed it—just.

Hone moved down the bed, parted her legs farther and lifted her to meet his lips. He licked the length of her slit.

Her muscles tensed. She shuddered as he settled in to tease her. He licked her entrance, pushed his tongue deep, the friction rougher than she'd expected.

"Hone, please."

He lifted his head. "Please what? I need your words. I'd like you to tell me what you want."

"In detail?"

"Yeah, I like a woman who knows what she wants."

"Make me come with your tongue. Slide your fingers inside me, or better yet, your cock." Her cheeks heated at voicing her demands, but she forced her thoughts to words, anyway.

"Perfect. When we're together, I want a lover who participates."

"I—I—what do you mean? Am I doing something wrong?"

"Hell, no. All I'm saying is I like honest reactions, and if you want something, I expect you to tell me."

"Then please hurry," she blurted.

"I didn't say I wouldn't delay gratification. I don't believe I ever said that."

"Oh."

His grin kicked up a notch before he resumed his licking and stroking. A moan of protest burst free, and his laughter puffed air against her sensitive clit. She jerked her hips and managed to frustrate herself further.

"Oh, please. Hone."

He was strong, his hands holding her lower body steady for each tormenting stroke.

Cassie swallowed, desperate for release, her heart beating so hard she thought it might explode under the strain.

A growl escaped Hone as her eyes closed yet again. How he knew they were shut, she had no idea.

"You taste good. Love your scent." Her juices coated his chin, shone in the late afternoon daylight as he licked his lips. "Is it me or is it getting hot in here?" He straightened and jerked off his T-shirt.

She'd seen his tattoos before—the tribal twist going up one arm and the snarling dragon on his back, but now she had a right to touch those inky scrawls.

"Let me explore your tattoos."

"Soon," he agreed, and she got the impression he was pleased with her request.

He bent again to lick between her legs, this time with skill and purpose. A low level buzz started at her core and slowly radiated upward in a wave. It kept coming and coming, and when he slid two fingers deep into her channel, twisting them a fraction, he hit the perfect spot and she exploded, the force of that wave crashing over her, consuming her, wrecking her and spoiling her for every other man.

Her muscles turned limp.

"Those pretty eyes are closed again."

She forced them open and found him grinning at her. "Your eyes are red." His pupils elongated and it was like looking at an alien creature. Sure her mind was playing tricks, she blinked, and when she studied him again, he appeared normal. Just those freaky red-brown irises, smoldering at her and banked full of passion.

"Red eyes, huh? How bad is your sight?" Humor lurked on his features, his full, sexy mouth quirking as if he held back a laugh—one of those rich belly laughs. A lusty all-is-right-in-my-day laugh.

"Shush. Let me up. I want to explore you."

"Don't think so." He dug around in his jeans pocket and pulled out a condom, which he set aside to fling off his footwear and the last of his clothes.

His body...it was fantastic. She'd seen him at the beach after swimming, with beads of water glistening on his sculpted chest and abs. This time she got the whole picture and a man comfortable in his own body. His cock stood to attention, full and big enough for her to wish her sight wasn't blurry around the edges.

"My turn," she said when she realized he was grinning again. A hard blink did nothing to zap away the redness. Made her wonder if she was about to fuck with the devil.

He barked out a laugh.

"Um, did I say that out loud?"

"Yep. I promise you, sweetheart. I'm not from hell, and all I want right now is to fuck you and give us both pleasure. Sound good?"

"Yes." A whisper-soft affirmation.

He ripped open the foil packet and rolled on the condom. "Spread those legs again, sweetheart. Let me see that pretty pussy."

She never hesitated and thanked the gods who'd whispered she should take extra care with personal grooming.

"Yep, pretty," he said, his red gaze raking her sex. He crawled onto the bed and caged her within his arms and body. "Put me inside you, sweetheart. I want to feel you gripping my cock."

Cassie chewed her bottom lip and didn't move. "I'd rather touch."

"Later," he promised. "Guide me."

Masculine determination. Smokin' hot body. Freaky red stare.

She wanted him, needed him so much. Her hand trembled as she reached between them to grip his shaft. He lined up against her entrance and pushed until the flared head stretched her.

He cursed softly. "I knew this would be good. It's also gonna be fast this first time. Okay?"

Her channel flexed around his cock head, wringing a tortured groan from him.

"Take me," she whispered and it came out throaty and suggestive. "I'm all yours."

He mumbled something—a bit like, *I hope you mean that*—then he was sliding into her wetness, stretching her inner muscles and firing her sex to red-alert. She hadn't thought she could climax again. Two quick strokes as Hone seated himself disabused her of that supposition. She clutched his shoulders, falling into rhythm with him and reach, reach, reaching for her second greedy orgasm.

"That's it," he murmured against her ear. "Feels so good, so fuckin' good being inside you. I could do this all day." One hand reached up to thumb her nipple and the sharp tweak of pain jumped to her clit in a fast echo of pleasure.

"Hone. Please."

"You do fuckin' please me so much. You're wet, so wet for me. Love your breasts and the way they overflow my hands."

Her hands ran down his back, gripping him to her. Her thoughts, usually full of her to-do list by this stage because her ex's lovemaking hadn't been that inspiring, centered on getting closer, getting off. Yeah, getting off again would be really good.

"Your eyes are closed again."

She spluttered out a laugh. "Maybe I'm afraid of seeing your demon-eyes. They might put me in a trance or do a tricky magical thing. Ohhh. Yes, right there. Do that again."

"Would never hurt you, Cassie. You're special." And he punctuated this surprising confession with a twist of his hips that broke her. Detonation. Implosion. The climax to end all orgasms. She felt her pussy tighten around him, felt the pleasure surge along every sensitive nerve. Hone plunged into her now. Short, sharp digs of his cock that kept the spasms igniting. She half-sobbed, the pleasure overwhelming. He groaned, thrusting deep and stilling, fully impaled while his cock contracted with hard pulses.

Cassie did open her eyes this time to his smiling face and perfectly normal brown gaze. Well, heck. "I'm obviously reading too many fantasy romances."

He rubbed his damp forehead against hers before kissing her lightly on the lips. "If I'd known how good the sex would be between us, I'd have pushed harder for this on day one." He kissed her again and withdrew.

Cassie wanted to protest at the separation.

"Fuck."

The harsh note had her bolting upright. "What?"

"Condom broke. I'm so sorry. That's never happened before."

"I'm on birth control. It's okay." Visions of Hone with other women, many other women with gorgeous figures, flooded her mind, but instead of acting in the responsible manner, asking pointed questions like an intelligent member of the Miller-Pope family, she remained silent.

"Stop what you're thinking. I always use condoms, and if you're worried, I can get tested. I'm clean, but you don't know that."

"I said it's okay."

"Okay." His eyes did that weird red thing. By the time she'd blinked to clear her fuzzy sight, she saw nothing out of the ordinary.

"I might have a shower," Hone said and held out his hand.

"Want to share?"

That damn broken condom had spoiled the mood between them. He couldn't exactly tell her the truth about taniwha and their immunity to human sexual diseases.

He was about to let his hand drop to his side when her fingers clasped his. He wanted to roar to show his relief, but instead, he tugged her off the bed and prowled toward the en suite bathroom.

Normally his dragon was like, *hey, sex. Good, now I can sleep.* Today, he'd created a disturbance. Hone had ended up seeing Cassie's splendid curves through a red haze for most of their loving. She'd noticed, but her glasses dependency had given him an advantage.

In the en suite, he flipped on the shower, silently approving of the tiled wet room without the usual shower stall. She had to be sore after the way he'd hammered into her at the end. "Does it matter if you get your hair wet?"

"It will dry." She shrugged, the movement of her shoulders making her breasts jump and shimmy.

*Nice.*

"Hey, you're ogling me."

"Yeah," he agreed. "I didn't have enough time before to explore all of you. You sore?" He almost laughed when she squeezed her thighs together.

"A bit."

But he was already reaching for a facecloth. He wet it under the warm water and wrung out the surplus. "Let me." He knelt before her, gently widening her stance so he could tend to her.

"I can do that."

She was like a skittish stray. "I know you can, but I want to make you feel better. After all, it's for my benefit too."

"You want to have sex again?" She sounded surprised—no bemused.

"I intend to make love with you and to you—as long as you're agreeable."

"I—okay. You said we were going to do a little sightseeing."

"We will," he promised. "But I can guard your sexy body easier if we're confined to one room. One bed." He grinned up at her, his taniwha humming at her answering smile.

"You make funny noises."

"I'm happy and content. Why shouldn't I purr?" Using the cloth, he cleaned her flesh then stood and gave in to his impulse to kiss her silly. The water poured over their heads, warm and relaxing. Normally, a rousing round of sex left him sated and relaxed. While happiness filled him and if he was any more relaxed, he'd be in a coma, he still wanted her, wanted to mark her inside and out with his taniwha. Taniwha didn't mark their mates as such, but they did mate for life. Once a taniwha committed to another—either taniwha or human—they seldom strayed. Until today Hone hadn't managed to fathom staying with one person for the rest of his life. His own taniwha had pushed him from the start, from the second he'd met Cassie. Resisting fate and his dragon had tied him in knots until his mind flip-flopped like a little girl. It was time to trust his beast in romance, as he believed and relied on him in other facets of his life.

Cassie required wooing to start her thoughts in the same direction as his…

"What will you do once you've finished your vineyard shows?"

"I'm not sure. I'm meant to be going to LA." Cassie reached for the shower gel. She opened the complimentary tube and squirted a dollop on the facecloth he still held in his hand, but she didn't add anything further to the conversation. "My manager wants me to put out another album and go out on tour to promote it. He'd like me to focus on a crossover to the pop genre. It's something I'm considering."

"Turn around. I'll do your back." She might leave. He hadn't considered that because of her grandfather's house. He'd assumed she intended to stay.

"Thanks."

Hone rubbed the cloth down her spine and over her shoulders, but his mind drifted elsewhere. Wasn't that damn ironic? He found one woman who did it for him, one that made him consider a future and there was a possibility that she mightn't stay in New Zealand.

For most people, that wouldn't matter. They'd follow their

woman, but for him there would be repercussions. Leaving his family support and the taniwha network would create problems. Hell, if it wasn't such a worry, he'd laugh off his arse.

Herbert hated puzzles, and even more, he disliked failure. Losing the couple he'd been tailing irked him. He drove around the streets in the area where they'd shaken him and still came up empty.

Deciding he'd function better with a full stomach, he drove south and pulled into the parking lot of the first McDonald's restaurant he saw. A burger, fries, and a cold shake, all consumed inside the air-conditioned restaurant, drove away his sluggishness. He pondered as he chewed. The motel. Yeah, he'd backtrack. He could book a room, say he was meeting his cousin and ask for her by name.

Nah, saying he was her cousin might raise suspicion, but he could check out the motel room. Learn if she'd checked out or he could, he thought with a flash of brilliance, watch the other girl—the friend who lived with the big, scary dude. Surly bastard, he was—the sort who'd act first and ask questions later. Worked for the private firm called George Taniwha & Son. He'd have to go under the radar to avoid detection.

He dabbed his mouth with a napkin and pushed away from the

table. His chair scraped along the polished floor, and he strode out the door.

He did enjoy overcoming a challenge.

## CHAPTER 15

# Wednesday, Papakura

H erbert strode into the motel office late afternoon, striking it lucky with the last room. It was the same unit the girl had occupied, which answered one question. She'd checked out after her clown scare.

But where had she gone?

An older Māori woman checked him in, her light eyes freaky with their intensity. Her nostrils flared and her gaze locked with his. He shook himself because it felt as if she were looking inside his mind. She slid the key over the desk. "Enjoy your stay."

He blinked, instinctively going for polite. "Thank you."

A young woman entered as he left. Bingo. This one was the other's friend, and eventually she'd lead him in the right direction.

She'd know Cassie Miller-Pope's location, and once he found the woman, he'd keep her off-balance enough that she wouldn't worry about anything happening on her land. She'd be frightened of her own shadow.

*Hotel at Matakana*

Sometimes Cassie made mistakes. Most people did, however picking up her phone without checking the caller identity—right up there amongst the big ones.

"Cassandra, I expected you to call me," her mother said. "You're twenty-six and should have outgrown this childish behavior."

Cassie tapped her finger against her leg and awaited her mother's next salvo. When it didn't come, she said, "Mother, I've been busy, and it's only been six days since I arrived."

"I can't believe you intend to live in your grandfather's house. If it were me, I'd sell it to—"

"I own the farm, Mother. Granddad left it to me. Please, we've had this discussion. Let's agree to disagree. How are you? How is Dad?"

"We're fine. Thank you."

"What do you want for breakfast, Cassie?" Hone called from the doorway. He'd gone for a run along the beach while she dallied with a coffee and the newspaper.

"Who is that?" Her mother's sharp tone peeved Cassie.

"A friend." Less said the better.

"A male friend?"

"Yes."

There was a pause, a huff of air. "I hope you're having safe sex."

"Mother, I am not having this conversation. It's good to hear from you, but I've been taking care of myself for a while." Thank goodness her mother wasn't in the same room because her cheeks had bloomed scarlet. Judging by Hone's grin, he'd caught the conversation.

"I suppose you're spending time with that girl?"

"If you mean Emma, then yes. She's my best friend."

"Who is the man?"

"Hone works with Emma."

"I see."

Cassie doubted it. "Mother, you might not approve of the way I live my life, but I'm healthy and content. Why can't you just be happy for me?"

"With your educational qualifications, you could be doing much more than working as an assistant to a singer."

Cassie gritted her teeth until the compulsion to tell her mother exactly how much wealth she'd amassed had passed. "Mum, I'm going to say this for the last time. I love you, but since I am an adult, you can't make my decisions for me. I am taking a break from my job for one month. Once that time has passed, I will make a decision as to what I'll do next."

"But how can you afford to take a month off work? Do you need any money? If you sold—"

"Did you get the Christmas present I sent you?"

"Yes, the gift box came, and it's lovely. Your father loves the two CDs you included. I didn't think I'd like this Katie-Jo person, but she's quite good."

Pride squeezed her chest. "I'm glad you're enjoying them. I hoped you would." She'd recorded her Dad's favorites in a friend's studio, knowing that her parents would never realize they were one-of-a-kind. "I'll ring you soon, as long as you promise not to harangue me about the way I live my life."

Her mother sucked in an audible breath. "I'm sorry, Cassandra. I didn't realize I was lecturing you. I only want what is best for you, to see you succeed. Your father keeps telling me I'll push you away, but you always listen to me. This is the first time you've told me to stop."

"I should have put my foot down earlier then," Cassie said lightly, wondering what had happened to her over-achieving parent.

"You remember Karen Ellingham?"

"One of your friends."

"Yes, she had a heart attack and passed away. She's two years younger than me. It's made me think. I've decided to scale back and delegate more. Your father has suggested it before, but I've always pooh-poohed the idea. He's taken up golf. Says it's all mathematics and angles, and I'd enjoy the challenge."

"Why don't you travel for pleasure? Try golf?"

"You're truly happy and you don't need any money? We could send you some."

"Mom! I'm going to go now before I lose my temper. Learn how to play golf. I'm hanging up now." Cassie ended the call and inhaled to deal with her surge of confusion. Her mother had apologized, even though it had been half-hearted.

"Everything okay?" Hone refilled her coffee.

"My mother. All my life my mother has lectured me about my poor decision making. She didn't approve of Emma, considered her a bad influence. She doesn't support me being in New Zealand. She worries I'm not making the most of my opportunities. Today she didn't make any digs about my weight, but she normally tells me I should have more self-restraint and diet. I love my parents, I do. They offered me opportunities while I was growing up. Because of Dad's insistence, I learned to play the guitar and the piano. I have a business degree as well as one in music. Mum had several miscarriages after me, and I get that she'd want to push me to excel, but a job in the business world...that's not me."

"Why haven't you told your parents you're a singer?"

"When I was a teenager, they sent me to boarding school, but during the holidays..." Cassie shuddered. "The holidays were awful, and as soon as I finished my schooling, I applied for a job in Nashville. The distance helped me get perspective and embrace my independence. My first job really was as an assistant to a music star. I met Kevin, and I had incredible luck. My employer was generous with his help, and I became successful. Every time I talked to my mother, she lectured me about my perceived wrongs. It was easier to remain silent. I don't deal with confrontations well. A flaw, I'm afraid."

"You're perfect the way you are." Hone leaned against the back of the couch, his tattoos drawing her eye. "I can't say I understand your silence though. I would've bragged of my triumph."

Cassie laughed. "Your family seems close. Because I attended boarding school, and my parents worked long hours, we didn't spend time together." Come to think of it, she hadn't explored his tattoos yet. Fingers or tongue or both? "My mother lectured me, informed me I did everything wrong. It was easier to stick my head in the sand."

Hone sipped his black coffee, his gaze on her. "Why the costume? The disguise? I've looked you up on the 'net. No one would recognize you if they didn't know your secret already."

"That started off as a joke. I had chronic stage fright, and Kevin suggested I dress up in a disguise. It sounds silly, but it helped, and I realized the anonymity would work in my favor too, so I developed my brand and stuck with it. As long as I'm careful, it means I can go shopping or out to dinner in the States and no one recognizes me."

"Huh, I'm fucking a beautiful country star and I can't tell anyone." Hone's grin and suggestive wink took away the sting of the harsh language. "Hey, don't freeze up like that. I didn't mean to upset you."

"You haven't," Cassie said, striving for a light tone. She thought she managed quite well. "You mentioned breakfast. I could eat."

"Want to go for a walk or order in?"

"Order in," she said without hesitation. "I still haven't had a chance to explore your tattoos. I could have fun with syrup."

"Deal, but we're both eating breakfast naked. If I'm getting sticky, so are you."

Not long after their breakfast, Cassie straddled Hone's hips as he lay facedown on the bed. She traced her fingers over the black-and-red dragon inked into his skin. A rumble came from him as she stroked down his spine. His entire body shivered beneath her touch. The man oozed sexual charm, and every single time he touched her, he rocked her world. She leaned down to press her lips against the head of the dragon.

"Your skin is warm."

"Because you're torturing me with your attention, your scent. You're wet and it's driving me crazy." He moved, twisting his body so fast, she almost toppled off the bed. His fingers banded her biceps, helping her balance until she leaned against the heaped pillows at the head of the bed. "I'm going to get another condom.

You sore?"

Her cheeks heated. "A little."

"I have lube. Got some when I visited the restrooms in the main building. Figured a new source of condoms wouldn't hurt, especially since we had the first one conk out on us." He grabbed a package off the right nightstand. "And since you keep disobeying me, I intend to blindfold you."

Color her intrigued. "Are you going kinky on me?"

"We can do whatever we want." He ended their conversation with a kiss that stole her breath and dulled her active brain. All she could focus on was the erotic duel of his tongue with hers and the shudder of helpless delight holding her in thrall.

He pulled back. "I happen to enjoy giving my lover pleasure."

"But it's still my turn. Let me taste you."

"I'd like to do that too, but not if you're sore. I need control."

Her tongue darted out to swipe her bottom lip.

He sucked in a quick breath, and she heard his now familiar yet strange rumbly purr. "Enough of that provocative behavior, Miss Miller-Pope."

She looped her arms around his neck and grinned.

Hone rose to dig around in his bag. He came out with a navy-blue scarf.

Some of her good mood faded. "Do you travel with blindfolds?"

"I packed it when you weren't paying attention."

"Oh."

"Cassie, look at me." When she did, his gaze had that reddish-brown glow. "It's true I've had other women. I like women, but right now, you have my full attention. I'm here with you because that's what I want. Okay?"

"Okay," she whispered, cursing herself. Stupid insecurities.

"You still want me to put on the blindfold?"

"Yes." She didn't hesitate this time. She trusted Hone. He wouldn't hurt her physically, not intentionally.

He sat on the edge of the bed, swept the hair from her face. His lids rested at half-mast and his lips curved in a faint grin. Her insides clenched, a spear of desire darting through her sex. She knew what awaited her and couldn't wait to experience his controlled passion again.

"I like your hair loose." He smoothed his hand over her hair and tucked a strand behind her ear. "Ready?"

"Ready." Her mouth dried. Silly, really. They'd made love three times throughout the night, each time heat-pumping good.

With quick competency, he tied the scarf in place. A pent-up breath whooshed from her, and she started when his whiskers rasped across the delicate skin of her neck.

"I want you on all fours. You okay with that?"

"Position me," she said, her pulse racing a little faster. Sex with Keven had been quick vanilla stuff in the missionary position. This—Hone—kept her off-balance.

He guided her into place. "You're beautiful. Sexy." His hand ran over one buttock without warning, and she let out a nervous laugh. "Widen your stance. Yep, perfect."

The mattress shifted and warm air blew down her slit. The action repeated and then his tongue licked and circled her nub. Sensations coursed to life. Her hips jolted, but Hone gripped them, forcing her to stillness.

"Not yet," he said.

She jumped at the sting on her right buttock. "Hey."

"Do as you're told." His gruff voice lit a flame inside her and expectation, anticipation, had her pulse racing, her breathing hitching. With her sight shrouded, every other sense overloaded her with information. She could smell his aftershave, hear her hoarse breathing while her pussy pulsed and craved friction.

He licked her again, keeping each stroke gentle against her tender flesh. She sighed and relaxed as much as she could to enjoy his attentions. Another lick teased her. She waited for more and nothing happened. Her throat worked, and she groaned.

"Easy, sweetheart. Just getting the lube."

A rustle sounded, the crackle of plastic and a sharp creak. The thumbing open of a lid?

Without warning, coldness struck her sex. She started, and Hone chuckled.

"I should have warned you, but I wanted to see you jump."

"Funny."

The second application didn't feel so bad. The lube heated from her body and the coolness eased her swollen flesh.

"I'm putting on a condom now, hopefully one that won't bust. Date's good. Nah, we're good."

"Pleased to hear it," Cassie said in a tart tone.

He laughed in that infectious way of his, the one where his entire face lit up, sometimes with that weird red glow in his stare. No idea what that was, but she'd already deduced if she saw that gleam, emotion had come to the fore.

Hands smoothed over her buttocks, the point of contact igniting lust in a big way. Condom. Contact. All engines go.

His cock prodded her entrance and pushed inside her. She winced and forced herself to relax. She hurt, but she wanted him so much.

As he pushed deeper, his finger glided over her clit. Instantly, pleasure pushed to the fore, desire and need. The warmth from his chest as he leaned against her, his cock fully embedded. Heaven.

He continued to move with slow, even strokes. It was magical. It was mesmerizing. It was stunningly beautiful the way he took his time. The man played her like a maestro, then upped the tension until she exploded with the ecstasy, with the joy and bliss of the moment. And as she toppled into orgasm, he increased his pace, driving into her now, flesh slapping flesh until his cock contracted and he reached his own completion.

Hone stilled, deep in her body. "I don't know if I can move. You've worn me out."

Cassie snorted a laugh. "Not you. You're insatiable."

He separated their bodies, and she mourned the loss of contact. "Be back soon."

Cassie waited a second, then tugged off her blindfold to stare after him. She wasn't stupid enough to miss the view.

His tattoo drew her attention. She blinked, sure she was seeing things. The dragon. She clapped her hand over her mouth before she made a fool of herself.

She could have sworn the dragon had been ready to leap from Hone's skin, its red eyes flaring full of fiery life.

Now…now it appeared as if it were asleep.

The water turned on and switched off. Hone wandered from the en suite with a washcloth in his hand, a big yawn splitting his face. He stilled on seeing her. "Something wrong?"

"No, but you're going to start me yawning soon. Someone kept me awake all night."

His grin told her that hadn't been a problem for him. "Spread your legs for me."

"Hone."

"Love the way you blush. Go on, babe. I've seen you now. Don't try to hide from me."

When she hesitated, he pushed her gently, so she fell against the pillows and used his free hand to tug her legs apart. She sighed as the warm cloth hit her swollen tissues and sighed again as the heat eased the lingering sting.

That done, he tossed the cloth aside and gathered her in his arms. "You up for snorkeling?"

"I need a nap."

"We can do that. A quick nap before we go for a drive to Goat Island. I organized a picnic basket when I walked over to the main building."

"I like a man with a plan."

Hone laughed as he tugged her against his chest and nuzzled her hair. She drifted toward sleep, her mind heavy. Life after Hone would be difficult, even if she was richer for their acquaintance.

## CHAPTER 16

# Thursday, Jack and Emma's house, Papakura

"Where is Hone and that friend of yours?" June Taniwha demanded. "I searched everywhere yesterday. Where is he? I demand you tell me."

Emma exchanged an alarmed glance with Jack and edged closer, needing his proximity. Spittle built at the corners of June's mouth, the matriarch of the Auckland taniwhas scary when her temper rose.

"Does Samuel know you're here?" Emma elbowed Jack in the ribs, and when he didn't move, she elbowed him again. It was his turn to speak.

"This has nothing to do with my mate." June's nostrils flared. "Where is Hone?"

"He's out on a job." Jack maintained his steady gaze, his body relaxed.

"Where?" June jabbed a finger at Jack.

"We signed confidentiality agreements for this job. We can't tell you," Emma said, wincing at the wisp of smoke coming from June's nostrils. "If you want information, you'll have to speak with George." Emma threw their boss in as a distraction. While it was true they'd signed agreements, June wasn't the type to spread gossip. The tribe matriarch took care of official business and ruled their people, so she was trustworthy, but Emma didn't like the blood-red haze discoloring her irises or her mottled skin. June's search for Hone didn't bode well.

"What about your friend? Where is the faithless hussy?"

Emma straightened her shoulders. She'd seen June in action, knew enough for apprehension to crawl up her spine. If June decided to slap her down... But she couldn't betray her friend or Hone. "I haven't seen her today."

June's lips pulled back, revealing pointy teeth as she inhaled. "Truth," she said slowly.

"If you think Cassie is a slut, then why are you so angry?" Emma demanded before good sense kicked to life.

"Manu showed interest in her. He's never looked twice at another woman. Your friend was meant for Manu and Hone has stolen her. I want my son settled. I want grandchildren. I want my dynasty underway, yet my older sons continue to play as if they have all the time in the world." She glided into Emma's personal space, her hands clenching and unclenching with each strident word.

"Emma," Jack warned.

Emma's teeth clacked together. Why wasn't she lecturing Manu and her other sons? This wouldn't end well. It was easy to decipher the watchful caution in Jack, almost if he were afraid to move and incur June's reprisal. She couldn't let June's behavior pass. It wasn't right for the matriarch to threaten Cassie, who was innocent of wrongdoing.

Jack's phone rang. He answered. "George. Right. Okay. Yeah, Emma and I have time to do the job. We'll come now."

"Emma can stay here with me," June said. "We'll have a cup of tea."

"She is coming with me," Jack said. "I won't have you threatening my mate."

"I *will* speak with the hussy."

"Stop calling Cassie that," Emma snapped. "She's my friend."

"Emma," Jack said. "Grab your camera."

"George said just you," June said. "Emma will stay with me."

Jack growled, low and mean. "Do your worst, June." Jack grasped Emma's arm and propelled her toward the exit.

"My camera is in the bedroom." Emma fought him.

"We'll pick up a spare at the office," Jack countered, implacable in his determination.

Emma glimpsed June over her shoulder, and her stomach hollowed out with a quick shot of fear. Jade-colored scales had formed on June's cheeks, and as Emma watched, June's pupils shifted into a dragon slant.

"Good idea." Emma hurried after Jack.

June wouldn't follow them immediately. At a recent conference of all New Zealand's taniwha leaders, the matriarchs and patriarchs of each tribe had decided it was too soon to come out to the human population. June wouldn't break the treaty they'd signed and appear in public with her dragon showing.

"Ring Samuel. Tell him June is out of control. Once you've talked to him, call Manu and tell him to put his mother straight about Cassie. Hone's taniwha wants her, and he'll fight June if she tries to interfere with his courtship."

Jack strode to his vehicle and Emma trotted after him, fear still pumping through her veins. She'd seen June angry but never to the point where she'd lost control.

"You didn't court me," Emma said.

"I didn't have to because you chased me." Jack started his work vehicle and backed from their driveway. "Ring Samuel now."

A loud crash sounded above the engine. Smoke poured from their kitchen window.

"Fuck," Jack muttered.

"Fire! Our house! Crap, what is she doing?" Emma hit speed dial, prayed Samuel would answer. "S-Samuel! June set our house on fire. You have to come. She's furious."

"Are you inside with her?" Samuel demanded.

"No, we're outside." Emma gaped at the flames licking across the window frame.

"She hurt you?"

"The house is on fire," Emma snapped.

"I'm on my way. Leave it to me."

"I'm calling Manu next. This is all his fault. If our house burns down, you will pay for a new one. I'm not claiming insurance for fire by dragon." She ended the call. "She won't burn our entire house. We should go back."

"It's too dangerous." Jack's grimace dug deeper, and he kept driving toward the office. "She's likely to hurt you if she's this out of control."

"I didn't do anything. I love our house."

"Don't worry. Samuel will calm the situation and pay us restitution."

"But it's our house," Emma wailed.

"I know, sweetheart." Jack's tone was grim. "I'll be voting for Manu to take over at the next tribe gathering. No one threatens my mate without consequences."

Matthew strolled through the paddocks, stopping now and then to check the buds on the female plants. They were in perfect condition, pest-free and ready for harvest. He rang Herbert.

"Harvest tomorrow," he said as soon as his employee answered. "This one is ready. The other crop needs a week before it reaches maturity."

Herbert grunted. "The woman has disappeared. Still can't find her. She has checked out of the motel."

"If she is with the man, that will work to our benefit. A romance will keep her busy." Matthew continued walking through the head-high plants. This weed should yield high prices. "Keep up the search," he ordered. "Tell me when you locate her."

"You don't need my help with the harvest?"

"No, I'd rather keep tabs on the woman. The harvest is organized. I can't see any problems. Talk to you later." Matthew hung up and shoved his phone in his pocket. Not long until his plan came to fruition, and he'd be free of his ex. He couldn't allow Cassie Miller-Pope to get in his way.

Two nights later, Cassie prepared for her spot at the show. Hone had said it was a short drive to the vineyard, and it was almost time to leave. Nerves—the good kind—bounced in her stomach. Pure apprehension would take over if she let it, but applying her stage makeup and dressing in her Katie-Jo clothes calmed her and helped her to don her stage persona. She became a professional singer. She slipped on her strappy sandals.

Hone had practiced with her several times and confidence soared within her, even though she intended to perform two new songs.

As if she'd conjured the man, he wandered into the bedroom.

He came to an abrupt stop. "I wouldn't recognize you if I walked past you in the street."

"That's the beauty of my disguise," Cassie said lightly. She swiped a final coat of mascara over her lashes. The heavier eye makeup and the lip gloss took her from ordinary to mysterious. The bright pink wig was an awesome touch. If she decided to go back to performing in the States, she'd keep this wig.

"Will I do?"

"You're gorgeous." Hone kissed her gently on the lips.

"You don't look so bad yourself." Black trousers. A pale blue shirt with an open neck. Black boots. "Very sexy."

Hone grinned. "You ready to rock 'n roll?"

Cassie picked up her guitar case. "Let's do this."

Crowds of people, male and female, young and old, queued at

the gates, picnic blankets and rugs in hand.

Hone slowed at the car park and wound down his window to speak to security. "We're performing. Katie-Jo."

"Right." The man removed a barrier. "There is a parking spot reserved for you up there. Someone is waiting for you and will escort you to the stage. Are there more coming or is it just the two of you?"

"Just us," Cassie said.

The man waved them through. Hone parked in a space marked with her name. An older man with long gray hair and wearing a white T-shirt advertising the Vineyard concerts straightened from his lean against a silver Nissan.

"I'll get your guitar. You take care of the other stuff," Hone suggested.

Cassie greeted the man with a handshake. "Hi, I'm Katie-Jo." On the other side of the vehicle, she saw Hone's quick surprise before he bent to retrieve their instruments. She grinned. She'd forgotten to remind him she played up her American accent while in her Katie-Jo role.

"Pleased to meet you," the man said. "Charlie Blake. I spoke to your manager. We appreciate you filling in for us."

"My pleasure," Cassie said. "I'm looking forward to it. This is Hone Taniwha, my musician."

The two men shook hands.

"I'll show you around," Charlie said. "You're third on the card, right before our main act, The Geraughty Rock."

"Thanks. I requested two tickets for my friends. They're going to ask for them at the gate."

Charlie consulted his clipboard. "Jack and Emma Sullivan. I have their name on the comps list."

"Awesome."

She was quietly impressed with their setup. The actual concert venue was a natural bowl set amongst the vineyards. Now that it was early evening, the heat of the day had dispersed and families, groups of friends and couples dotted the grassy area. Excited chatter and laughter floated on the air.

"You hungry?" Hone asked once Charlie left them alone in the employees' lunchroom, which he'd commandeered for his performers. "I got the kitchen to pack us a sandwich."

"I never eat before a show," Cassie said, her fingers strumming chords. "You go ahead and eat if you're hungry."

"No, I'm good. Anything you need? Want a bottle of water?"

"Got one," she said, indicating the bottle sitting beside her. Hone prowled the room and repeated his circuit, his hands clenching and unclenching at his sides. A realization slapped her over the head. "You're nervous."

"No. A bit." He turned to her, scowled and his eyes glowed red. "Aren't you?"

"A little. As soon as I start singing, I'll be fine. You don't have to play for me."

"I want to share this part of your life with you."

"Oh." Warmth curled through her veins. "No one has ever said anything like that to me."

"Your manager?"

She shrugged. "It's his job. He doesn't attend my concerts."

"He have other clients?"

"Half a dozen or it might be more by now. My contract with Kevin ends at the end of this year. He wants me to sign on for another three years."

Hone's expression froze, and she couldn't read his mind.

"I—"

"Katie-Jo. There you are."

Cassie turned at the familiar voice, felt her brows rise and her mouth fell open. She clacked her teeth together. "Kevin, I didn't really believe you'd come tonight."

"I thought I'd visit my country star. Where are your musicians? You told me you'd organize them."

"No, I said I was going for an unplugged atmosphere for my segment. I want the songs and the vocals to shine."

"I see."

"This is my friend Hone. He's helping me with the music."

Kevin offered Hone a nod but didn't extend his hand in greeting. Cassie frowned, not liking or understanding his unfriendly attitude.

"See you later." Kevin left without another word.

Cassie grimaced at his suit-clad back then at the wooden door. That had been fun. She felt as if she should apologize to Hone for Kevin's rudeness.

"Katie-Jo, are you almost ready?" Charlie asked after a knock at the door to announce his presence.

She stood. "Hone, can you mind my water bottle? I'll signal when I want it."

"Sure." Hone picked up his guitar.

Cassie grinned at him. "Ready?"

"As I'll ever be." He paled as the crowd cheered when Charlie introduced Katie-Jo.

Cassie sucked in a deep breath and strutted onto the stage. The usual anxieties tap-danced harder than normal. Not difficult to guess why. Her pride rode on this concert. She refused to dwell on the right or wrong of her new songs, but if they flopped with the crowd, especially with Kevin's presence, she might cry.

Aware the crowd had quieted, she lifted her right hand in a wave and stepped up to the freestanding mike on the platform.

"Hi. I'm Katie-Jo." Once again, she emphasized the American part of her heritage. "You probably haven't heard of me, but the country fans over in America think I can sing a little." Her fingers strummed her guitar and behind her, Hone started to play the intro bars with her. "I thought I'd start with a song that everyone informs me is a Kiwi classic. You might recognize it. It goes like this."

She glanced at Hone, taking in his extreme paleness, although his fingers didn't falter as he blinked back at her with a flash of fear—no, maybe insecurity. That made two of them. She turned back to the audience, embraced her apprehension and started singing.

"Boss, I might have found her." Herbert stood at the rear of the crowd, watching the pair on stage.

"What do you mean *might have*?"

The boss sounded cranky, but Herbert understood the importance of getting this crop through to maturity. "I'm in Matakana. The two friends are here and the guy that hangs around her is up on stage. The girl singing. It could be her. She looks different, sounds different, but the body shape...it could be her."

"Is it or isn't it? I need her location. I can't have her snooping around, seeing things she shouldn't."

"I'll see if I can get closer to the stage and send you a video. You've seen her up close and talked to her."

*Come on, boss. Don't lose it now. I'm counting on a good payday after we harvest the last of the weed.*

"That's an excellent idea," Matthew agreed.

"All right, boss. My gut tells me it's her. It might take me a while to get back to you. I don't want to draw attention."

"Thanks, Herbert."

Herbert hung up and studied the crowd. He needed to stay away from the friends. They were near the front. Damn, this Katie-Jo person could sing. He'd Google her later, check his favorite online music store.

He skirted the crowd and found a position close enough to zoom in for a photo. While the quality and lighting wasn't ideal, it might be enough for the boss to ID. And if not, he'd follow the guy onstage with her once he left the vineyard. Either way, he'd find Cassie Miller-Pope and make sure she didn't learn they were using her property to make illegal income.

## CHAPTER 17

"**Y**ou were brilliant," Hone said and, unable to help himself, he hugged her while they were both still holding their guitars. He stepped back with a grin but kept hold of her free hand. "The crowd loves you."

"Thanks. I have to admit, I was worried about the new songs."

Hone led her backstage and tugged her from the path of the musicians loitering behind the scenes, ready to play.

"Katie-Jo!"

The manager guy—Kevin—glared at him. Interesting. Obvious he disliked Hone hanging around Cassie. Too bad. He'd had his chance and mucked it up. Cassie wouldn't forgive and forget his betrayal. Besides, Hone was certain she liked him a little now. This Kevin joker wouldn't get his way this time.

*Unless Cassie decided to sign another contract with him.*

Hone pushed aside the concern and his taniwha's snarl—luckily hidden amongst the rockin' beat coming from the headline act who'd taken the stage.

"Kevin, what did you think of the segment?"

"The songs were good. Not your best, but they went down well with the crowd."

Hone found himself gaping as her manager tried to undermine her confidence. He opened his mouth to slap the man down but Cassie beat him to it.

"Bullshit, Kevin. What are you drinking? The crowd picked a new song for my encore."

"Because they don't know you here. They haven't heard your songs before. This isn't a good test. You're better going the pop route. I think—"

"You know what, Kevin? I don't care about your opinion, and this isn't the time or place to discuss it. I'll give you a call and make an appointment to see you when I get back to Los Angeles. You coming, Hone?" She stomped away, and both men stared at her retreat.

"You won't keep her," Kevin snarled.

Hone forced himself to meet the other man's gaze, forced his taniwha to behave, forced calmness to his tense muscles and gestured with a hand shrug. "Hey, I'm just the music man."

He ambled after Cassie. The last thing he wanted was for the man to hurt Cassie again. After all, he'd discovered jealousy could make a taniwha do stupid things. A human male was probably no different.

His phone buzzed as they exited the performers' room. Fresh air washed across his face as he answered. "Hey, Jack. Did you guys catch me playing?"

"Is that Jack and Emma?" Cassie asked.

"Yeah." He raised his hand in a hang-on motion. "Wait. What? Crap. You okay?"

"What is it? What's wrong?" Cassie demanded.

"Okay, we'll meet you at the gate. Just a sec." He lowered the phone. "Do we need to hang around for much longer?"

"I'd like a quick word with Charlie about the show next week. We can leave after that."

"Yeah, we won't be much longer."

"Why don't we meet them at the pub we passed? The one just down the road. That way we can grab something to eat. I'm starving. A sandwich won't cut it tonight."

"Good idea. Jack. There's a pub called The Thirsty Cricket. You should have seen it on the way to the vineyard. Yeah. We'll meet you there. Grab menus. We're both starving." He hung up. "We have a date. You were great out there. I am in awe of your talent, and the crowd loved your songs. All of them. Don't let that fool manager of yours pierce your confidence. If you don't believe me, ask Jack and Emma. They were in the crowd and will have ground-level feedback."

Cassie beamed and darted close to press a quick kiss to his lips. "I was excellent tonight. Don't worry about me. I don't understand the game Kevin is playing, but I won't fall for it. The man is an ass."

"That's my girl."

"I need a shower. Do I smell?"

She smelled like him, not that he intended to impart that knowledge. "You're good." He nuzzled her neck. "You smell like flowers and woman. Perfect. Let's go and find Charlie then we can have dinner."

Charlie found them. "Thank you, Katie-Jo. The crowd loved your segment. Several people have told me they enjoyed the unplugged aspect because it helped your voice shine. I have to admit I was hesitant because you were an unknown quantity. I researched you, of course, but..." He gave a shrug. "If it's all right with you, I'll give you a longer segment next weekend. Enough for two more songs."

"I'd love that," Cassie said.

She beamed and looked so beautiful Hone wanted to drag her back to their room. Eating was overrated.

"Excellent. I'll see you there. Call me if you have any questions. You have my number."

"Thanks, I will. See you next weekend."

Charlie left, and they made their way to the car park.

The moon hung low on the horizon, a copper red in color. Some would say a portent of bad tidings. Hone suppressed a shiver, even though he knew the red glow was likely due to the bushfire they'd had up here this week.

"Is something wrong with Jack and Emma?"

"You could say that. I'll let them tell you. Why don't you text Emma and tell her we're on our way?"

Hone seemed tense and had done since Jack had rung. Actually, he'd seemed strained since Kevin had approached her after the show. Slimy worm. Her manager, not Hone.

Hone...

Visions and memories of their last bout of sex, slow and gentle then fast and crazy as lust had overtaken them both made her smile.

Best. Weekend. Ever.

She tapped a quick message to Emma before shifting her thoughts back to Kevin. He'd done this before—tried to undermine her confidence. In hindsight it was always when he wanted her to do something. *Gah!* He'd turned her into a needy mess of a woman who relied on others instead of trusting her instincts. She'd changed. All it had taken was one decision to come home because no matter what her mother said or tried to tell her, New Zealand *was* home. Once she'd arrived, spending time with Emma had been all she needed to straighten her mind.

Kevin used manipulation to steer her in the direction he wanted.

No more.

"You've got your fierce on. What's the problem?" Hone whipped into a parking spot.

"I was pondering which songs to add for next weekend." Liar. A quick glance told her he'd bought her line.

"Do you have more new material?"

"A couple, but they're rough."

"Work on them. Even if you only add one new one and a cover, the audience would be pleased. You were incredible tonight."

"Thanks."

"If you don't believe me, check with Emma. She won't lie to you."

"No, she won't."

They walked into the pub hand-in-hand. She hadn't expected Hone would be a demonstrative lover, but he seemed to savor the contact. He made those weird purring sounds that made her tummy roll in a good way. Unlike Kevin, he didn't have secrets and agendas.

"They're over there," Hone said with a jerk of his head.

"Good timing," Emma said as they neared. "They said the kitchen was closing, so we decided to order for you."

"Did you enjoy the show?" Cassie asked, the suspense killing her. She thought the show had been good, had been pleased until Kevin.

"I wish you could have heard the comments from the crowd,"

Emma said. "Tell her, Jack."

"You've made new fans. The ones sitting near us intended to download your music online." He grinned at Hone. "You thinking of changing professions?"

Hone snorted as he slid into the booth beside her, effectively trapping her against the wall. Their thighs brushed and suggestive tingles roared to life in Cassie.

"I was scared shitless. I didn't think I would be, but I had to force myself to walk on stage. I don't know how Cassie does it."

"Both of you were awesome. I enjoyed the show," Emma said.

"Thank you. That means a lot to me." Cassie studied her friend, then her attention slid to Jack. "What's wrong?" Despite Emma's enthusiasm and Jack's words of encouragement, both of them seemed off.

"Our house burned down." Emma snuffled, and a tear rolled down her face. "We...we've lost everything. The fire brigade couldn't save it."

"What happened? How?"

Emma did some silent husband-wife communication with Jack, shrugged. "Maybe an electrical fault."

"You're insured?"

"Yeah," Jack said.

Emma sniffed. "It's only stuff, but...but..." Her lip wobbled and Jack growled in the same way Hone did when he became emotional.

"Why don't we visit the ladies' room before dinner arrives," Cassie said. "I wouldn't mind checking my makeup. I didn't have time before I left the vineyard."

Emma sent her a grateful glance.

Hone stood and brushed his fingers over her cheek. "Shout if anyone gives you any problems. Jack and I will be there in a flash."

"We're just going to the restrooms. We'll be quick because the smell of that food is divine."

The minute he and Jack were alone, Hone pressed for details.

"June set your house on fire?"

"She wanted you and Cassie. When we refused to tell her anything, she ceded most of her control to her dragon. God, Hone. Smoke was coming out her nose."

"Where was Samuel? Manu? They usually rein her in when she loses her temper."

Jack grimaced. "Not this time. We left before they arrived."

"She still searching for us?"

"As far as I know. I haven't contacted Manu in case June learns something she shouldn't. Hone, I've never seen her like this. She is out of control."

"Manu needs to step up."

"Yeah," Jack said grimly. "He has to stop playing inventor-boy and acknowledge he's next in line to rule."

"He doesn't want to lead."

"Too bad." Jack scrubbed his hands over his face before he met Hone's gaze. His expression told of his anguish, his taniwha bleeding through the human half of his psyche. "Fuck, I thought we were going to die. June considered it. I saw it in her body language."

"Do you have somewhere to stay tonight?"

"Not yet. I decided it was best to get out of Auckland. I rang your father to tell him what happened. He suggested we stay under the radar." Jack frowned. "George sounded worried. Without saying it, he told me to guard both you and Cassie."

"Crap." His father always remained calm under pressure. Always hard to read, he gave away only what he wished to reveal. "Stay with us. There's a spare room. I'll square it with the management. Did you save anything?"

"We have our vehicle plus the clothes on our back. Fuck, if she has hurt my cat..."

"Tom will be fine," Emma said, appearing beside them. "He's a tough tomcat." Emma had fixed her makeup although her bloodshot eyes gave away the fact she'd cried. She squeezed Jack's shoulder before she slid into the booth.

A sliver of fear worked through Hone. If June hurt Cassie, he didn't know what he'd do. "Where's Cassie?"

"Two fans stopped her for autographs and pictures."

"Fuck." Hone jumped to his feet and was at her side before he'd decided what to say. Photos. Social media. A big, fat hell no. "Hey,

C-Katie-Jo. Your dinner has arrived."

"Just one more photo," a young woman pleaded. She snapped a selfie with Cassie before Hone could stop her. "Thank you," she gushed.

"Dinner." Hone gripped Cassie's forearm and led her to their booth.

"You didn't have to be so rude."

"With all the weird things happening you shouldn't publicize your whereabouts."

"But I'm in disguise."

"Hone is right," Emma said, cutting through Cassie's argument. "You can't be too careful. Our house was set on fire. What if it's all connected?"

Cassie plonked onto the seat, her cheeks paling. "You think this is linked?"

Hone was certain it wasn't, but if Cassie became warier, all the better.

"We don't know for sure." Emma swallowed. "We'll have to wait for the police reports."

"I'm sorry. I didn't think," Cassie said, sounding miserable.

The waitress rocked up with their meals. Jack and Emma had ordered him a steak while Cassie had fish and chips with salad.

"Where are you guys staying tonight?" Cassie asked.

"They're staying with us," Hone said.

"Great," Cassie said. "Hone said we could go to the Matakana farmers' market tomorrow and we're going snorkeling again."

"No swimsuit," Emma said.

"Actually," Jack said with a hint of smugness. "You're in luck. I put your swimsuit in the vehicle yesterday. We have swimsuits and towels and the clothes on our backs."

Later that night, Cassie snuggled up to Hone. "I'm too wired to sleep."

"Excellent," Hone said. "What should we do?"

"Play tiddlywinks?" A smile tugged at her lips in the darkness.

"I can see those pearly whites, Cassie Miller-Pope."

Her grin broadened as she sought his lips. She missed, but it didn't matter. She—plump and with no drive or ambition, according to her mother—was naked and in bed with a total hottie who delighted in her curves and thought her musical talent rocked. He'd told her so. A lot to celebrate.

Her mind drifted to Emma and her jubilation faded. Poor Emma and Jack. Maybe she could offer them her house as long as they wouldn't mind her living there too. She'd suggest it tomorrow.

"Hey, where have you gone?"

"I'm right here, silly." She pressed a kiss to his chin because she could. His stubble tickled her lips, and that was enough to bring on the happy again, her body language broadcasting her feel-good mood.

"Your mind is busy. I can hear it ticking over."

"I was thinking I'd offer Emma and Jack the use of my house as long as they wouldn't mind me staying in one of the rooms. I won't be there for long."

"You leaving?"

His sharp tone made her tummy tingle. Did he not want her to leave? She didn't want to go, but Hone wasn't forever material, not with his track record. The best she could hope for was to stay friends.

"Cassie?"

"I'm not sure what to do, to be honest. If I sign with Kevin again—"

"Why do you have to sign with him? Aren't there other managers who wouldn't treat you like crap?"

Another manager. Holy crap. "I must be slow because that hadn't occurred to me. I'll check it out tomorrow."

Hone exploded into action, rolling her under him and sealing her shriek of surprise with his lips. "I have the solution to stop that busy mind of yours."

"You do?"

"Yeah."

He kissed her, the tempo slow and sexy and toe-curling good.

A sigh tickled her throat as she opened to him and accepted the thrust of his tongue, the bite of sharp teeth at her bottom lip. That bite—his bite—shot down her body to land between her legs.

One thing was true. His talented touch turned her into a wanton, and she'd never had as much fun with a man. Oh, she watched the envy on other women's faces. Easy to see their astonishment. Emma suffered through the same thing, yet Jack didn't notice anyone except his wife. That gave her hope...

Aw, who the hell was she kidding? Hone was a player who quickly became bored with one woman, and she...she had a music career in another country. New Zealand didn't rate as the land of musical opportunities, as much as she'd love to stay. Her home here could only ever be a vacation home.

"Cassie, you're denting my pride," Hone whispered, a thread of pique winding through his words. "If you're tired, tell me, and I'll roll over and go to sleep."

"Huh! You're having as much trouble sleeping as I am."

Hone rocked, his cock rigid against her stomach. "That's true, but with me it's sexual frustration."

"Poor baby."

"Now you're mocking me. Do you know what happens to women who misbehave?"

"No. What?"

He moved so quickly she hung over his knee in the time it took to process his action. A second later, he applied his hand to her butt. Smack. Smack. *Smack*.

"Ow!"

"Jack and Emma will hear." He punctuated his words with three more smacks at different angles and progressively nearer to her pussy. His big hand cupped the sex and rubbed it. Arousal took her by surprise, rendered her speechless. A finger burrowed between her legs, dipping into her heat.

"Focused. Totally focused."

His satisfied chuckle tugged at her funny bone. The man was a menace to women. A menace and right now, he was her menace. Something fractured in the region of her heart, a frisson of pain, a smidgeon of lust and a gossamer thread of love blossomed.

Well, hell.

Hone smacked her again, the whoosh of heat no longer taking her by surprise. He smoothed his callused palm over her tender skin and dipped his finger close enough to her clit to make her gasp her delight. Not only was she enjoying the heck out of her time with Hone, she was learning about her sexual self. She didn't mind a hint of pain with her loving. It ratcheted up the sensations.

"More," she demanded.

Hone smacked her, striking her where butt and upper thigh met.

"Not there. I feel empty. I need that big cock of yours."

"Why didn't you say so?"

He moved again, lifting and rearranging her body with ease.

Doggy-style. He seemed to favor this position, and while she'd never enjoyed it before, Hone made the sexual journey fun.

"Condom," he muttered. "Where did we put them?"

"In the side pocket of my handbag."

"Don't move," he ordered.

He returned in long seconds, the cracking and ripping indicating he was donning the condom. "See what you think of this," he said, seconds before he applied cool gel to her flesh. It coated her clit, and he stroked it into her channel with his finger, first one and then two.

"Ow! Cold."

"Stop complaining." He slapped one buttock.

"You try it."

"I put lube on my dick."

"Condom-covered dick," she pointed out.

He stroked his finger inside her, tickling her nub enough to make her pay attention. The gel heated with her body and continued heating until her flesh burned, her clit burned, the flames of arousal burned.

"Oh."

"I see I have your attention now."

His cock nudged her entrance, and he pushed deep with an unhurried stroke. "Damn, that's good."

Too good. That burning sensation had every thought, every sensation, every particle of her being focused on the flesh between her legs. A shudder rolled through her as Hone's cock caressed her clit with each thrust. "Faster. Please, Hone. Faster."

He laughed and pushed into her again, his strokes coming more often and striking her in exactly the right place. Of course, his talented finger with its precision work on her clit didn't hurt. She gasped, briefly considered holding back to savor the sensation. Hone didn't let her. He upped the pace of his strokes, the prick of his fingernails at her hipbones anchoring her in the moment.

Up, up, up she rose until she toppled over and shattered. She gasped hoarsely, the pleasure prolonged and intense. Hone plunged into her now, his strokes fast and choppy, his hands gripping her tight. He cried out, stilling as his cock pulsed deep inside her.

A sharp thump on the wall made her giggle. Hone grunted, the sound coming close to laughter.

Emma would tease her in the morning and Cassie didn't care. She yawned once he withdrew and dealt with the condom.

"I might sleep now."

"Me too," Hone agreed as he wrapped his arms around her.

Cassie yawned again. How much longer would this last? One week? Two? Best she not worry about the future. One day at a time. That was the best way to go.

One day at a time.

## CHAPTER 18

# Three days later

The days away from Auckland had left her rested and full of enthusiasm to get her grandfather's house ready for occupation. However, something perturbed Jack and Hone. She kept disturbing the two men in a huddle. Sometimes with Emma, which left Cassie uneasy. Secrets. They had them. She didn't.

Cassie applied paint over the last part of the spare bedroom wall and stood back to survey the new decor. Rich, decadent cream. Not bad. She set down her roller and wandered out to see what was keeping Emma.

"Hey, do I have body odor or something? The three of you whispering secrets is enough to make me paranoid."

Emma rushed into speech. "Fire-related stuff. The insurance

company is refusing to pay out. They're calling it arson and dragging their feet."

"But even if it is arson, that's not your fault," Cassie said.

"Insurance companies have their own set of rules." Jack shrugged, a tiny jerk of shoulders that spoke of disheartenment and frustration and irritation. "All we can do is keep up the pressure. There's a vehicle outside."

"Might be the plumber," Cassie said. "I rang him to sort out the kitchen and make it useable now that the new units are in place." Cassie hurried to meet them, but Hone intercepted her, drawing her to a halt.

"No, I'll go. You wait here with Jack and Emma."

"It's not necessary, but okay. If it's the plumber, tell him I want him to fix the taps in the bathroom, too."

"The house is looking good," Emma said. "Are you sure you don't mind Jack and I moving in?"

"It's fine. I need to decide soon. I don't want to leave the house empty again and I know you and Jack will care for the property. I'll have to decide what to do with the land."

"How many acres?" Jack asked.

"Just over ten. I haven't even had a chance to check out the paddocks. There is a creek and a swimming hole we used to spend time at when I was a kid. It's probably full of debris by now. Grandad used to clear it at the start of each summer."

"Jack and I can do that. You could lease out the land to a local farmer. What's the fencing like?"

"I have no answer to that either. With all that has happened since I've been home I haven't bothered. I figure it will keep."

Voices in the kitchen indicated Hone's return.

"Can I go and speak with the plumber now?"

"No wonder Hone spanks you," Jack muttered.

Emma let out a guffaw, quickly covered by her hand. Her blue gaze danced with hilarity.

"No comment." Cassie pushed her glasses up her nose and marched away before telltale mortification blazed in her cheeks. Hopefully, the house would be ready soon, and Jack and Emma could move out of Hone's place. They'd all have privacy again.

While Cassie spoke to the plumber and issued orders, Hone had a discussion with Jack and Emma.

"I rang Dad. He says everything has quieted down with Auntie June, but we should keep our distance."

"Is it okay for us to lower security on Cassie?" Emma asked.

"Dad says as long as one of us is with her at all times, that should be enough. He thinks Auntie June burned out her anger at your house, and we don't have to worry about death by dragon."

"She destroyed our house," Jack growled. "Now the insurance company is quibbling about payment and trying to say our occupation attracted a crazy. Someone needs to repay our losses."

"Dad says Samuel has promised to make good on the damage.

Manu has his mother locked down, and she seems to have accepted she went too far."

"So Manu is acting leader?" Emma asked. "I understood he didn't want the responsibility."

Hone slapped at an audacious fly buzzing around him. "He didn't have a choice. He must be frothing at the mouth having to deal with this when he'd rather be in his lab."

"You guys in a huddle again?"

Emma didn't miss a beat, thinking faster on her feet than him and Jack. "We're discussing furniture and the best place to buy it. Now that the painting is almost done, we can move in as soon as we have a bed and kitchen stuff."

"The electrician is coming tomorrow to sort out the wiring in the kitchen. If we order a stove today, you'll have the basics. Where is the best place?"

Emma rearranged her ponytail, pulling it tight. "Probably Manukau. We'll start there. You guys coming?"

"Dad wants us to drop by the office to discuss a new job," Hone said. "I want you to watch everyone around you and listen to Emma. Okay?"

"Sure," Cassie said. "Believe me, the first clown I see, I'll scream loud enough to wake the dead in this town and the next one over."

"Not funny," Hone said, concerned yet unable to justify an order for her to remain at home, out of sight. "Everything has been quiet, but I want you to be extra careful." Despite their audience, he drew her close and kissed the tip of her nose. "Promise?"

"I promise."

Her words should have relaxed him, but his dragon rumbled, writhing beneath his skin to highlight his uneasiness. Emma was a trained operative. He'd trained her himself, and Jack had helped. She was good at her job and would inform him if anything seemed wonky.

"Right," Emma said. "Practicalities. Will a king-size bed will fit in the spare bedroom?"

"It will be a tight squeeze, but not if you and Jack take the master. I'll get a double for the spare room and keep the smallest bedroom as a music room. Don't worry," Cassie said, tapping her head. "I have the measurements in here."

Hone gave Cassie a quick kiss and shunted her toward the doorway. "We'll wait until the plumber finishes."

As she and Emma pulled out of the driveway in Jack's vehicle, a late-model sedan drove past. The driver waved, and Cassie returned the greeting. "That's my neighbor. That must be his son."

"At least he's not the nosy neighbor type," Emma said. "Do you think he'd be interested in leasing your land?"

"Maybe. I've got a bit of time. Once the house is sorted, I'll walk the boundaries and see what needs doing. It was never an economical block. Maybe Matthew wants to grow Christmas trees on it. I wouldn't mind having trees on the place. It might be nice."

"Are you leaving?"

"Probably," Cassie said.

"What about Hone?"

"Weren't you the one who warned me about him? Said he didn't do anything except casual?"

Emma's hands clenched and unclenched on the steering wheel. "He seems happy, less restless with you around."

"Doesn't mean he's ready to commit," Cassie said even though her heart ached as she forced out the truth. Her phone buzzed, and she frowned at the screen. "Kevin. I should take this."

"Go right ahead. With this traffic, it will take a while."

"Kevin," she said. "How are you? You still in New Zealand?"

"Leaving tonight. Have you signed the contract yet? We need to make plans for this year. We've left it too late already. Probably won't be able to book much in the way of concert venues."

Cassie opened her mouth to blast him for his negative attitude, aware that in the past she would've let it slide. As it was, she bit back her retort. "I'll get on the contract tonight."

"Good, I need you to sign and get it back to me by the end of the week. Clock's ticking." He hung up before she could reply.

Cassie pulled a face. "Kevin is an asshole."

"So why are you signing with him?"

"I don't think I will, but I'd be silly not to consider his offer. Two months ago, I wouldn't have hesitated."

"Because you were a couple?"

"Yeah, and in the glow of togetherness, I failed to see he was using me. Trying to control me."

"I like this new Cassie."

Emma pulled up outside a store that sold everything from electronics to washing machines and bedroom furniture.

"I even told my mother to stop pushing me around when I spent time with them over Christmas." Cassie laughed at her friend's wide-eyed expression. "She didn't take me seriously, but I reiterated when she rang me a few days ago. Still not getting it. I might have to resort to telling Dad exactly what I do to get her off my back."

"If she learns you're a well-known singer—"

"She'll probably lecture me and try to shove me toward the opera genre."

Emma giggled and the infectious gurgles enticed Cassie to join in. They were still laughing when they walked into the store.

"I have a list." Cassie plucked it from the handbag slung over her shoulder. She scanned it to refresh her mind. "Beds first."

"Jack said we should pay for the furniture. I agree."

"Emma, you guys lost everything in the fire. Use your money to buy clothes and... Look, you buy linens to go on your bed. I have no idea of your preferences. You'll need a few towels. Would that salve your pride? You're my best friend, and I've saved my money rather than spend it on stuff. It makes me happy to share with you."

Emma's eyes were moist as she flung herself against Cassie and hugged her hard. "Thank you. I'm sure the insurance company will pay out eventually, but things are tight right now."

"Furniture today. Perhaps linen if we have time. What about dinnerware?"

"Samuel and his sons have arranged a collection for us." Emma's expression tightened, a flash of fury.

An instant later, her face cleared and Cassie blinked. Imagination. While it was good in songwriting, her vivid inventiveness saw things that weren't true in real life. After all, why would a charitable act make Emma angry?

"Okay, let's do this. Now that the main work is done in the house, the sooner we furnish the rooms, the quicker you can move in properly."

"I'm over sleeping on the floor," Emma agreed.

With efficiency, they commandeered an employee, picked two beds and mattresses, a couch and two easy chairs, a kitchen table and chairs, a fridge, stove and microwave plus a dishwasher. Cassie arranged for delivery the following day.

"We have time to visit the department store for bed linen."

Emma raised her chin. "Let's do this."

Cassie hurried out of the store, jazzed by everything they'd achieved. Immediately, her skin prickled, and it wasn't the change in temperature from air-conditioning to the muggy outdoors. "Is it my imagination or is someone watching us?"

"Maybe they're ogling our sexy bodies," Emma said as she unlocked Jack's vehicle and casually scanned the car park. "I can't see anyone obvious. You?"

"No, let's go to our next stop and keep an eye out." She craned her neck and scrutinized the area behind them.

Emma spluttered out a laugh. "Well, you'd make a good private eye. Can you be more obvious?"

"Sorry. Isn't that Manu?"

"Where?" Emma's voice was sharp.

"It is." She waved, and he lifted a hand in acknowledgment. "He's coming over."

"Hi, Manu. What are you doing here?" Emma asked. "I understood work was keeping you busy."

"Not too busy to escort my two favorite ladies for coffee," Manu said.

"We're off to the department store," Cassie said. "But we could do coffee. You want to meet us at the mall?"

"I might as well come with you." Manu opened the rear door and slid inside.

"Don't complain if you get bored shopping for sheets and towels." Cassie winged a wink toward her friend. "Emma? What's wrong?"

Emma clenched the steering wheel, and she studied the parking lot with an intensity that was scary.

"Bit of a headache," Emma said.

"You want me to drive?" Manu asked.

Cassie frowned, gazing from Emma to Manu. Manu seemed off too and didn't wear the same easy-going attitude he'd sported when she first met him. Now that she looked closer, he bore shadows beneath his brown eyes, exhaustion hovering over him like a ghost.

"No, I'll drive," Emma said. "Where is your vehicle?"

"It's at the mall. I needed computer parts and saw you come out of the store."

Cassie frowned again, knowing something wasn't right, but unable to pinpoint what or why Emma and Manu were suddenly behaving strangely. Maybe it was her imagination again. "So, what color sheets are you going to buy?"

"Pink with flowers," Emma replied without missing a beat.

Manu chortled from the rear seat. "Does Jack like pink?"

"Jack will like whatever I buy," Emma snapped.

An uncomfortable silence fell, and Cassie struggled to fill the gap. Had they argued? And if so, why didn't she know about it?

In the department store, they headed straight for soft furnishings floor.

"You get your sheets, and I'll grab pillows and towels. What color towels?"

"A dark color that will go with the bathroom," Emma said. "Darker is better with Jack around. I tried white and had to replace them."

Cassie strode away to fulfill her mission. When she turned into the towel aisle, she glimpsed Manu and Emma in whispered conversation. Tense because Emma was jabbing him in the chest with her forefinger. Manu stood there and took it before wrapping Emma in his embrace. Not a romantic one, more comforting and friendly. None of her business. Besides, Emma might tell her what was wrong during the drive home.

Long years of friendship had taught her that Emma stewed and processed when she became angry or upset about something. Shrugging away her concern, Cassie grabbed a cart and started her assignment.

Cassie studied the colors and quickly chose a selection of towels. The pillows took a bit longer, but she grabbed six. She also tossed in a package of tea towels.

"All done?" Manu asked.

Emma remained silent, her arms full of packaged sheets.

"All done."

Half an hour later, after a quick and uncomfortable coffee, Cassie was glad to be on the road back to Clevedon.

"Emma, is something wrong?"

The healthy color fled Emma's hands as she gripped the steering wheel tighter. "June isn't well. Manu is worried about her."

"I see." An understatement. She didn't understand at all. If June was unwell why would Manu want to spend time with them? "Why was Manu shopping and not with his mother?"

"He said his brothers made him take a break."

"Oh." Well, that made sense, but it didn't explain Emma's mood. Anger pulsed off her, and she hadn't been like that when they left Jack and Hone.

The built-up suburbs gave way to the green countryside, and Cassie let her mind drift to her music. Other managers. Who could she contact? She needed someone with knowledge of the country music bigwigs and who could be flexible about the changes she wanted to take with her career. A sensible person would continue to put out Katie-Jo country songs to make use of her fan base. Perhaps she could use another name for her new stuff and start over as an indie. A lot of musicians were taking the independent route these days, and there was no reason she couldn't dabble on the side. Of course, she wouldn't be able to handle a full-on concert tour if she did that. Maybe a month of concerts. Yeah, she could handle a month, and maybe, just maybe, she could return home to New Zealand to relax. Something to consider.

Cassie pulled a notebook out of her handbag and started making a list of what she needed to research. She glanced up and stared, surprise making her blink. "Stop the car."

"What? What's wrong?" Emma turned fierce, her tone no-business.

"What is a young kid doing walking down a country road all alone?" As soon as Emma stopped, Cassie hopped from the car.

"Wait. Don't get out."

"It's a kid, Emma." She ignored her friend's protests and walked to intercept the child. Not very old. A little boy. He wore a red-and-blue Spiderman suit and had a small bag tucked over his shoulder. His mouth formed into an O when he saw Cassie, then he grinned. Wow, he'd be a heartbreaker once he was older, although right now, he couldn't be more than five or six. Certainly not old enough to wander down the road on his own.

"What are you doing?" she asked.

"I'm running away from home," the boy said.

"Why?"

He wasn't crying and didn't seem unhappy. In fact, excitement pulsated from him as if he were on a grand adventure.

"Daddy read me a story about a boy who ran away. I decided to see if I had the same adventures as Sam."

"Oh." Cassie restrained her burst of humor. He didn't appear tired or dirty, so he couldn't have wandered far. "Does your daddy know you've run away?"

"He was busy in his office."

"Okay. I'm Cassie. What's your name?"

"Dillion."

"Hello, Dillion. It's very hot. Would you like to have a cookie and a cold drink?"

He cocked his head and studied her before giving a decisive nod. "The boy in the story met a lady and had cookies."

"Right." The boy had to live on this road. She'd ring

Matthew—no, wait. "Is your daddy's name Matthew?"

"Yes."

Good. At least she knew where he came from and he hadn't walked far. She'd give Matthew a call and drop Dillion back after his cookies.

"Come on," she said. "We'll give you a ride home."

"I'm not allowed to ride in cars with strangers," Dillion said.

"That's good advice," she agreed. "How about I walk back to my house with you? It's right next door to your house."

"I only live with Daddy sometimes."

Ah, so that explained things. Matthew shared custody of Dillion. He seemed like a good father if he read stories to his son. He was probably frantic. Back at the vehicle, Emma seemed relieved.

"This is Dillion, and he lives next door," Cassie explained. "He's run away from home."

Emma gawked at her.

"We're going to have cookies," Dillion told Emma.

"Let me grab my phone. Dillion, quite rightly, doesn't want to get into a car with a stranger. I'll walk back to the house with him and ring Matthew so he doesn't worry."

"Oh, but—"

"It's not far. We'll be ten minutes tops."

Emma scanned the road behind them. "All right," she said, her tone grim. "See you soon."

*Weird.* Emma was behaving plain weird. Probably the strain of the fire.

Cassie rifled through her handbag and found the business card she placed in the side pocket.

"Hello? Matthew? This is Cassie Miller-Pope. I have something that belongs to you."

"Pardon?" His tone was frosty and unwelcoming.

"I found your son on the side of the road, not far from my place. He said he was running away from home."

# CHAPTER 19

Hone's nerves bounced up and down the entire time Cassie and Emma were away. His taniwha wasn't much better with his restless growling.

"Thank god," Jack said. "Here they are now."

Hone was halfway out the door before he registered the action. "Where's Cassie? She's not with Emma." He sprinted to the driver's side demanding answers. "Where is Cassie?"

"She's walking. We found a young boy on the side of the road and she insisted on walking back with him. What was I meant to do? I can't tell her the truth—that a fire-breathing dragon wants to punish her. She'd say I was crazy."

"Hone." Jack grabbed him when his taniwha pushed past his restraint and shook him. "It's not Emma's fault. We're doing our best."

"I talked to Manu," Emma said. "June has disappeared. Samuel and the boys are hunting for her."

"Crap. I'll go and get Cassie," Hone said, taking off at a sprint.

Fear cramped his guts, the itch to shift strong. He kept running, scanning the air for signs of June. Surely she wouldn't fly over in daylight and put the entire race at the risk of discovery?

Damn, where was Cassie? He still couldn't see her.

Ah, there she was. A dark-haired child walked at her side, both chattering away and not paying attention to their surroundings. Typical humans. So unaware of the dangers.

He slowed and gave his taniwha a mental shove. *It's all right. She's safe. If June comes, we're here to protect her.*

"Hi," he called before he reached them.

"Hone." A brilliant smile flashed across her face and his heart drum-rolled.

God, she was so beautiful. He couldn't lose her, not to June. He couldn't live without her. Nothing had prepared him for Cassie, yet his father had been right. The moment the right woman walked into his life, he'd leave his tomcatting ways behind.

Hone studied the kid. Cute in his Spiderman suit.

"Is he a stranger?" the kid asked Cassie.

She laughed in the musical way of hers that never failed to stir him. "No, this is my friend, Hone. Hone, this is Dillion. He lives next door, and he's coming to visit until his father picks him up."

"What cookies do you have?" the kid asked.

"We have shortbread and chocolate chip. I couldn't decide which ones to buy, so I got one packet of each."

As Hone fell into step with them, the pair continued to chatter. It was so easy to imagine her with his child, and that told him, more than anything, that he couldn't let her leave. It meant he'd have to tell her about his dual nature as a taniwha, but he thought she'd accept all of him. At least, he hoped she would. He couldn't marry her without letting her in on the truth, yet he risked everything if she rejected him and left to pursue her career.

"That's an awfully big frown. Are you doing heavy-duty thinking over there?"

"Work stuff," Hone lied, and the falsehood cut him. No, he didn't enjoy lying to her.

They turned into the driveway and found Emma had set up outside with an umbrella to keep off the sun. That would also help screen them from June if she went crazy and decided to fly during the day.

Unless she had one of Manu's devices...

He cursed under his breath. "I should call Manu to see what's happening with Auntie June. Evidently she hasn't been well."

Hone strode indoors, plucked his phone from his pocket and face-timed his cousin. "Manu, has your mother got one of your devices?" he demanded without preamble.

"No, I keep them locked up when I'm not working with them.

She tried to get at them and failed. Emma said you guys are at the house in Clevedon."

"Yeah. It's probably safer in Papakura, given the larger population, but none of us can think of a reason good enough to persuade Cassie it's less dangerous in town. We've tried, believe me, but she said she is surrounded by private investigators and couldn't be more protected. And she said it's easier to spot strangers out here. It's taken her a few days to settle after that clown episode."

"God, what a mess. I have no idea what to do, Hone. If any other dragon ran amok like this, we'd put them down for the greater good, but this is my mother. The matriarch of the tribe. She's out of control, but I don't know if I can do the right thing."

"I'm sorry." Hone's throat tightened, hearing his cousin's grief. He got it. He truly did, but June was trying to kill Cassie when none of this was her fault. She hadn't dumped Manu. They hadn't had a relationship. Cassie had said it and Manu had confirmed they were nothing more than friends. Cassie slept curled in his arms, not his cousin's. "I'll help."

"No, you need to say with Cassie. My brothers will help me." He swiped his hand over his face, exhaustion like a feather cloak draped over his shoulders. "Don't look like that. None of this is your fault. You and Cassie are good together, and I'm happy you've found someone."

"There's a car coming. I think it's the neighbor, but I want to check."

"I'll inform you when we find Ma."

"Okay." Hone hung up, his heart heavy. None of them would win. June's actions had already ripped the tribe apart, and he had no idea how they'd recover.

Outside, a late-model car pulled up and a tall, slim man dressed in business clothes stepped from the driver's side.

"Dad!" The kid ran to him, and Hone's shoulders relaxed on seeing the joy and relief on the man's face. He loved his kid. "Cassie likes playing dress-up too. She wears a pink wig. I told her I make a good cowboy."

"Yes, you do, son. Thank you for picking up Dillion and ringing me. My ex..." His expression tightened as he spoke to Cassie. "She would have used this to change our custody schedule."

"It was no problem."

"Can I come and visit again?" Dillion asked.

"As long as you ask your father first," Cassie said. "Get your father to call me to make sure I'm home first, okay?"

"Okay." Dillion took a huge bite of his cookie. Cute kid.

"Hi," Hone stepped forward, his hand outstretched. "I'm Hone Taniwha, Cassie's boyfriend."

"He might as well piss on her," Emma whispered to Jack.

His buddy barked out a laugh, and Hone glared at them both, thankful that neither of the human adults heard.

"Matthew Jamieson," the man said.

For a businessman, he had callused hands. Maybe he worked on his farm during the weekends instead of hiring people. Christmas trees, Cassie had said.

"Thanks again. Nice to meet you all."

Cassie, Jack and Emma started to unload the vehicle, and Hone jogged over to help them, while keeping an eye on Matthew and his son. The man was a good father, and it was obvious the kid adored him. When they drove away, Hone heard the kid's excited chatter about running away, and the father telling him he could only run away if he was with him. Strange thing to say, but it made sense.

"Hell, did you girls buy out the shops?" Jack asked as they dumped parcels and bags on the new kitchen counter.

"No, we left stuff for other customers," Cassie said without missing a beat. "We didn't want to be greedy. The beds and other furniture will arrive tomorrow afternoon, so tomorrow night you can sleep in a proper bed instead of on the camp bed in Hone's spare room. We should have a barbecue to celebrate. I'll buy one in the morning."

"No, ours survived the fire," Jack said. "Everything in the garden shed was okay, so I'll bring out the mower, my garden tools and the barbecue tomorrow morning."

"We should visit your swimming hole. The weather forecast is for another humid day," Emma suggested.

"Can you guys sort out the packages?" Cassie asked. "I need to start rehearsing for the next vineyard show and work out which songs to sing. I have to make a few phone calls to the States later and want to reread the contract Kevin sent me."

*Crap.* "Can I help with anything?" Hone asked.

"Yeah, how are you at contracts? I need a fresh set of eyes to tell me I'm not imagining things. Kevin has clauses in there I don't like."

"I can do that," Hone said, thankful his father had insisted on him taking business classes and finishing a degree before he joined the firm fulltime.

"We can all read it through if that would help," Emma said.

"Have at it," Cassie said, pointing at a pink folder. "There are two copies in there. I've taken notes and made a list of what I want, but not many of the matters are addressed in the contract."

Hone growled. "He trying to rip you off?"

"He would see it as business, but it's not good business for me. Anyhow, thanks. I'll be in the other room with my guitar. Holler if you need me."

Hone's phone beeped, and he scanned the text. "Samuel has found June. She's at home under lockdown."

"Good. We can relax a bit," Emma said.

Jack peered into a bag of towels. "I don't envy Manu. He has a tough decision to make."

Hone sighed. "Hope it doesn't cause a ruckus with the Waka family. They've made no secret of the fact they think they should be in charge."

"Will the Waka brothers make trouble?" Emma asked.

"Yes," Hone said.

"Yup," Jack agreed. "Manu will have to fight to keep leadership, and he'll have to deal with June first."

"Won't Samuel—"

"No," Hone interrupted Emma, "If June becomes too unstable, Manu will do the right thing. He won't put his father through the anguish of taking his mate's life."

"Hell, what a mess. I can't believe June wigged out over Cassie and Manu." Emma leaned against Jack and sighed when he wrapped his arms around her waist. "She has always tried to find her sons mates and talked about more grandchildren, but it seems silly for her to go over the top about it. She's..." she shrugged. "She's never shown any signs of instability that I could see. She seemed like a fair leader."

"Manu is broken," Hone said. "I offered my help, but he said his brothers would assist if necessary."

"It's murder," Emma blurted.

"Is it murder if you're saving a hundred lives? The general population aren't ready to learn of our existence yet, and if June catches up with Cassie, she'll kill her without blinking," Jack explained. "She is that furious. This situation isn't black and white."

## CHAPTER 20

# Late afternoon, the next day

"I've read your contract, Cassie. Kevin is trying to diddle you out of merchandizing and his management fees seem high." Emma slapped the contract on the new kitchen table and pulled out a chair to join Cassie where she pondered her list.

"I've contacted three other possible managers. Two men and one woman. All of them manage other artists I trust and come highly recommended." Cassie studied her notes on each of the managers, scrawled during last night's calls.

"You've decided on one."

"Yes, I think so. They were all top-class, enthusiastic and okay with the plan I'd sketched out for the next two years."

"You're still leaving." Emma's lips drooped at the corners.

"Yes." She didn't tell Emma the rest of her plan. She would, but not until she finalized the details and set her plan in motion. No jinxes for her, thank you very much.

"What about Hone?"

Cassie frowned. "What about Hone?"

"You intend to walk away without regret." Now Emma sounded disapproving.

"You were the one who informed me he wasn't husband material. It sounds as if the boys are back with the barbecue." Relieved at the interruption because she didn't want to discuss Hone, even with her best friend, she jumped to her feet. "I have beers in the fridge. We deserve one."

Emma followed her outside, and Cassie could literally feel her friend's disapproval prodding her in the back. Of course she liked Hone. If she were honest, she was halfway in love with the man. Walking away would hurt, but she had to do the adult thing. She'd made a plan she could live with. She'd tell Hone about it first—before Emma. Give him a chance to tell her where she stood in his life.

"Where do you want the barbecue, Cassie?" Jack asked.

"You and Emma are going to be living here. You decide," Cassie said.

"You're leaving?" Hone's sharp gaze, tinged with that weird red, speared right through her, but she couldn't decipher his thoughts on the subject.

"Eventually," she said, not ready to supply answers because she wasn't certain of her future path yet. It depended on which manager she chose. While she had a clear favorite, she had a few more questions for each of them before she made a final decision. "Anyone want a beer? I've got steaks marinating, made garlic bread and the salads are ready."

"I could go for a beer," Hone said.

"I'd like to check out the swimming hole," Emma added.

"Oh, good idea," Cassie said. "Why don't we do that after a beer? We can eat once we get back."

Half an hour later, Cassie led the way, over a rickety style and down a narrow, overgrown track, populated with blackberry bushes.

"Ouch." She paused to untangle a prickly branch from her sandal. Beads of blood formed on her foot.

Hone put his hand on her shoulder. "Let me go first. My hide is tougher than yours."

"Not gonna argue. The track goes around to the left for a bit. We should be able to hear the creek soon."

"I'll bring the slasher next time," Jack said from behind them. "It won't take much to clear the track."

Hone rounded the corner, pausing to hold back blackberry branches for her. It was better with him going first. Quicker too.

He paused at the top of a rise.

"There," she said, pointing. "It's not as bad as I suspected. I remember a bigger pool, but I was a kid the last time I swam here."

"We could make it bigger," Jack said.

Emma scanned their surroundings with approval. "It's nice and private with all the trees around."

Cassie pulled a face and held up her right hand in a stop motion. "Emma, I know exactly where your mind has gone."

Hone barked out a laugh. "Is it a crime? Mine wandered there too. It's the perfect spot for skinny dipping and other stuff."

"It won't take long to clear the visible logs and check for hidden debris," Jack said.

"Let's go." Hone led the way down the hill, walking easier now that the path had widened.

Cassie stopped and frowned. "I thought that the farm was bigger. I don't remember those pine trees there. I remember Granddad telling me his plot was a perfect rectangle."

Pine trees of different sizes grew along the straight boundary before taking a dogleg left.

The wind picked up, bringing the fresh scent of pine.

"We can check it out on the way back," Emma suggested. "Walk up the fence line."

In silent agreement, the foursome waded into the pond, working together to remove branches and debris.

"It's deeper than I imagined," Jack said.

"Not deep enough for diving, but good for cooling down," Hone agreed.

Despite the lateness of the day, mugginess clung, the air heavy as if it might rain.

Cassie's stomach let out an undignified rumble. "I'm ready for food. I worked through lunch on a new song."

"I could eat," Emma announced. "But let's walk up the fence line. The walking will be easier since it's clearer."

Hone led the way, picking through thistles, more blackberry bushes and thick grass. It was a relief to reach the fence where the walking presented fewer prickly obstructions.

"Hold," Jack said without warning.

Cassie froze.

"What is it?" Emma asked.

"Hone, to your right at ten o'clock. Is that an alarm?"

Cassie scrunched her brow, mystified by their discovery. "But why would there be an alarm—"

"Drugs," Hone muttered. "Now it makes sense. That's what I can smell. I couldn't work out what it was, but yeah. Cannabis. Someone is using your land to grow weed."

Matthew watched his sleeping son, his heart aching with love for the small being he and his ex had made together. Happier times, before she showed her bitchy side, the side that liked variety in her men.

His phone vibrated, and he answered it absently as he left his son's bedroom. Should he take Dillion now and not worry about the last of the cash crop? He'd prepared Dillion as much as possible, obtained false passports and had organized a private plane to Fiji. From there, they'd catch a commercial flight and zigzag their way to Central America. Originally, he'd planned on South America, but ultimately, he'd felt Central America was safer and language became less of a barrier. No one would comment on a father and son living in a cottage on the beach.

"Boss, the silent alarms at sector C are going off."

"Wait. What?" His mind jerked back to the present.

"Sector C alarms are going."

"Hell, probably the neighbor exploring her land. It had to happen." Matthew considered the angles. "All evidence of our crop has gone. I checked the area myself before we planted the new saplings. The crop is on the neighbor's land, so we'll play dumb. Herbert, if you want to risk it, go down and harvest some of the buds and sell it to my contacts. Keep the sale proceeds for yourself, but be careful because if you get caught, I will deny everything." He paused, planning his future actions. "Nail up a few of those clown masks, but away from the silent alarm. Hopefully, they won't find that."

"Okay, boss. What's the plan?"

"Deny everything and move up my schedule. You still have the post office box?"

"Yes," Herbert said.

"I'll send your final pay there. It's best if we don't contact each other again. I'm going to destroy this phone."

"Don't stiff me, boss," Herbert said as if he were uttering a pleasantry.

"Have I ever?" Matthew demanded, his tone icy.

"My point is this isn't a good time to start." Now his right-hand man sounded defensive.

"I have too much to lose to screw this up." If he were in Herbert's shoes, he'd have misgivings. "Check the box once a week. Heed my words about the crop. Act fast and don't be greedy." He hung up, his lips twisting. Kind of ironic he'd utter those words when it was greed that had led him to using his neighbor's land.

His other phone rang. The number on the screen had him scowling, tense, girding his parental loins for an ex-wife custody discussion battle. "Maureen." While he aimed for pleasant, his instant tension bled through his greeting.

"Josh and I are going to The Mount for the week. You'll have to bring Dillion home now because I won't be here tonight."

Bitch. Always changing their custody agreement on a whim. He'd played along. Mr. Nice. He'd let her call the shots, going along with her orders even though they grated.

Hell, who was he kidding? He'd like to wring her bloody neck. "Would you like me to keep Dillion for the week?"

There was a silence. A pause. "What about your work? I won't have you leaving Dillion with sitters."

Matthew held back his snort with difficulty. According to Dillion, Maureen left him with the neighbor on a regular basis. "No, I'm working from home this week. I'll make sure I confine my work to the evening when Dillion is in bed or if he's napping during the afternoon. I have three or four visits arranged, but they'll be short and I can take Dillion with me."

"I'll want to talk to Dillion every night," Maureen warned.

"No problem. Will you ring at the usual time? Around five?"

"Yes," she said slowly. "Don't make me regret this, Matthew. I won't give you a second chance."

"Thank you," Matthew said. "I appreciate this, Maureen."

"You can drop him off next Sunday night at six."

"Okay. We'll be there."

Maureen hung up halfway through his sentence. Matthew disconnected on his end, triumph blooming as he pumped his fist in the air. His stupid bitch of an ex had played right into his hands. Kismet or what?

His phone went again, and his stomach bucked with misgivings. Hell, had Maureen changed her mind already?

"Yes."

"This is Cassie Miller-Pope, your next-door neighbor. My

friends and I went for a walk and discovered a cannabis plot on my land. Were you aware of this?"

"Pardon?" Matthew wanted to chortle, so great was his relief that Cassie was on the end of the phone call rather than his wife. "Did you say cannabis?"

"Yes. You haven't noticed anything strange?"

"No. I walk through our trees, checking for signs of pests, but other than a bit of a pruning once a year, we leave our trees to do their thing. Where is this plot? Do you think that is why you had vandals in your house?"

Her gasp was audible. "That would explain things," she agreed. "I have had rather a lot of bad luck."

"Have you rung the cops?"

"Not yet," she said. "I wanted to check with you first."

"Where is the plot?"

"It's on our common boundary but is growing on my land. Whoever owns the plants has tried to disguise them with a border of pines, the same variety as yours."

He considered, consulted his watch. Herbert should have had time to harvest the buds by now. "Would you like me to pick you up and we can visit the local police together to lodge a complaint?"

"No. It's all right. I'll contact the police. Thanks for the offer."

"You're welcome," Matthew said. "If there is anything I can do to help, you know where to find me. And thank you again for intercepting Dillion for me. He's the light of my life, and I'd be devastated if anything happened to him."

"He's a great kid. It was my pleasure to entertain him. Sorry to interrupt your evening. The police will probably contact you, anyway."

"Give them my number," he said. "I'm fine with that."

Matthew hung up and wanted to do a celebratory cheer. He didn't, instead going to his room to pack and to pull out the disguises he'd prepared for them to leave New Zealand.

Once he told Dillion they were running away, he'd be excited and eager to get into his latest character. The kid was a natural when it came to acting and voices. They'd be long gone before Maureen decided to exercise her right to phone her son. If she played true to form, she'd be giddy with the fresh, new relationship, and her son and everything else would come second best until she became bored.

Lady Kismet smiling, indeed, and doing a saucy hip waggle.

## CHAPTER 21

"He denied knowledge of the plants," Cassie said.

Emma's forehead puckered in a frown. "Did you believe him?"

"Yeah, I did. He asked me if I thought the people who planted the crop were the ones who had broken into my house. I hadn't considered that angle."

Hone exchanged a skeptical glance with Jack. "If that's the case, the alarm would have alerted them. They'll be here soon."

"It's possible they've been watching and trying to scare you off," Jack added.

"Ring the cops. You've reported getting run off the road and the clown incident. Ring the cops now before someone tries to pin this on you," Emma said.

"But I knew nothing about the plants."

"Difficult to prove that," Jack said.

Cassie plucked the local cop's card from her handbag. The phone rang for a long time before the man answered. She explained about what they'd found.

"I'll be straight there."

When the cop arrived, they walked down to the plot they'd discovered. The cop took photos and rang for a team to clear the plants.

Cassie walked the edge of the plot with Hone. She brushed past a shoulder-height pine and came face-to-face with a clown. A shriek emerged, echoing under the trees before she calmed enough to realize it was merely a mask nailed to a post. She patted her chest, her breathing fast and choppy. "Man, I hate clowns."

Hone slipped his arm around her shoulders and hugged her against his side. "You okay?"

"Yeah." She peered closer at the smirking clown mask. "The mask is brand new. It's not weathered by the sun or rain." She walked a few steps farther. "Someone has harvested the plants in a hurry. See. And look. Footprints." She pointed them out to Hone.

"Hey, I'm the private investigator. Give me a chance."

Cassie wrinkled her nose. "I can't believe this was growing here all the time."

"A sophisticated operation," the cop commented, taking yet more photos. "You said you'd spoken to your neighbor?"

"Yes, he's a businessman with a young son. He said the trees on his land don't need much in the way of care, and they don't check on them often."

"Do you have his number?"

"Yes, he said to give it to you."

"I'll speak with him and the other neighbors. Ask around and see if anyone has noticed anything."

"Someone managed to vandalize my house without attracting attention. Most of the properties are down long driveways with plenty of trees to ensure privacy."

It was nearly two hours before the police left, taking the plants with them for disposal. Cassie watched the last vehicle pull from the driveway with something like relief. "Well, that should be that. If the plants are no longer there, hopefully the owners of the crop will leave me alone. It should be safe here now. Anyone for a drink? I'll bring out the chips and dip. I'm starving."

"Fire up the barbecue, Jack," Emma suggested. "I'm hungry too."

The scent of steak cooking on the grill had Hone licking his lips. He crunched on a vegetable hunk loaded with dip and sipped his beer straight from the bottle.

"Food always tastes better outdoors." Emma waved a carrot stick in front of Jack's nose. "Even the healthy stuff."

Jack growled and showed his teeth. Cassie didn't see the hint of taniwha but longing sprang to life in Hone. Did she really intend to leave? And how would she react to learning of the existence of dragons? He liked to think she'd take the truth in her stride and accept him, want to stay with him in New Zealand, but who knew?

Kind of funny. Fate and his previous girlfriends would die laughing.

"What's the time?" Emma asked.

Hone checked his phone. "Eight-thirty."

Cassie placed a lettuce salad and a potato salad on the outdoor table. "No wonder I'm hungry."

"Steaks are done." Jack used a pair of tongs to transfer the meat to a platter held by Emma.

"I'll get the garlic bread," Cassie said.

Hone watched her arse until she disappeared from sight, and Emma dug him in the ribs.

"You said you didn't do serious."

Hone turned to meet her gaze. "So everyone says."

"And?"

"Cassie is different. I like her. She makes me laugh. She makes me happy."

"She says she's leaving," Emma said.

"Yeah."

Emma nudged his ribs with her elbow and almost lost a steak.

"Watch the meat." Jack rescued the platter and placed it on the table.

"Well, what are you going to do about it?" Emma demanded.

"Not sure yet," Hone said. "We haven't known each other long." He shifted his gaze, Jack's jerk of head warning him of Cassie's return, not that he needed the heads-up. His taniwha kept him appraised of Cassie's whereabouts. "The garlic bread smells good."

"My mother's recipe. She uses herbs along with the garlic and tasty cheese. Mum doesn't approve of me eating it." Mischief lurked in the curve of her mouth, the tiny dimple digging into her cheek. "I might have more than one piece tonight."

"I like your curves," Hone said. "Although it smells so good you might have to arm wrestle me for seconds."

Her laughter filled the air, and Hone had never felt happier.

*You can't let her leave.*

He and his taniwha were of one accord. His phone vibrated, and he almost didn't bother answering in favor of eating first. He followed the others to dig into the food before guilt and curiosity got the better of him. His phone ceased its summons. A missed call. Manu. He stood back and let the others fill their plates while he rang his cousin.

"What's up?"

"Ma's gone. She was here and seemed back to normal, bossing us all around. I left for two minutes to take a phone call. Dad was with her. He relaxed his vigilance and Ma disappeared. Hone, she's vanished. Her vehicle is still here."

"Is she walking?" *Please let her be on foot.*

"I think she's flying."

"Does she have one of your inventions?"

"No."

"Crap." A range of possibilities raced through his mind. Foremost, would June be stupid enough to shift and fly here? His aunt didn't lack intelligence. If she hadn't learned of Cassie's location already, it would be easy enough to guess. Surely, she wouldn't continue her crusade against Cassie? "What do you need us to do?"

"Stay where you are. I'll call if I need you."

Jack and Emma were watching him. Cassie, thank goodness, was serving up two plates of food. One for him. Her generosity and care filled him with pleasure, but the idea of June on the loose overrode the feel-good factor. Terror slashed him, gripped his chest, checked his breathing. He struggled to center himself, fighting the snarl of his taniwha. "Anything you need, Manu. Jack and I are here for you."

"Thanks."

The knowledge of what Manu must be going through muted his fear and anger. No matter what Manu did, he couldn't win.

He lowered his voice. "We'll keep an eye out, contact you if we see anything. If you need us, we're there."

Jack sidled closer while Emma distracted Cassie. "What's up?"

"June is on the loose again."

"How?"

"Manu didn't say exactly, but Samuel is between a rock and a determined dragon. He was watching her and let down his guard."

"Does he need us to help?"

"Manu said to sit tight. He didn't say it, but June might still be angry at Cassie."

"You can't go home with her tonight," Jack said. "You need to stay here with me and Emma."

"Safety in numbers." Hone sighed as he caught a glimpse of the rising moon. Blood red again. Given the circumstances, it was creepy and apt. "I might ring Dad. He'll want to know and might be able to help."

"Hone, your dinner is ready." Cassie turned, a plate of food in each hand. His woman. *His*. His heart practically turned over in his chest, and his taniwha gave a tiny groan before transmitting messages of lust to every corner of his body. His dick twitched.

Jack shook his head. "You're gone, man."

"You can talk," Hone replied, not even trying to deny the truth.

"You'd better get over there. I'll ring George."

"Thanks." Hone strode over to Cassie and leaned close to kiss her cheek before accepting a plate. "You didn't have to get my food for me."

Her cheeks flushed. "No problem."

He followed her over to where Emma sat at a second picnic table, one he and Jack had rescued from Jack's place.

"What's Jack doing?" Emma asked, her gaze sharp and her

shoulders tense. She mightn't have taniwha genes but she'd developed good senses from working as an investigator and spending time with him and Jack.

"A work thing," Hone said. "He's talking to Dad."

Cassie helped herself to garlic bread. "You guys work long hours." She crunched into the bread and moaned.

Emma laughed aloud. "That sort of ecstatic groaning should only come from the bedroom."

Hone snorted. "Have to agree, sweetheart."

Cassie swallowed a mouthful of bread and waved the rest of the piece in the air. "Please. We're eating dinner," she admonished.

"What's so funny?" Jack asked.

"Cassie is making love with her garlic bread," Emma said.

"If it tastes as good as it smells, I might do the same."

"See," Cassie said, giving an approving nod to Jack. "Someone who appreciates the good things. Who wants another glass of wine or a beer?"

"Stay there. I'll get the drinks." Emma bounded up and trotted inside the house.

"Do you think my problems have ended now that the police have taken away the plants?" Cassie asked.

"I hope so," Jack said. "I noticed one thing when we visited the second time."

"Some of the plants were gone and the alarm system had been ripped out."

Cassie froze. "I noticed someone had plucked off parts of the plants, but I didn't notice the alarm. Why didn't you tell me?"

"We're telling you now," Hone said.

Cassie frowned. "What does that mean?"

"It means we suspect your neighbor had a hand in this. He was the only one close enough. The alarm system was meant to give him warning," Hone said.

"But he denied it. He sounded... I believed him. The cop said he was going to speak with Matthew."

"The man is intelligent," Jack said. "The cops won't find anything on his property."

"But shouldn't we say something?" Cassie asked.

"There's no proof. Did you notice he had sheep grazing in some areas but others were fenced off?" Hone received a head-tilt of agreement from Jack. "The fencing around the plants on Cassie's land was built to keep out the sheep."

Jack forked up potato salad. "Yeah. If the cops realize and ask, he'll have an excuse. That he's rotating the grazing or something similar."

"Cassie, don't worry. Sometimes, the bad guys get away. Nothing anyone can do about it. The owner has lost his plants, and that will hit his pocket."

Cassie gaped at them. "But I liked Matthew. He has a son."

Hone chuckled. "Takes all sorts, sweetheart."

Emma returned and dispersed drinks, and the conversation

drifted to Cassie's music.

"Have you decided which songs you're doing for the show next weekend?" Emma asked.

"Yes, I was going to ask if I could run through the songs tonight. I want to check the timing."

"Dinner and free entertainment. Score." Emma lifted her glass of wine in salute.

Cassie cocked her head as she stared past Emma. Her brows drew together. "What is that? Do you see it?"

Hone turned in the direction she indicated. Horror interfered with his breathing. He speed dialed his father. Crap. *Answer the phone, dammit.* "In the house. Cassie. Emma. Jack—"

Jack was two steps ahead, phone in hand. "Manu, June is here in Clevedon at Cassie's house." He rattled off the address. "Hurry. Inside. Cassie, now."

"But what is that? It looks like..." she trailed off as Emma grasped her upper arm and propelled her indoors.

George Taniwha took longer to answer. "Yeah?"

"Dad, June is here, at Cassie's place."

"Dragon form?"

"Yes." Hone didn't take his gaze off aunt. June in taniwha form was a fearsome sight, her jade hide gleaming, her scales and horns glinting under the early moon. She let out a roar, flames shooting from her giant maw as jade green wings brought her ever closer.

"Hell. Where's Manu?"

"On his way." Hopefully. As a water taniwha, Jack could shift, but he didn't have fire in his arsenal. His abilities were swimming and close combat fighting. It also took him longer to return to human form.

"Leaving now," his father said.

Hone ran inside to check on Jack and the girls. Emma clutched a permitted gun while Jack closed windows and curtains, searching for the best place for cover.

Hone's dragon fought for escape. He couldn't contain the growls and rumbles. June intended to hurt his mate. Not gonna happen. He ripped off his shirt and kicked off his sandals.

"What are you doing? What was that? A dragon? But that's impossible..." Cassie trailed off, frowning. "Hone, what is up with your tattoo? It's glowing red."

"Stand back, Cassie," Emma snapped.

Hone knew he should shift, but he hesitated. "Cassie." He embraced her before giving her a swift kiss. "I love you, Cassie. Do whatever Emma and Jack tell you."

Walking away was the hardest thing he'd ever done.

Cassie pressed her fingers to her lips. "What's going on?" Jack and Emma jumped into action, expressions tense as if they were preparing for war. "Why are you brandishing a gun? I didn't think guns were legal in New Zealand. What is Hone doing? Did you see his tattoo?" She wandered toward the door. "I saw a dragon. It *was* a dragon. Did you see it?"

"Cassie." Jack's sharpness had her freezing three steps from the door. "We'll explain everything later. Right now you need to stay with us. Get behind those chairs."

A high-pitched shriek filled the air. Spine-chilling. The tiny hairs at the back of Cassie's neck lifted, and when the screech repeated, she took half a step back. Second thought, she didn't want to know.

"What if she burns down the house?" Emma asked. "It's not safe in here either."

"Who? What are you talking about?" Cassie demanded.

"She'll pick us off one by one if we're outside where she can see us. Hopefully, Hone can keep her busy until Manu and his brothers arrive."

A roar thundered through the air, deeper and fiercer than the first shriek.

"W-what is that?"

"They're both in the air now. Emma, you remember where to aim?"

"The head, between the eyes."

"Good. Don't take any risks, babe. And don't shoot Hone by mistake."

"I won't. I've been practicing."

"Cassie, stay behind us and out of sight. I don't want Hone distracted," Jack ordered.

"But—"

Emma gripped her upper arm with her gun-free hand. "Promise, Cassie. This is important. *Promise.*"

The tension in the room grew, and Cassie dragged a jerky hand through her hair. Something...a d-dragon...

"Cassie!"

She nodded mutely at her friend. Hone's dragon tattoo...

Jack strode for the door, and Cassie realized he carried a gun too. Emma trailed him, alert and weapon at the ready. A harrowing scream rippled over the landscape and trepidation liquefied her limbs.

Cassie staggered, gripped the kitchen counter and swallowed hard. What the hell was happening?

Jack and Emma disappeared.

A shot rang out.

Cassie winced. She couldn't stay here, wondering what was happening. She inched toward the door, switching off the light at the last second. Twilight had fallen, and it took a few seconds for her to focus.

Jack and Emma had separated. Emma stood against the wall of the house to her right. She couldn't see Jack since he wore dark clothes and blended with the evening light.

Another of those horrid shrieks—enraged and frustrated—had every hair on her body standing to attention. Her gaze rose skyward, seeking the source.

She blinked. Once. Twice.

Two, no three dragons battled in the skies above her property.

Her breath burst in and out, and she pinched herself. No. Still there.

*Freakin' big dragons.*

The jade dragon she'd seen first, a black-and-mainly red dragon and an inky black dragon she hadn't noticed initially.

Fire spurted from the jade dragon's mouth. The other two dragons separated. The black dragon zipped closer and nipped the jade dragon on the tail. The red dragon screamed as the flames struck its flank. It faltered slightly and plummeted before beating its wings again. Another dragon entered the fray. This one also black. Together, the three dragons attacked the jade one. Heavy drops of rain fell to the ground.

Jack appeared at her side. "I told you to stay out of sight. You'll make things worse."

"Me? What's happening? Why aren't you and Emma surprised? No, wait. What did you put in my drink? Did I inhale some of those drugs?" Words and questions tumbled from her, but Jack didn't answer, his attention on the fight in the sky above her house.

Emma appeared on her other side. "Why are you outside?"

"I didn't think cannabis was that strong," Cassie muttered in reply.

It started raining again. Cassie stared at the drops, splattering the ground.

She gasped. "T-that's blood."

"Hell, there's Samuel," Jack said, tension radiating from him. "His presence will make things more difficult."

"Where are Manu's brothers?" Emma scanned the sky.

Cassie gaped as two new black dragons blinked into sight. Together, they muscled a black dragon away from the fight. Flames lit the evening sky, the rumbles and roars reminding Cassie of thunder. A furious scream rippled through the air, and she clapped her hands over her ears. A fight to the death. Cassie didn't know for sure, but instinct told her this was serious.

"That is Manu and his brothers," she whispered, aghast.

"The whole family is there," Jack acknowledged.

"Hone?" He'd said he loved her. Her eyes widened as she replayed his words. He'd thought he might die! She turned to Jack and yanked on his shirttail. "Is that Hone up there? The one raining blood."

"Let me concentrate," Jack snapped.

Dragons. *Fire-breathing dragons.* The fire spurting from their giant maws reduced. Maybe they were tiring. Dragons. Great big fictional creatures, right in front of her. The jade dragon seemed strong and agile. The creature whipped its tail, maneuvered so fast the other dragons flew past. Then the jade dragon flew at the red one, claws outstretched. They collided mid-air, the impact sending the red dragon plummeting.

Cassie gasped.

The jade dragon cackled, the hoarse reverberation making

Cassie flinch. Adrenaline pulsed through her veins, her fear as real as the dragons soaring through the sky. A scream formed in her throat, fighting, struggling for release. She held it back as the red dragon hit the ground.

The jade dragon screeched in triumph and swooped. Three black dragons barreled after the victorious creature.

"Samuel is trying to interfere," Emma cried.

Another dragon hurtled through the air, coming from nowhere. Black scales glittered. It...he—the dragon's fierceness implied a male...maybe... Cassie shook herself. One of the black dragons cut off the new arrival, driving him back.

A keening cry pulled her attention to the dragon on the ground. She took two steps before Emma grabbed her and wrenched her to a halt.

"Don't let June see you."

"Why?"

"She blames you."

"Blames me for what?"

"Breaking up with Manu."

Cassie gaped at her friend. "What are you talking about? Manu and I are friends." Her gaze sought out the fallen dragon. "Is that Hone? Watch out!" she screamed.

The jade dragon swiveled its head, big glowing jade stare turned in her direction. They blazed with fury. The creature landed gracefully and prowled toward her, tail swishing in rapid beats.

Cassie backed up rapidly. Run. *Run!* She turned to flee and flames rushed past her, near enough for the heat to sear her skin. The grass and a tree danced with sparks.

A black dragon landed. Fingers grasped the waistband of her trousers.

"Cassie." Jack shoved her behind him. Emma stood at his side and both of them fired at the jade dragon.

"Stand. Out. Of. The. Way." The jade dragon roared. "*Give. Her. To. Me.*"

Emma and Jack kept shooting. Bang. Bang. *Bang.*

The jade dragon screamed and tossed its head. Blood splattered to the ground, but the beast didn't hesitate. It smirked, long, sharp teeth protruding from its jaws. Cassie couldn't rip her horrified gaze away. Scary beautiful. The beast snorted, drew in a deep gust of air.

"Don't do this, June. Don't hurt Jack. I love him, and this will be murder," Emma shouted.

"Move. Away." The whispery words emerged separately. Menacing. Determined.

Jack fired, shooting high to miss. Cassie thought it was a warning. "No, June. You'll have to kill us to get to Cassie."

Cassie gasped. This was because of her. What had she done? Wait. They'd said June was angry. She hadn't realized the depths of the woman's fury.

The dragon sucked in a huge breath. Smoke curled from her

nostrils. The surrounding air sizzled as flames shot to their right.

Oh, god. This dragon—June—was sending her own warning.

"We're not moving," Jack shouted.

Tension radiated off Emma.

The hostility emanating from Jack went off the charts. "Fire," he shouted.

Cassie flinched. Unable to help herself, she peered past Jack's shoulder. One by one, the dragons landed behind June. Two of the black dragons muscled another away. Angry snarls filled the air.

June, the jade dragon, sucked in another breath. "Last. Chance."

Fear paralyzed her, and Cassie couldn't move. The red dragon struggled to its feet and staggered closer, but the black one turned its head and snarled ferociously. Without warning, light glowed around his shadowy body, and a very naked Manu stood in the dragon's place, brandishing a sword.

Cassie clapped a hand over her mouth. Jack and Emma didn't budge, holding their united front.

"Don't do this, Ma. Cassie didn't do anything wrong."

June—Cassie had accepted this was June—dragged in more air. Smoke whooshed from her nostrils and she let rip with flames.

## CHAPTER 22

E mma screamed.

Jack fired.

Heat seared Cassie's skin. Move. *Move.* Her legs refused to obey her brain.

Pain seared across her forearms. Tiny blisters formed.

Emma groaned, slumped to the ground.

Cassie's knees gave way. Horror clutched her throat, her chest. Using her dress, she smothered flames dancing along her friend's left leg.

Jack cursed. Yanked at his T-shirt. Stifled the flames on Emma's clothes, scooped up her friend and retreated into the house. He moved so fast, Cassie gaped. The last thing she saw was the tattoo dragon on Jack's back. The tattoo reared, fury etched into its snarl.

Another roar almost deafened her. The red dragon struggled toward her. Terror held her in position.

Naked Manu didn't blink as yet more flames poured from the jade dragon. He swung his sword, a strange power rippling through the air. Her skin prickled. She gasped, her throat parched, her skin throbbing from the heat.

The air dried. Smoke poured from June's nostrils.

Cassie tensed for the flames. A roar filled the air, filled her head, filled her ears, deafening her to everything else.

The red dragon kept coming. Sharp teeth glittered. Terror, the like of which she'd never known, rendered her legs useless. A sob escaped.

This was the end.

She was gonna die.

In that instant, she realized how much she wanted to live. She gulped and gathered her strength to leap to either side, before the jade dragon crisped her. *Emma.*

A faint croak escaped Cassie. Was Emma all right?

Heat sizzled in the air. A roar sounded. A gurgle. Drops of what sounded like rain, felt like wet rain pelted the ground. Splattered her body.

Silence fell.

A pregnant hush.

Cassie dragged in huge breaths, trying to fill her starving lungs.

Time slowed.

Black-and-red filled her vision. Sweat beaded on her brow. Her heart tried to burrow from her chest, the fierce clamp around her ribs squeezing her to the point of dizziness. She blinked. Once. Twice. Three times. Black-and-red scales. A mean growl vibrated through the air, but not directed at her. Not her? The dragon was standing guard. Protecting her?

Cassie swayed a fraction before she forced her limbs to function. She shuffled to the right and peeked from behind her dragon sentinel.

Manu stood in front of the jade dragon, sword grasped in his right hand. The blade glittered, even in the faint light. What looked like blood splattered Manu's body and his head drooped. She couldn't see his face, but she could see the sagging dragon tattoo depicted on his back. His head bowed too, and were those tears?

Cassie took another unsteady step.

She gasped, biting her lip to stifle her horror.

A dragon head lay on the ground.

The jade dragon—June—was dead.

She took off her glasses, wiped the lenses on her clothes, replaced them. Nope. Not imagining things. This was scary real.

The red dragon turned its big horned head toward her. His gaze narrowed in what appeared disapproval.

One of the three black dragons snarled, struggled to push past the other two.

"Shift," Manu snapped.

The black dragon in the center shimmered before it transformed to a naked Samuel.

Cassie lifted her gaze to his face and fixed it there. Fury rode his features.

"You killed your mother because of a mere human," he boomed. "You chose *her* over your own blood?"

Cassie backed up and tripped. *Holy heck*! Only she could trip over a dragon's tail. The red dragon shifted its stance, putting himself between her and Samuel's wrath. His red nostrils flared and wisps of smoke spiraled free.

"I had no choice," Manu said in a flat voice.

"You had a choice. That human or your mother," Samuel roared, his face turning mottled scarlet.

"It would have been murder," Manu said. "Cassie didn't do anything wrong. We're friends. That's all. Ma's insistence on grandchildren and furthering the family line has caused this. Ma's mind snapped. She would've killed an innocent."

"You murdered your mother."

Manu straightened his shoulders, lifted his chin. "She gave me no choice."

The two black dragons shifted. Manu's two brothers each grasped their father's arms.

"You agree with your brother?" Samuel demanded.

Cassie didn't hear the reply since Jack exited the house. "Is Emma all right?"

"She has burns on her right arm and leg, but they're not as bad as I feared. She's in a bath of cold water. She's going to be okay. The baby too."

"B-baby?"

"Yes," Jack said curtly.

Hone sighed with relief as Cassie ducked into the house.

"Vehicle coming," Jack snapped.

Manu snapped to attention. He strode to his mother's body and stabbed her with the tribe's sword. His low murmur rippled with power, and his mother's body faded to dust. He repeated the action with her severed head.

Hone willed his dragon to shift and prayed like hell Samuel could hold his shit together because the motor roared in the same manner as the one belonging to the local policeman. Yep, the cop who had a crush on Cassie.

His dragon stood to attention, pushing a rippling growl through Hone's mind. *Quiet.*

"Clothes," Jack snapped, thrusting clothes at him and another set at Manu. Enough to cover the worst of the blood on their bodies. "Put away the sword."

Manu seemed to snap from the dark place in his mind, and the sword melted into his human body. He yanked on the pair of track pants Jack gave him, and when he presented his back, Hone saw the sword resting in the hand of Manu's dragon tattoo.

The cop car pulled to a stop. The door slammed as the driver climbed out.

"Is anything wrong, officer?" Jack asked, taking the lead.

"We've had reports of gunfire and strange flames in the sky," the cop said.

"We did light our bonfire," Jack said and gestured at the pile of tree clippings that had caught fire during June's rampage. "I'm afraid it smoked a lot. Some idiot chucked a paint spray can in there because it scared the crap out of us when it exploded."

The policeman scrutinized their faces, studied the fire. Tension radiated from his rigid frame. He didn't believe Jack's story.

"Where is Cassie? I mean Ms. Miller-Pope."

"Inside," Jack said.

"I'd like to speak with her."

"I'll get her," Hone said.

Before he could go to the woman his dragon had claimed, the woman he'd come to love and admire, she appeared in the doorway.

Cassie's hair was wet, and she wore a different dress with a lightweight cardigan covering her arms. Smart lady.

"Hi. Is there a problem?"

"A neighbor reported gunshots. I was worried the owner of the drugs had returned."

"No, no problems," Cassie said. "We did have a fire." She frowned, and Hone saw some of her tension recede. "A barbecue."

Hone smothered his flash of dark humor. A barbecue. *Right.*

The cop hesitated. "Okay. If there are any repercussions pertaining to the drugs, I'm a call away."

"Thank you," Cassie said. "I appreciate that."

The strained atmosphere remained until the cop car disappeared.

"You can come out of hiding now," Manu called.

His two brothers emerged from behind a clump of bushes, dragging Samuel with them.

"Murderer," Samuel spat. "You've brainwashed your brothers. No one in the tribe will accept you as leader."

"They already have. Ma had become unstable. You know it. You just don't want to admit the truth."

"No, it was that human's fault."

"Take him away," Manu ordered. "Take Hone's vehicle. Leave me a unit."

Kahurangi plucked a unit from his wrist and tossed it to Manu.

"Keys are inside," Hone said.

"You'd better sleep with one eye open," Samuel roared as Kahurangi and Tane led him away.

Manu stood strong, his chin up and shoulders straight until Hone's vehicle disappeared from sight and the engine noise faded. Then, he crumpled, his shoulders rounding, his head bowing in misery. "I had no choice. Ma had lost it."

Hone strode to him, wrapped his cousin in his arms and gave

comfort in the only way he knew how. Manu would forever have his support because his cousin's actions had saved Cassie. Jack and Emma had put their lives on the line to save her too. He owed them big time.

A soft hand touched his arm. "Bring Manu inside. He needs rest."

*Cassie.* Hell, he'd thought she'd run from him after the ferocity she'd witnessed. She stepped back, and instantly, he missed the physical contact. Was she okay with his otherness? He couldn't tell. If he lost her after all this, he wouldn't function.

"Manu can take the couch. It's man-size and should be comfortable enough."

"Thanks." Hone waited until Cassie disappeared inside before half-guiding, half-manhandling Manu.

"I need a shower," Manu said in a low voice.

So did he since blood and gore irritated his skin as it dried.

"This way." Hone saw Cassie had planned ahead, and a pile of fresh towels sat on the vanity counter. He started the shower and nudged his cousin toward it. "I'll find you something to wear."

Half an hour later, when Hone walked into the kitchen, Manu was sound asleep in the lounge, a lightweight blanket over him.

Jack and Cassie sat at the kitchen counter, each with a drink. Whisky by the smell.

"Emma sleeping?"

"Yeah. I put our healing salve on her burns. She said she was okay and told me not to fuss." Jack choked up, and Hone got it. He felt the same way about Cassie.

"I'm sorry," Hone said. "You're gonna be a father."

"Yeah," Jack said. "I never thought I would."

"You should have told us." Cassie gulped. "You and Emma—you p-protected me. You risked everything. For me."

Hone reached for one of Cassie's hands and fitted their fingers together. She didn't pull away and relief flooded him. His otherness might not be a problem. "And for me," he said.

"You would have done the same for us. Both of you," Jack added. "Don't deny it."

"But your baby…" Cassie trailed off, her eyes bright with unshed tears. "And Manu…h-he…I—" She broke off and swallowed hard. "You could have lost everything."

"It was the right thing to do," Jack said. "I…we would make the same decision again."

Cassie turned to him. "Want a whisky?"

"Sure."

Cassie stood to get another glass from the cupboard. She scooped up the bottle of whisky and after filling his glass, she placed it at her elbow. "So, dragons. Were you going to tell me anytime soon?"

Jack downed his drink and set the empty glass on the counter. "I'll leave you to it."

Cassie waited until Jack had disappeared before she let loose her curiosity. "How do you become a dragon?"

"Taniwha. We're born this way."

"All the myths and legends about taniwha are true? I thought they were part of Māori folk tales."

"Every myth or legend starts with a hint of truth."

"How many of you are there? Is Jack one? Emma wasn't surprised. She knew. How come you didn't tell me?" The questions poured from her quick and fast. "What about children? If Jack is a dragon...um...taniwha, will their baby be one? Do you howl at the moon or anything? Wait. Are werewolves and vampires real?"

Hone suppressed a flash of humor. "Jack is a water taniwha. He is in his element in the water. His shift is different from ours in that he's stuck in his form for a longer time before he returns to human. My family and relations are the flying, fire-breathing type. Like werewolves, we are ruled by the moon. We become highly sexual at full moon and to keep our human shape, we need a lot of sex at that time of the month. If we don't, we're forced to shift, a problem in these modern days." Hone paused to sip his whisky. "Emma and Jack's baby will have taniwha genes. From what I've learned, it depends. Some half-taniwha can shift. Others can't."

"Have you met any vampires? Any werewolves?"

"There are a few vampires around, but not many because of New Zealand's small population. Werewolves, yes. Feline shapeshifters too."

"Wow." She rubbed her hands together in excitement. "Just wow!"

"You can't tell anyone, Cassie."

She prickled like a hedgehog. "I wouldn't. I won't. You're my friends."

"I want to be more than a friend, Cassie. I wasn't kidding earlier. I love you."

"I...oh." Pink colored her cheeks.

"I don't want you to leave."

"We haven't known each other for long."

"No, but once a taniwha develops feelings, he or she is unwavering. My dragon considers you our mate. I haven't looked at another woman since I met you. I wouldn't. I'm not interested in anyone but you. You complete me."

"Oh, Hone."

Hone moved before his brain issued the order. He jerked her into his arms and held her tight. "I thought I was going to lose you."

# CHAPTER 23

Cassie leaned against him, and his taniwha sighed and purred with satisfaction. Having her here felt like home. Another purr vibrated in his chest.

"Is that your taniwha?"

"Yes."

She struggled against his embrace and pulled away a fraction when he relaxed the hug. Her gaze was serious, and something in him fractured at her expression.

"I have commitments. Meetings planned after I finish the last vineyard concert."

His purring ceased. Instead, fear chilled his skin. "So you're leaving despite everything?"

"Yes."

Hone swallowed down a growl when he wanted to howl his anguish.

"For one month, maybe two, and then I intend to come back to New Zealand."

Hope flared in him. "To me?"

"We'll see." She beamed and blurted, "There is a good chance."

Hone grinned back at her, his heart lightening at her words. "Are you ready for bed?"

"More than ready," Cassie said. "It's been a hell of a day."

In the bedroom, Hone stripped and Cassie did the same. No matter how exhausted, he intended to make love to her. His mate. She mightn't accept it yet, but that didn't make it any less true.


Dragons were real. Her best friend was married to one. *Dragons were real.* Flying, fire-breathing freakin' dragons.

Hone kissed her and her toes curled. She kissed him back before breaking their lip-lock.

"Is it easy to fly?"

"It's a learned skill. We have to reach sixteen human years before we're allowed to try."

"Interesting. How do you manage to stay hidden from humans?"

"It's becoming more difficult all the time. We have scientists working on ways to allow us to travel unseen in dragon form. We have our own doctors and medical staff."

"Do you guys get sick a lot?"

"No, we're incredibly healthy."

"Could you take me flying?"

"That is only allowed if you fully accept me as your mate."

Cassie frowned. "Being with you is right, but after Kevin, I don't trust my own judgment. I mean, you don't exactly have a good track record. Everyone warned me about you."

"Everyone?"

"Emma. Jack."

"Hell," Hone muttered. "Don't I get a chance?"

"I'm giving you a chance," Cassie said and grabbed him by the shoulders to focus his attention. "We'll spend time together before I go, and I said I'm coming back. Don't you trust me?"

"I don't trust that manager of yours. I didn't like him. He wants you back."

"No, he's worried he's going to lose his source of profit. He didn't appreciate what he had, and now he's concerned. Enough talk." Her fingers went to his ears, and she yanked them.

"Hey," he protested, freeing himself.

"Just getting your attention. This has been a horrid day. Kiss me. Make me forget."

"I could do that if you stop talking." Challenge emanated from his stare.

She struggled to contain an improper giggle and made a buttoning motion against her lips.

"Good," he said and kissed her.

Instead of an aggressive kiss, she received gentle. Every nerve in her body seized, relaying messages. She sighed and wrapped her arms around his neck. Hone was right. They'd almost died tonight. Celebrating life was a much better than dwelling on June...

She shuddered, recalling the crazed expression, the determination. And Emma. *God*!

"Stop thinking."

"I...June...it's hard to switch off my brain."

"Then I'm not doing a good job."

His busy fingers tweaked her nipple.

"Excellent moves, mister."

"Pleased to be of service." He continued to kiss and fondle her before moving down the bed and parting her thighs. "Let's see if this rings your bell."

A half-laugh emerged as he tongued her folds, grazing her clit with his tongue. Just enough to send her crazy. A puff of warm air had her mind readjusting, her thoughts realigning with his.

With fingers and mouth, he drove her high and fast, but not enough to let her come. She lifted her hips for more stimulation, not above pleading. "Hone, please."

"You taste sweet," he whispered. "So sweet. You please us both so much."

"Us?"

"Me. My taniwha."

"Oh." She glanced down at his cock. It seemed normal enough. "You don't have a weird cock, do you? I haven't noticed any barbs."

Hone barked out a laugh, the warm air feeling great puffing against her swollen flesh. "You've seen me, touched me, tasted me. Am I any different?"

"Now I'm not sure. I'm second guessing every bit of knowledge."

Hone chuckled again, the hoarse sound bringing a wash of humor to her.

"I'd better check." She wriggled from beneath him and crawled over him. With a laughing grunt, he allowed her to push him onto his back. "My, what a nice erection," she purred. "Better get a condom, so I'm not wasting time." After pulling a foil packet from the strip on the nightstand, she gripped his shaft, measuring the breadth with her hand. "Feels like a cock." With her gaze on his, she licked the bulbous head. "Hmm, tastes like a cock."

"It acts like a cock too," Hone said as a drop of pre-come beaded at the top. "Therefore, it must be a cock."

Cassie took him into her mouth, sucking and licking. Tasting and savoring the amusement and rightness that bubbled through her. *Therefore, it must be a cock.* She snorted through her nose, and Hone jumped.

"Hey, watch the teeth."

She pulled off him. "Sorry."

"Put on the condom," he ordered.

She puffed out her chest, noticed the way it distracted him and purposely did it again as she unwrapped the condom. She rolled the latex down his shaft.

"On top. I want to watch you. Guide me into place."

Cassie didn't like going on top. Kevin's fault, because he'd criticized her body. Hone didn't do that. His gaze roved her, but pure appreciation shone in his expression. She positioned herself and sank downward, savoring every instant of him impaling her. He filled her, made her happy, so happy.

And that was all that counted.

She rose and fell, her hand going between her legs to touch her clit. She went slow. She went fast. She varied the angle.

Hone groaned, his gaze holding hers. A hint of red showed and his pupils did a weird slitting thing before reverting to normal. His taniwha. Wow.

She squeezed her internal muscles, and Hone's hands shaped her hips, guiding her motion. Up. Down. Fast. Slow. The slight prickle coalesced to a shining blast of pleasure. She groaned, her finger sliding across her slippery clit. It was too much, not enough. Another slide of her finger and she exploded, her world one of satisfaction and bliss. She was vaguely aware of Hone's shout, the frenzy of movement before she sagged against him. Their lips met in a blast of passion. So much passion and pleasure, and in that moment, she thought maybe she loved Hone too.

*The next morning*

Cassie slept later than normal, and the birds sang outside when she finally woke. She was alone in the bed and the faint murmur of voices came from the kitchen. She threw her legs over the edge of the bed, smiling until she remembered.

*Dragons.*

June had wanted to kill her because apparently, she'd cheated on Manu with Hone.

Sober now, and still full of questions, she dressed quickly in a floral blouse with a fifties vibe and a pair of jean capris. Barefoot, she padded to the kitchen.

Jack and Hone were sitting at the kitchen counter and the scent of coffee enticed Cassie to grab an empty mug.

"How is Emma? Is she awake? Can I go and see her?"

Hone stood and gave her his bar stool. Instead of moving away, he placed his arm on her shoulder, the heavy weight comforting and welcome. His touch suffused her with joy because Kevin would've stood over the other side of the room, even after a night of intimacy, and he'd be all business. He'd criticize her style of dress.

*Why don't you wear something modern and trendy? You need to lose weight.*

Hone loved her curves. Jack loved Emma's curves. Must be a dragon thing.

"I gave Emma pills to make her sleep."

"Is that safe for the baby?" Cassie asked.

"Yes, I spoke to our medic. She assures me the medication won't harm the baby," Jack said.

"Emma's burns?"

"The salve helped control the pain. She'll have scars on her arm and leg." Jack growled, the vicious sound making Cassie squirm closer to Hone. "I wish I could kill June myself for hurting Emma. She knew Emma was more fragile than us and she didn't care."

"Where is Manu?"

"He'd gone when I got up to make coffee," Jack said.

He'd seemed broken last night. Heck, he'd chopped off his mother's head with a big ass sword. He had to be hurting. "Will he be all right?"

"I hope so," Hone said. "His brothers understood there was no other choice, but Samuel will be a problem."

"Anyone want breakfast?" Cassie asked. "I'll cook something once I check on Emma." She wandered off, coffee in hand. She pushed open the bedroom door, expecting Emma to be asleep. Instead, she found her struggling to get dressed.

Cassie rushed to the bed and set down her coffee on the nightstand. "You need help?"

"I don't have a sleeveless blouse," Emma said in frustration.

Cassie sucked in a harsh breath on seeing the pink skin. "Is that sore?"

"A little tender. I was lucky Jack applied the salve straightaway. It's a dragon thing, I guess."

"I've got a tunic top. Be back in a sec." She hurried away, rifled through her wardrobe and picked out two different sleeveless tops. "Here you go. I found two that should work. So, a baby, huh? I'm gonna be a sort-of auntie. That is so exciting."

Emma beamed. "Jack and I had just found out. We wanted to savor the secret for a few days."

"Are you feeling okay?"

"I'm fine. The dragon medic said I'm in perfect health. Jack wants me to go back to see her today."

"You should," Cassie said. "That's not the only secret you've been keeping from me."

"Cass, I couldn't tell you about dragons. I promised Jack. And you saw June. She is...was scary. No way I'd blab and have to face her wrath."

"I won't tell. Pinky swear."

They grinned at each other.

"Want breakfast?" Cassie asked. "I'm going to cook for us all, but first, do you need help to get dressed?"

"No, I'm good."

"I'll send Jack just in case," Cassie promised.

Jack appeared in the doorway. "We have company. Cops," he

said in a terse voice.

"What now?" She scowled at the thump on the front door and stomped down the passage to answer it. "Yes, can I help you?"

Another police officer stood with the community constable.

"Have you seen your neighbor Mr. Jamieson?" the community constable asked.

"No, not since the day before yesterday. He and his son were here for afternoon tea. What is this about?"

"I'm sorry. We can't say," the second cop said. "Did they say they were going on a holiday?"

"No, but nothing like that came up in our conversation. We talked about books and movies and the weather," Cassie said. "We ate cookies. That's it."

The constable exchanged a skeptical glance with the cop. He turned back to Cassie. "If you hear from Mr. Jamieson, please tell him we'd like to speak with him."

"Will do." Cassie closed the door and returned to the kitchen, where she found the others. "Did you hear? What do you suppose is happening?"

"At a guess, I'd say custody problems," Jack said. "Of course, he might have had something to do with the drugs. I don't believe his denials about the crop."

"Agreed," Hone said. "There's no proof of the drugs belonging to him, but I noticed a newly planted area on his land. The seedlings hadn't been in the ground for long."

"Huh," Cassie said. "You got all that? Must be why I'm a singer rather than an investigator."

Her phone rang, and she snatched it off the counter. Excitement bubbled through her on seeing the identity of her caller. The manager at the top of her list. "I've got to take this. Won't be a minute."

Hone saw her exhilaration, the brightening of her eyes as she skipped away to find privacy. "She's going to leave."

"Have you told her how you feel?" Emma asked.

"She knows, but I can't hold her back. New Zealand doesn't have the same opportunities. She loves to sing, and she's good at it. If I told her I wanted her to stay, she'd come to resent me."

"You can't be sure—" Emma broke off when Cassie skipped back into the room.

"I have a meeting with Henry Girven. He's a top manager. I'm so excited. I'll have to book a flight. He said he'd fit me in as soon as I can get to Los Angeles."

Hone fought to keep calm. He wanted to protest, beg her to stay, but he remained silent. He had no right to impose his wishes on her, to corral her dreams. Perhaps she would come back to New Zealand.

His taniwha whined. *Whined*. Hone suppressed him with ruthless intent. He couldn't trample on her talent.

*A week later*

Hone managed to hold it together until Cassie disappeared through the passenger-only zone at the airport. His taniwha writhed, and his skin strained to contain his form. He strode through the airport, intent on going home.

Three-quarters of an hour later, he peeled into his driveway and skidded to a stop. Damn, he'd forgotten Manu would be here. Too bad. He needed a drink.

His door slammed as he marched to his kitchen and his booze cabinet. He'd known this day would come, but it didn't make it any bloody easier.

Manu sat at the kitchen table, a drink before him. Pain squashed him, made him seem less while fatigue highlighted his bloodshot eyes. Hone bit back a frustrated snarl. He understood his cousin's mood. Understood exactly the torment-ripping emotions, the helplessness, the unasked for thing called vulnerability.

Hone plonked onto the opposite seat. He poured himself a drink. "What are you drinking? Whisky?"

"Yeah."

Hone topped up Manu's glass.

"Dad challenged me to a fight," Manu said.

Hone lifted his head, met his cousin's bloodshot gaze. "Cassie has gone home to the States."

"She left you?"

Hone snorted. "Kind of ironic, huh?"

They drank in broody silence, each mired in their own misery. Day turned to night. The level of the whisky bottle reduced steadily, but neither of them became drunk. Stupid dragon genes. Couldn't even get a good alcoholic buzz.

Finally, Hone got up and staggered to bed to sleep. He didn't sleep, couldn't sleep when all he wanted was Cassie.

# CHAPTER 24

They wanted her to stay in the States, suggested a new album and setting up a tour. Cassie said she'd consider it. Initially excited about signing with a new manager who agreed to let her have a huge say in how her career ran in the future, now flatness filled her.

She missed Hone.

So much. An empty space throbbed inside her and not even a pasta meal and a chocolate dessert from one of her favorite restaurants sealed the gap.

She thought about him in the morning when she was first awake. She turned to him a million times during the day to tell him something. But the nights...the nights were the worst. She ached to feel his arms wrapped around her, ached to feel his kiss. She plain ached, so she didn't sleep. Not even makeup managed to hide the shadows on her face.

Tonight was no different.

She tossed and turned and finally gave up. With a glass of wine in hand, she wandered to her hotel balcony and stepped outside into the cool evening air.

She'd changed.

Cassie returned to the bedroom. She'd arrange a meeting with Henry tomorrow and would tell him her problem. Hopefully, if he didn't tear up her newly signed contract, he might have a solution.

The next day, Henry's secretary fitted her into a five-minute gap between appointments.

On the threshold, she hesitated, her chest heavy with dread. This could go so badly wrong. She twisted her hands together and stepped inside.

The grizzled man in a navy-blue suit looked up from his paperwork, cocked his head. "Something wrong, Cassie?"

"Henry, I appreciate everything you've done for me. So much. But I can't stay here in Los Angeles. I feel smothered and I-I miss my friends. All night, I lay awake worrying about it. Singing and working with you is my dream, but I n-need to go home to New Zealand." Her voice trembled, and she bit her lip, terrified that she might give in to the tears burning in her eyes. "Please."

"You still have several songs to write to fill your album. Correct?"

"Yes."

"Go home to New Zealand. Write your songs and send my secretary a weekly report. Send videos of you singing so I have an idea of how you're going and can advise you. With modern technology, there is no reason why you can't work from New Zealand and commute back and forth as necessary. You might need to spend one or two months at a time back here while we're recording in the studio. Depending on the type of promotion we decide to go for, you might have to tour, but I can't have you unhappy here in Los Angeles. For now, base yourself in New Zealand, and we'll try to make it work. Okay?"

"Y-yes." She gaped at him as she replayed his words. It was that easy? "Yes! Thank you. Thank you."

"Cassie, I'm not an ogre. If there is a problem, you need to let me know so we can fix it. We're a team, and we need to work together."

Cassie peered at him for a frozen second. Did he mean that literally or figuratively? Because if dragons were real, maybe ogres...

"Cassie?"

She jolted back to her business head, tucking away thoughts of the supernatural. "Thank you, Henry. I won't hesitate next time. The contract is so new, and Kevin—"

"I've heard about the way your ex-manager operates." Distaste coated his words. "Go home to your friends. You'll do better work if you're relaxed and happy."

Forty-eight hours later, she was on a plane. She landed at

Auckland International Airport at six in the morning and, after formalities, took a cab to Hone's house in Papakura. Hopefully, he was there. If not, she'd hunt him down.

At seven-thirty, she pounded on the door, her heart thumping in concert. What if Hone had moved on? What if he'd found someone else?

She swallowed as she heard footsteps, and the door flew open. Manu.

"Um, is Hone here?"

"In his bedroom." Manu blinked at her with tired, bloodshot eyes. He'd lost weight since she'd seen him last.

"I-is he alone?"

Manu snorted and stood aside. "He's in his bedroom."

Apprehension bounced through the pit of her stomach, nerves transmitting to her hands and fingers. She wiped her clammy palms down her wrinkled dress. Maybe she should have taken the time to shower and change.

Her footsteps slowed. What if he didn't want her?

She sucked in another breath and pushed open the door while bracing for the worst. The room was stuffy and dark and smelled of alcohol.

"Hone?" She fumbled for the light, relieved—so relieved—when she found only Hone in the bed.

He rubbed his face and blinked at her. "Cassie? Am I imagining things?"

"I-I missed y-you." She swallowed the hard lump in her throat that was making her stutter. "I can't sleep."

"Oh, god, Cassie. Is that really you?" He bounded off the bed, and heedless of his naked state, wrapped her in his arms.

Tears pricked at her eyes as she sank against his hard chest. Hone drew back and kissed her, and she felt as if she'd come home.

"I can't believe you're here." Hone kissed her nose, her chin and nuzzled her neck. "I missed you so much. How long are you here?"

"My new manager says I can base myself here for most of the year. I'll have to travel a bit, but I shouldn't be away for longer than a month, maybe two, at a time."

A slow grin flourished on Hone's face, highlighting his haggard appearance. But his irises glowed that reddish-brown, and she understood she was seeing his taniwha. "I love you, Cassie. I've been so miserable without you."

"Hone, I love you too."

He kissed her and drew her to the bed. Her clothes faded away, and she sighed as their naked bodies moved together in perfect synchronicity. His hands shaped her breasts, plucked her nipples even as she stroked his chest.

He left her to get a condom, then they slid together again. He pushed into her, stretching and filling the empty spaces inside. They held each other, shattering into climax and lingering in the aftermath.

"Cassie, will you marry me? I love you. My taniwha has already claimed you. We both want you more than anything."

"Yes," she whispered. "Yes, I love you—both of you. Oh, Hone. Yes."

Their next kiss contained passion and acceptance, commitment and joy.

Best kiss ever.

Best day ever.

Forever.

# EPILOGUE

# Cassie's house, Clevedon, two weeks later

**"I** can't thank you enough for letting us live here at the house," Emma said. "Right, Jack?"

"You don't have to keep thanking me. This house is yours for as long as you want it. Hone and I are fine living at his place in Papakura. Besides, I'll be away for a month here and there when I have studio and publicity commitments."

Hone wrapped his fingers around hers. It gave her a buzz, sent pleasure coursing through her veins every time. "We're going to be away for a month here and there," he amended.

She shared a grin. "That's true." They'd set a date for their wedding. Something small and intimate with just Hone's family and hers—although her mother was still doing her best to run Cassie's life. Even though she hadn't met Hone, she didn't approve of her daughter getting married in such haste. Too bad. Cassie had no intention of changing her mind. "You haven't had any trouble here?"

"It's quiet. Peaceful. Not a single clown or trespasser," Emma said.

Jack turned the steaks on the barbecue, and the scent of cooking meat made her stomach rumble. "The cops have been around a few times, asking about your neighbor. Evidently, he's done a runner with his kid. The community constable didn't say much, but we got the impression they have no idea of his whereabouts. There is no record of him or the kid leaving the country."

"Matthew loves his son." Cassie picked up a piece of garlic bread and waved it in front of her as she spoke. "It was easy to see when they were here together. Dillion loves his father too."

"Oh, that reminds me. A letter came for you in the mail earlier in the week. It's propped behind my recipe book." Emma started to get up, but Cassie stayed her with a hand.

"I'll grab it. Want another soda? Hone, Jack, another beer?"

The letter bore a Hawaii postmark, and she didn't recognize the handwriting on the envelope. She tucked it under her arm and carried the drinks outside. "I've no idea who it's from." She squeezed in the gap between Hone and Emma and put the letter in her jacket pocket for later.

"Steaks are done." Jack placed the platter on the table.

"What did Kevin say about you signing with a new manager?" Emma asked.

"Huh! It's a wonder you didn't hear him shouting out here. He said I was an ungrateful bitch and I'd regret it, then he hung up on me. I haven't heard from him since."

"He was trying to take advantage of you," Hone snapped. "Bastard. If he decides to visit you in person, I'll give him a knuckle sandwich with a punch to wash it down."

Jack snorted and Emma echoed the sentiment.

"I might let you," Cassie said. "Wow, I hang around you guys for a while and turn into a bloody-thirsty wench."

"My wench," Hone said with satisfaction.

Emma chortled. "I never thought I'd see the day."

"I like him," Cassie said and winked at her man...ah, dragon. "Will you take me flying?"

"We'll have to get permission from Manu because I'm not sure if his units will make you invisible," Hone said.

"This is so exciting. I'm learning about this new, mysterious world. How is Manu?"

Hone frowned. "Not good. Samuel is doing everything he can to provoke him."

"Samuel wants to die, and Manu is the only one who can give

him death."

Cassie set down her knife and fork. "How?"

"The sword," Emma said. "Now that June is gone, Manu is the tribe leader. He bears the responsibility for every dragon within the Auckland region."

"If June was the leader, how come Manu had the magic sword?" Cassie asked.

"The sword chooses the leader by melting into their body. It rejected June and accepted Manu before June flew here. Kahurangi said that was the final bit that made his mother snap," Hone said.

"Fascinating, but scary too." Cassie pushed her plate away and retrieved the letter. She ripped open the envelope and scanned the contents. "I don't believe it. Listen to this."

She started reading aloud.

*Dear Cassie,*

*Although we didn't know each other well, I feel as if I owe you an explanation, and Dillion wanted to say hello. No doubt, the police have already contacted you to ask if you've seen me. The drugs belonged to me, and when your land and house remained vacant, I decided to risk an extra planting on your land. The attacks and the clown thing happened because of me. I wanted to scare you away until the crop was ready to harvest. Unfortunately, my ex-wife and your discovery of the crop forced me to escalate my plans. No matter, since everything turned out in the end. Dillion is safe, and we have a new home, a new life, and new opportunities.*

*Thank you for being so good to Dillion. You were amazing with him, and I will be forever grateful.*

*Best wishes,*

*Matthew Jamieson*

"Is there a postmark?" Hone asked.

"It was posted in Hawaii almost two weeks ago. I doubt they're still there," Cassie said.

"Are you calling the cops?" Jack asked.

Cassie folded the single sheet of paper and stuffed it back into the envelope. "No, I don't think so. They could be anywhere by now. Besides, the cops probably assume Matthew has fled New Zealand. They'll already be following leads and searching outside the country."

Hone picked up her hand, seeming to take delight in the physical contact. "At least we can relax our guard, and you're no longer in danger."

"I wish we could help Manu," Cassie said. "He saved me. You all saved me."

"Because we understood what you meant to Hone," Emma said.

"It was easy to see."

"I had no idea," Cassie said indignantly. "Why didn't anyone tell me? It would've saved me a lot of heartache."

Hone squeezed her hand. "You needed to choose me, sweetheart. Accept that we were meant to be." He leaned over and kissed her.

"Ew," Emma said. "We're still at dinner."

Cassie laughed against Hone's lips. She was right where she wanted to be with the man she loved.

Silver linings.

Eager to learn what happens to Manu? Read **Black Moon Dragon** to learn more about Manu's fate. (https://shelleymunro.com/books/black-moon-dragon/)

Would you like to read more of my romances? Sign up for my (https://shelleymunro.com/newsletter/) to learn about upcoming releases, receive free books and short stories tied to my series plus contest and special promotion news.

Enjoy!

# About Shelley

USA Today bestselling author Shelley Munro lives in Auckland, the City of Sails, with her husband and a cheeky Jack Russell/mystery breed dog.

Typical New Zealanders, Shelley and her husband left home for their big OE soon after they married (translation of New Zealand speak - big overseas experience). A twelve-month-long adventure lengthened to six years of roaming the world. Enduring memories include being almost sat on by a mountain gorilla in Rwanda, lazing on white sandy beaches in India, whale watching in Alaska, searching for leprechauns in Ireland, and dealing with ghosts in an English pub.

While travel is still a big attraction, these days Shelley is most likely found in front of her computer following another love - that of writing stories of contemporary and paranormal romance and adventure. Other interests include watching rugby (strictly for research purposes), cycling, playing croquet and the ukelele, and curling up with an enjoyable book.

### Visit Shelley at her Website

https://shelleymunro.com

### Join Shelley's Newsletter

https://shelleymunro.com/newsletter

# Also By Shelley

**Paranormal**

*Dragon Investigators*

Blue Moon Dragon

Blood Moon Dragon

Black Moon Dragon

Snow Moon Dragon

*Middlemarch Shifters*

My Scarlet Woman

My Younger Lover

My Peeping Tom

My Assassin

My Estranged Lover

My Feline Protector

My Determined Suitor

My Cat Burglar

My Stray Cat

My Second Chance

My Plan B
My Cat Nap
My Romantic Tangle
My Blue Lady
My Twin Trouble
My Precious Gift

### *Middlemarch Gathering*

My Highland Mate
My Highland Fling
My Elusive Mate
My Valiant Princess
My Highland Wedding
My Highland Billionaire

www.ingramcontent.com/pod-product-compliance
Lightning Source LLC
Chambersburg PA
CBHW031159020726
47499CB00002B/423